GREEN
FIRE

🎧 Hear the music

🔊 Listen to extracts

at

www.dekaydence.com

GREEN FIRE

Susie Cornfield

GARRET
BOOKS

Green Fire
Published by Garret Books in 2009
ISBN 978-0-9552279-3-6

Garret Books Ltd Reg. No.: 5647052
Registered address: Suite 210, Maddison House, 226 High Street, Croydon, CR9 1DF,
Surrey, England, UK
www.garretbooks.com

A CIP catalogue record for this book is available from the British Library

Designed and typeset by Caroline and Roger Hillier, The Old Chapel Graphic Design
www.theoldchapellivinghoe.com

Copy editors: Ros Lavine; Margaret Histed
Readers: Isobel Rapoport, Maggi Ovink, Pat Shalhoub and John Kippen

Printed and bound in Great Britain by Bookmarque Ltd, Croydon, Surrey

For God,
if you're still there,
because as a child I worried that,
amidst the darkness, prayers, pleas and tears,
no one ever brought you laughter.

Also by the author

Fiction
Black Light; a satirical thriller, first in the series The Chronicles of Dekaydence (Garret Books, 2008, ISBN 978-0-9552279-2-9), produced originally as *The Sticky Rock Café*

Non-fiction
Farewell, My Lovely; a collection of tributes to much-loved departed pets. Original paperback (Garret Books, 2006, ISBN 978-0-9552279-1-2); hardback, revised and extended edition (Garret Books, 2009, ISBN 978-0-9552279-4-3)

History
The Queen's Prize; the story of the National Rifle Association of Great Britain (Pelham Books, 1986, ISBN 0 7207 1751 5)

Susie Cornfield trained as a journalist on a local newspaper before joining the staff of *The Sunday Times* where she was the paper's radio critic. She went on to become a columnist for the *Sunday Telegraph Magazine*, a writer for BBC TV and a presenter/producer for United Artists TV.

What they said about *Black Light*:

A racy, pacy, crazy book. Like Philip Pullman on speed!

Piers Plowright

Exciting and cool ... funny, weird and offbeat ... A can't miss book!

Andrew Weatherston, *Teen Titles*

A very exciting read . . . had me on the edge of my seat.

Benjy Taylor, *The Independent*
(round-up of the best five books in the year's
boys' own adventures)

A wholly innovative teenage thriller.

John Lloyd, Waterstone's

*Lock up this author until she gets the next book out – if it's as
barmy and brilliant as the first!*

Francis Rossi

*Mould-breaking characters ... a plot thick enough to stop bullets
... Black Light is not to be missed.*

S. Clark, review on Amazon

CONTENTS

DRAMATIS PERSONAE

Angelica Nera *Ruby Q's mother*

Bianco *teenager who works for GeeZers and Dekaydence*

Bodkin *Dekaydence laboratory assistant*

Cage Martin *a 19-year-old, the Martins' eldest son*

Cataract *senior partner at the accountants Cataract, Cyclops and Mote*

Catgut *composer of avant-garde music*

Claud Canapé *internationally renowned designer*

Comprendo *leader of gang of three young men*

Edwina Gardening-Fork (pronounced Spade) *Editor,* Shed Monthly

Elsa D. Cooper *Ruby Q's grandmother*

The Face *leader, the GeeZers*

Grout *Dekaydence laboratory assistant*

Hilli *the Face's minder*

Hunky Doré *US pop star*

Indigo *the King's granddaughter, Will's cousin*

Innit *a teenager, working for Dekaydence*

Jack Martin *a 17-year-old, the Martins' third son*

Jarvis *gofer on Dekaydence's* Daily Unigraph

Jezza *Innit's girlfriend*

Kane Martin *an 18-year-old, the Martins' second son*

The King *constitutional monarch of Great Britain*

Lady Catgut *wife of the composer Sir Harrison Catgut*

Lars Sparks *internationally renowned photographer*

Lily Nera *Ruby Q Cooper's aunt*

Lord Lorenzo di'Abalo *head of the Company of Dekaydence*

MacCavity *head of Dekaydence Security*

MacGluten *head chef at Dekaydence*
MacMinor *Red Tartan guard*
MacNoodle *Red Tartan guard*
McCarbon *deputy head of Dekaydence Security*
Meryl Martin *a 20-year-old, the Martins' elder daughter*
Mr and Mrs Martin *parents of Taylor, Jack, Kane, Cage and Meryl*
The Minister *the Union's Environment Minister, also a turkey farmer*
North, South, East and West *regional leaders of the GeeZers*
Petty Masters *avant-garde fashion designer*
Phlegm *Lord di'Abalo's butler*
The Phoenix *a freelance activist with the Real GeeZers*
Piccolo Smith *a 17-year-old runaway musician*
The President *elected head of the Union*
The Professor *head of Dekaydence Research & Development*
Rallan Cooper *a drummer, Ruby Q Cooper's father*
Randall Candelskin *Signor di'Abalo's right-hand man*
Ruby Q Cooper *a 16-year-old journalist on the* Daily Unigraph
Schneek *rollerblading assistant to Petty Masters*
Sinus *the King's butler*
Spiky Hair *Editor, Dekaydence's* Daily Unigraph
Taylor Martin *a 13-year-old, the youngest in the Martin family*
Mr and Mrs Treasure *Elsa Cooper's housekeeper and gardener*
Waat *half-sister to Innit*
Wiggins *a King's Counsel, brother to Cataract*
Will *a 17-year-old, the King's great-nephew*
Young Miss Burgess *right- and left-hand woman at* Shed Monthly

The Chronicles of Dekaydence begins in book one, *Black Light*. This is the story so far ...

The GeeZers, peaceful eco-terrorists, are being superseded by Real GeeZers who see violent action as the only way forward to save the planet from environmental meltdown and political corruption. They are prepared to die for the cause. Now one they call the Phoenix is prepared to kill.

Will, the King's great-nephew, Ruby Q, a journalist, and Piccolo Smith, a rock musician, continue their own fight to save the planet. And they, too, face the growing power of Lord Lorenzo di'Abalo's evil global company of Dekaydence, which manipulates food, fashion, music and now the whole shopping experience, as well as religion. And there's the White Room from which youngsters return happy but mindless.

Can things get worse? Of course they can.

People are disappearing mysteriously from the streets where crazed bloodthirsty liz'oids, such as Colin, roam. There's the imprisoned former politician, Randall Candelskin, who'll do anything to be back in his designer underwear. The cracker-addicted designer Petty Masters and the pop star Hunky Doré, who's a six-packed handful, to put it mildly. And whatever the skills of the Professor, Innit and Bodkin, modern technology appears to have a mind of its own. As does, increasingly, the young Grout.

SUMMER

1 MANY HANDS ... AND LIGHT WORK

The King stared aghast: Hunky Doré, the pale, blond pop star dressed in his characteristic gold lamé catsuit, who'd run on to the stage in the Royal Marquee and burst into an extraordinarily wild set, was playing bass, rhythm *and* lead on a three-necked guitar. Somewhere along the way, the young man had acquired two extra pairs of hands. Hairy black hands at that, at the end of long, thin hairy black arms.

"Amazing," murmured the President of the Union.

"Just what I ..." The King halted, realising the President's attention was drawn not to Doré's handy-work but to the unusual abundance of glittering lights in the marquee.

"Marvellous idea, turning political hot air into electricity," said the King, "then to achieve it by imprisoning MPs and Lords permanently in Parliament ... Someone deserves a medal. Or canonisation."

"Dekaydence is a miracle worker," said the President, graciously acknowledging the numerous VIPs bowing to him rather than to their monarch.

"I do hear the House of Lords' contribution is negligible," said the King, ogling the Dekaydence delicacies on the just-out-of-reach tray of a passing waiter.

"Free thinkers," the President said, tersely. "They have

a tendency not to be free talkers. Show 'em a fence and they'll spend a decade ruminating on the quality of the wood before they even begin to debate which way to sit on it."

Suddenly, the lights went out.

The music stopped abruptly.

The midsummer's night party guests were thrown into darkness. Someone in the crowd stifled a scream. The King sensed an unease; hardly surprising, given the recent bombing of Number 10 Downing Street by a Real GeeZer, which had killed the President's wife and son. The young blighter was still on the run. Who knew what he or any of the other teenage eco-terrorists might do next?

"Your Majesty, Mr President, ladies and gentlemen," a voice boomed from the speakers. "Apologies. A technical hitch. A rare outbreak of speechlessness in both Houses of Parliament. Resolved speedily by the Company of Dekaydence ordering an immediate cut in politicians' salaries, expenses and time off. So, Mr Doré, play on!"

There were cheers of relief and applause: the King thanked his god who watched over him from an adjacent throne; the crowd, and the President, bestowed their support on Hunky Doré who stood sullenly centre stage under a powerful spotlight before embarking on a new handily hectic set.

Not long ago, the King mused, the fad had been for implants and extensions; was it now for the growing range of Dekaydence techno-scientific combi-creations?

"The world is becoming a strange place," the King pondered. "At least Dekaydence has all but rid us of those young eco-idiots, the GeeZers, blocking motorways with dustcarts to save a planet the rest of us know is in excellent health."

The President emptied his glass of Dekaydence champagne, ignoring the ramblings of a monarch whose family ranked madness high in its genetic inheritance.

"Perhaps," the King continued to muse, "if I took drugs instead of tea I might discover what young people are about nowadays."

"I beg your pardon," said the President, unable to swallow a startled belch.

"And now there's the problem of Real GeeZers," the King continued.

"Not to worry," said the President, "Dekaydence is on the case, as we speak."

"More Sticky Rock Cafés?" the King enquired.

"Oh, no," said the President, a knowing smile slithering into its familiar place. "Something much stronger. Something, how shall I say ... dark and tartany?"

"Understand," said the King, who didn't but welcomed anything that ensured the security of his throne.

"Hurrah for Dekaydence," he added with mild enthusiasm, turning to peer through the driving rain, the bewigged footman turning too, to ensure the Day Crown, a coronet set on a bowler hat hanging from a golden pole, remained above the monarch's head.

An Eye-Spy flew high above the river, its myriad camera lenses scanning and transmitting information to Dekaydence HQ, within the Palace of Dekaydence, a few miles to the east on the south side of the river.

On the opposite riverbank stood the massive new Dekaydence 24-hour shopping mall, protected by a web of anti-personnel rainbow-coloured laser lights, which was due to open ... well, no one quite knew when. The King shuddered. He'd been assured the prevailing wind would carry the noise, if not the stench of crowds and food, away to the east but ... He sighed; he so loved his home and garden.

He turned, the footman echoing his steps, and saw in the crowd his great-nephew, Will, his dark handsome features as impenetrable as ever.

The young Highlander was a strange lad to be sure – always had his head in a book – but the King consoled himself that he might be of use. The Royal Press Office was working to turn him into a popular pin-up, for in these troubled times it paid for the monarchy to be celebrity, as well as asset, rich.

Nevertheless, if the lad ever stepped out of line ...

2 SPIT AND RUN

"Sorry to be late. The sat-nav sent us in the wrong direction, right into some bloody underground railway system. Bloody postal service, I 'spect," said the Face, marching into the Victorian chamber deep below the river Thames, a minder in tow. "Nearly had him."

The minder blushed.

The eight GeeZers, huddled together on the floor, each with a minder behind and a lit candle in front, murmured their sympathies.

"OK, you each know your escape plan?" the Face enquired briskly, squatting beside them, setting up a candle and collating nods and verbal assents. "They've learnt of this meeting but not the location. I'll get a message instantly should the situation change. But let's keep it brief. So, North, why the urgency for this meeting?"

"I'm quitting," said North.

"What?" The Face stared at North in disbelief.

"I've worked hard for the cause, Face," said North, "but we're no nearer to saving the planet. I'm losing GeeZers every day to Dekaydence, either brainwashed by Sticky Rock Cafés or taken from the streets for experimentation in the White Room or wherever. I'm quitting and joining the Real GeeZers; so is my number two. And there's no one prepared to take on our roles."

"So, you discard peaceful protest for the violence of the Real GeeZers," said the Face, disdainfully. "And their blood and guts."

"As I see it, Face, being a peaceful GeeZer is wasting time, and lives," said North, quiet yet firm.

"What about the rest of you?" The Face challenged the other seven.

"We're down to single figures," said West. "There's not much fight left in us."

"We're split down the middle," said South.

"And you?" said the Face.

"We are few but we remain loyal to you, Face. Always will," said East.

"And you lot?" the Face enquired of the four central Union delegates.

Their spokesperson gave a Gallic pout and shrug.

"Ze debate continues, Face. But given our hot Latin blood ..."

"So, division and done deals behind my back," the Face said, reflectively, extinguishing the flame with spittled fingers, pocketing the candle, and standing up. "I counted you all as friends as well as colleagues. My mistake. For safety's sake, I declare this meeting over. To the enemies of peace, I say farewell. To friends, adieu, we'll meet soon. But take heed, all of you: the power of Dekaydence grows stronger."

The Face turned from the assembly and, with the minder, strode to the designated tunnel, climbed a rope ladder and disappeared with it inside.

East snatched at a candle, and stood up.

"Traitors and feeblings!" East snarled at the remaining GeeZers and stormed off to a tunnel with the minder.

Suddenly, they heard footsteps. Running, fast approaching the chamber. Those seated sprang to their feet. A few, with their minders, sprinted to their escape tunnels. Others, despite their minders' urging, froze in uncertainty. The Face had said no one knew their location; besides, GeeZers were guarding all the entrances.

In the tunnel, the Face had turned back to watch.

Out of the darkness, a young man, a look of terror on his face, ran into the hazy vision of those in the chamber.

"Get out!" he cried, as soon as he saw them. "They're here! Get out quickly!"

A flash of light shot across the room.

The young man dropped to the floor.

"Move!" The minders screamed. "Move!"

Minders and GeeZers began shouting and running in all directions.

A GeeZer, who'd gone to aid the fallen youth, was trying to shake off a minder when a dozen powerfully built, armed Black Tartan guards, their eyes hidden behind red-tartan sunglasses, stormed through the entrances, firing huge exploding balls of blinding light into the dark chamber.

"Hit the floor, NOW!" a Scots voice boomed above the mayhem, as the crazed metal liz'oids, restrained by RasaLasa guns, yowled and screeched for GeeZer blood.

Those who didn't obey would be immobilised in an instant by the RasaLasas or suffer a bloody fate from the released liz'oids.

In the tunnel, before the minder got his way to move on and fast, the Face watched the scene with growing despair and anger. Cursing and wondering what had happened to the highly reliable "mole", the Face realised the young man on the floor, who'd signed up underage to the GeeZers' cause, was lying in a pool of blood. Someone would have to inform his family.

"No one tells me that violence is the way to go," the Face muttered to herself, before hurrying after the minder through the maze of tunnels to safety.

3 THE PHOENIX RISES

The young man, codenamed the Phoenix, who had the body of an athlete and the courage and heart of a metal tiger, waited among the trees of the country estate, alert to the sounds and smells of night and nature, including the rain gouging puddles on the gravel driveway and pounding on the roof of the Georgian mansion close by.

Hearing an approaching car's engine, the young man breathed in slow and deep, willing energy to course through his body.

A black limousine scrunched across the gravel, passing him in the shadows, and pulled up outside the house. A chauffeur leapt out of the car, opening an umbrella, which was grasped by a tall distinguished-looking man in evening dress, his expensively coiffured chestnut locks sitting neatly above his Roman forehead. As he stepped out of the back seat the man dismissed the chauffeur who drove off swiftly, already tasting the whisky waiting for him in the flat above the garage.

The Phoenix crept closer.

Fumbling and failing to find his keys, the tall man cursed and reached for the doorbell, catching sight of something out of the corner of his eye. He turned to see that the something was flying fast towards him.

He was about to cry out, to wield his umbrella as a shield, but it was too late. The Phoenix's RasaLasa gun had hit its target. The man stood immobilised, his open jaw full of a silent scream, his eyes frozen wide in shock and horror.

4 WILL'S WAY

Will disliked having to attend these frivolous royal functions, and dreaded the fact that more were scheduled into his diary. He was desperate for answers to scientific questions but the more he researched, the more he found ISPs blocked, websites shut down, and relevant scientists unreachable at their universities or research centres.

He scanned the crowd, meeting the mesmerising blue-green eyes of Lord Lorenzo di'Abalo, head of the Company of Dekaydence. Did the man know of Will's imprisonment inside the company's HQ? Luckily, the scar on his ear where the Dekaydence rainbow stud had been was fading and, in any event, was covered by his long locks. Luckily, unlike others, he'd escaped, thanks to Piccolo, who ...

No! This was not a time for friendship. This was a time of war.

Politicians and powerbrokers played dirty, he realised increasingly. They might mouth concern about issues such as climate change but, at base, they sought only to maintain their political power or increase turnover.

Thus he saw that Dekaydence was seducing teenagers from eco-worries with the techno-magic Palace playgrounds and the trendy Sticky Rock Cafés, with the consequence that the numbers of GeeZers, peaceful or otherwise, was shrinking drastically.

He knew also that the Number 10 bombing had been carried out not by a Real GeeZer, his associate, Cage, as the authorities wanted everyone to believe, but on the orders of Lord di'Abalo himself.

Rumours abounded as to why but, whatever the truth, one thing was for sure: The Age of Dekaydence had begun.

Everywhere he looked, Will saw authority corrupted: the King would do anything to safeguard his throne, Candelskin was driven by money, and di'Abalo ... Ah, there was the rub. Was it power alone? Will couldn't be sure.

He was sure, however, that the GeeZers, including his own brother, Tommo, fighting to save the planet from global meltdown, with a stubborn commitment to non-violence, had achieved nothing. And that his big, beautiful, kind-hearted generous brother had died, or been murdered, for nothing.

That act had decided him six months ago: change would come only through dramatic, violent action. It was the reason he'd joined the Real GeeZers, the reason he'd agreed to become their leader. Tonight would be a test of his leadership, for tonight the Real GeeZers launched their first major assault.

The problem was, as he read and researched, he had growing doubts about the causes of climate change.

5 WEB TRAP

The man held in the web-bond was being dragged across his own property of muddy fields, bramble and woods, heading he knew not where. Or why. Who was the young silent kidnapper, about the age of his son? What did he want? Money? A new car? Free fuel permit? A curfew pass? The stuff his son demanded.

The man was furious: he had to be up early for tennis, before the car took him to the TV studios. Before that, he had vital work to do, massaging his demanding ego.

As the Union's Environment Minister he'd announced that night a raft of "green" policies at a Guildhall dinner. Of course, by design, the policies were ineffective and the questions rigged, but the Minister prided himself on preparing elegant, amusing, albeit vacuous answers and wished to revisit and relish them before retiring. (He also had to check with his accountant as to how much money he could expect to make when the laws were passed. Money which, of course, would be placed offshore, thus saving him the nuisance of paying taxes he could well afford.)

The Minister was sure that by now his wife would've checked with the chauffeur and alerted the authorities. And once those Dekaydence chappies got on the case, well ... He might be uncomfortable for a while longer but in a few hours his young captor would wish he'd never been born.

The Minister's clothes were sodden and he was shivering, any warmth from the evening's alcohol having evaporated long ago. He wanted to say something cutting to the young man but the RasaLasa imprisoning his body had gagged his vocal cords.

They reached a barbed-wire fence.

Inwardly, the Minister gave a smug smile; he'd spent a small fortune upgrading the security system (well, he'd pay, as and when his lawyers had argued down the costs and/or bankrupted the company). He then watched the young man uncover a new, neatly cut hole.

As he was dragged through, the Minister caught his bare hand on the wire but his cry of pain remained stoppered in his throat. His mind was racing. Why hadn't the alarm gone off? Why hadn't the security lights come on?

He started to sweat.

They were heading down the hill towards the vast warehouses. The Minister sensed relief. His business ran 24 hours a day, seven days a week. The early shift would be starting soon; someone would see him.

By now Dekaydence would be on the case. Soon he'd be showered and tucked up in bed, watching himself on the news. What a story he'd have to tell Tom and Tony at tennis tomorrow. How they'd laugh as he made light of it all. He might even buy them a coffee. No, no, that was going too far.

A thought occurred to him suddenly: would this incident make his son feel for him anything other than ill-concealed apathy or, as more recently, positive dislike?

6 BUBBLE TROUBLE

"Have a nice Dekaydence Day! Press buttons 3, 2 and 6 simultaneously if you're contacting us between March and May! Attention! Any non-ticketed passenger will be executed at the next stop! Ha! Believe that? You'll believe anything, fools!"

Boy, when an Orbobubble breaks down, the Voice Guard really cracks up big time. At least they've got Hunky Doré and the Studs and Sluts on the radio.

Their music's great, isn't it? But even Orbees can't be immune from this kind of deluge. Did you know, we've had our annual rainfall in the past 48 hours?

You don't say?

People are dying in houses in the new towns built on old flood plains. Thousands have abandoned their homes because rivers are bursting their banks. Trains and planes are cancelled, schools are closed, businesses are washed up and there are food and drinking-water shortages ... How can anyone deny climate change? Or ineffective government? And now there are Real GeeZers threatening violence!

Ruby Q Cooper, you've been on your soapbox ever since this heap of technology broke down hours ago, making us late for the Royal Garden Party.

Yes. And as you reside in my head, I'd like your support, please. Otherwise I'm going to start charging you rent.

Won't get you far. I don't do money.

A drawback, I agree. So, instead ... I'll stop talking to you.

You can't. I'm all you've got. Your dad's still missing, there's been scant news on your mum in nine years. And now lover-boy Jack's gone off to join the GeeZers.

Stop it! Jack and I are good friends. End of story. And I'm doing all I can to find out what's happened to my parents. Whether they're alive or ... It's not easy, you know, I'm dealing with Dekaydence at every turn ... I do have a grandmother.

How can I have overlooked Elsa, the self-centred, egotistical author?

OK, OK, but there are the Treasures.

Yes, whenever you're in need, the good ol' Treasures are there for you. Quite why two such nice, sane people continue to work as housekeeper and gardener for Elsa, I do not know. In fact ... Hey, what are those youths doing out after curfew, with liz'oids on patrol?

Oh, no, there are the liz'oids! They've seen them! Look at their jaws! Oh ...

The liz'oids are backing off. How weird is that? And now the youths are attacking that man locking up his shop!

We've got to stop them ...

What's that noise?

It's the Orbee. It's moving. But we must help ...

"Fasten your safety belts, please. And have a nice Dekaydence Day!"

"Excuse me, Voice Guard ..."

"To your right, the Palace of Dekaydence, renowned playground," intoned the Voice Guard on the intercom. "You, there! No slouching, sit up straight!"

Watch it, Voice Guard, she's with me and I'm not slouching, I'm ...

"Please, Voice Guard, we must get help. Look over there ..."

"Sit down, missy madam! Else there's no nice Dekaydence Day for you!"

It's all right! The thugs have lost interest in him. He looks OK, but—

Oh, no, the thugs are heading this way!

They're throwing stuff!

Watch out, Ruby Q!

They're all wearing masks, with the same face.

Get down, Ruby Q!

Oh! I'd recognise that dimple anywhere. Only, I don't understand. Why are the thugs wearing masks with Cage's face printed on them?

I dunno, maybe it's a trendy anti-hero fashion statement. Whatever, duck!

"Have a nice Dekaydence Day! You and me, and a friend or three ..." sang the Voice Guard.

Cage may be a fool, joining the Real GeeZers, but he's not a murderer. But with his picture everywhere, they're bound to catch him soon and what'll they do to him? And what will that do to his family? To Taylor and Jack, Kane and Meryl, and poor Mr and Mrs Martin?

Look – one of the thugs has taken off his mask. He's waving at you, Ruby Q.

It's Innit!

Great, you've got friends who throw things at you!

Don't you remember? Innit's tried to "sort me out" in the Palace of Dekaydence.

Oh, yes.

Even his sister warned us about him.

Yes, she was a nice girl. What was her name? Which? Where?

Waat, actually.

Yes. So, what's Waat's brother doing out on the streets?

What he likes best, causing trouble. Duck!

What was that noise?

It's the Orbee! It's fighting back.

"Get this, bum-rags! Have a Real Nice Sticky End to a Dekaydence Day!"

The thugs are running away!

Why am I not surprised? Hit by a tsunami of raspberry ripple ice cream, nuts and glacé cherries, I'd do the same.

7 COLD TURKEY

In the vast windowless warehouse some 25,000 screeching weeks-old turkeys, many dying, many more wounded or sick, fought and clambered over each other and the Union's Environment Minister who was kneeling, near-naked in their midst, on the wet, soiled and stinking floor, trussed, and with a long feather of red and gold stuck securely between his buttocks. Over the airwaves wafted the soothing refrain of "By a Sleepy Lagoon".

The Minister's head lolled on a dislocated neck trussed between his knees, his trouser belt held his ankles tightly together. The expertly coiffed chestnut locks – now awry with straw, sweat and dirt – straggled across the Roman forehead. Blood trickled from his mouth, his clipped nose, and the raw stumps that had been his toes. He was dimly aware that several turkeys were pecking at him, that one had a beady eye trained on his, and that he was kneeling in shit and semen that included his own.

In the depths of pain, with any sense of dignity erased, he knew he'd received the exact same treatment meted out to his birds.

For the first time in 50 years, the Minister prayed with a vehemence he'd never felt before, demanding of God that the young man's fate would be worse than his. As he prayed, he tasted the bitter awareness that even if help did arrive soon, he would never wear the peer's ermine promised him for the money he'd donated secretly to the President's Party from the fortune amassed from the cheap meat he produced but refused to eat himself.

Rather, the feathers now falling on his back like snowflakes would be his shroud.

8 PICCOLO AT PEACE

In the boathouse, beyond the house and the increasingly waterlogged lawn, Piccolo Smith sat comfortably slumped on the upper level above the bobbing boats, devouring pasties and cider, made from ingredients produced in indoor greenhouses. As well as a resourceful gardener, Lady Catgut was an excellent cook and a devilish brewer. He'd never had such tasty, wholesome meals. At home, it'd been any rubbish past its sell-by date; imprisoned in Dekaydence along with the other kids, they'd been guinea pigs trialling junk food, processed meals, puddings and sweeties galore.

After escaping Dekaydence, after quitting the in-fighting GeeZers, Piccolo had sought refuge with Sir Harrison Catgut, hoping that, despite the conductor's tetchy, arrogant manner, he'd learn from the man knighted for his services to loud, modern music. Here, he'd hoped, for the first time in his life, he'd have the peace he craved in order to compose and play.

Catgut had opened the door to him, smiled vacantly and wandered off, humming. It'd been Lady Catgut who'd invited him in and then, discovering that he too was a musician and didn't drink tea from the saucer, had offered him dinner and then asked him to stay and help care for the confused man her husband had become.

"What am I thinking of?" She'd given an embarrassed laugh. "It'd be frightfully boring for you, we're miles from the nearest ..."

"I'll stay!" Piccolo had said firmly.

It was bizarre: Catgut recalled nothing of the experiences he'd shared with Piccolo the previous year. Not the underground imprisonment at Dekaydence HQ with members of the Imperial Orchestra of the Union. Or being forced to compose pop music for the Sticky Rock Cafés. Not the explosion. Or the contrived story put about by Dekaydence media that the musicians had had a miraculous escape from a plane crash in South America.

Catgut was a changed man.

True, he looked much the same: tall, spare, with long flowing hair. And he wore the same old cricketing trousers, loose shirt and a voluminous dark blue velvet cloak. But this Catgut was gentle and kind, his words and deeds coming from a quieter, deeper world, the opposite of the waspish Catgut of old. Piccolo savoured the change.

He accompanied Catgut on walks through the surrounding countryside, in a silence broken only when the conductor stopped to marvel at a flower, a tree, or the song of the thrush, or to talk about music. This new Catgut shunned modern music, listened intently to Bach, and spoke passionately about Elgar, Vaughan Williams and Delius.

Later that night Piccolo waded back to the house and found Catgut alone in his study, listening to Delius's "On hearing the first cuckoo in spring".

"Don't become my Eric Fenby," said Catgut, when the piece had concluded.

"What does that mean, man?"

"If I end up like Delius, blind and crippled, relying on someone to take dictation, you must get away, Piccolo. Leave, and make your own music."

"Ain't nothing goin' happen to you," said Piccolo. "You's one tough ol' bird."   Catgut stared at the ceiling.

The sound of drumbeats in the rain distracted Piccolo. For the first time in his life, he realised he'd found stillness within himself. The kindness and care shown him by the Catguts encouraged him to contain his sadness and anger. If he recalled the abuse he'd suffered as a child or thought of Will, his first ever friend who he'd known for too brief a time, the pain was there – but as a tender scar rather than a septic, open wound.

He was a distance from happiness but, for the first time, he heard melodies deep within music, within the wind and the trees, and within the silence of companionship. He began to compose again. Sometimes, he felt his heart soar like a lark ascending a summer sky.

9 UNCLOSE ENCOUNTERS

The King had quit the royal party but no one else had as the food, drink and music continued to flow freely.

Commanded by His Majesty to remain until the end, Will cursed inwardly. Terse with anyone who tried to engage him in conversation, he searched for the only person he wanted to talk to: the young Dekaydence reporter who secretly passed on information to the GeeZers. She was on the VIP guest list but where was she? Where was Ruby Q Cooper?

It was late into the evening when he saw the familiar mass of unruly dark red hair and the tortoiseshell glasses, as she made her way determinedly through the crowd towards him.

"Miss Cooper," he said, trying to contain his enthusiasm. "It's a pleasure ... "

He stopped, seeing the anger in her dark green eyes.

"They've found the Union's Environment Minister trussed up in his own turkey shed," said Ruby Q, ignoring his proffered hand. "There's already film on the illegal websites, showing him and the disgusting way he keeps his birds. Oh, and they're blaming the Real GeeZers and somebody called the Phoenix."

Will wanted to throw a punch at the sky, but he

remained calm.

"Who's the Phoenix?" He noted the ease with which he was now able to lie.

Ruby Q's eyes narrowed.

"Great act, but don't bother for my sake. I know you're mixed up with the Real GeeZers. But I wonder if you and your lot ever stopped to think what might happen if the Minister dies? All hell will break loose on GeeZers, Real or otherwise."

"What else can happen to GeeZers that isn't happening already?" Will replied, coolly. What did he care about the fate of another lying, cheating politician, and one who was prepared to see his children die on a wasted planet?

"It's those yucky royal press releases about you working for peace," she continued. "They convince me you've sold out to the Real GeeZers. Like Cage has."

Will tried to remain calm. He needed this young woman on side.

"Miss Cooper, I work for peace because I believe it's the way forward."

"Oh, yes?"

"Aye, I do. But I *am* intrigued by the Real GeeZers' commitment to attack only those responsible for irresponsible actions against the planet."

"So Real GeeZers are to be judge and jury? Like the thugs on the street tonight who decided to beat up someone just because they felt like it?"

Will forced himself to remain calm.

"Thugs wearing masks with Cage's face printed on them," Ruby Q continued.

"What?" Will was genuinely surprised.

"Cage face masks. They appear to be all the rage among happening thugs."

Will frowned.

"I think you've been duped, Miss Cooper," he said.

"What d'you mean?"

"Ask around. I think you'll find those thugs are mercenaries, hired recently by the government to give Real GeeZers a bad name. And it appears they've succeeded."

Ruby Q stared at him.

"No doubt the mercenaries get a password to call off any stray liz'oids," he said, adding bitterly, "Shame the masks don't show the faces of those truly responsible for the deaths of the President's wife and son."

"Who are ...?" said Ruby Q.

He regarded her, steadily.

"You're the journalist, Miss Cooper, go find out."

"But you know?" Ruby Q persisted.

He shrugged.

"Ideas, like everyone else."

"Care to share them?"

"Maybe. If you tell me everything you saw in the White Room."

"So your Real GeeZer friends can blow it up and kill dozens in the process?" Ruby Q retorted. "I think not."

"As I said, I don't encourage those kinds of contacts,"

said Will, quietly.

"So why ...?"

"I need to know because ..." He hesitated, savouring his mastery of a dramatic pause. "Tommo, my brother, was killed last year, probably because he'd learnt something about the Company of Dekaydence."

"The papers said ... But then ... " Ruby Q floundered.

"Precisely," said Will, "and with due respect, even you can't believe everything you read. So, you see, that's why I have to know. I have to find out."

"I understand," said Ruby Q. "But I can't – I won't tell you if you have dealings with the Real GeeZers, because I don't 'do', let alone understand, violence."

Will looked her full in the eyes.

"I swear to you on my brother's life that any contact I have with Real GeeZers is to help me find out what happened to my brother. If you'd lost someone ..."

Bull's-eye! He knew from Cage about her search for her parents and now he watched the "hardened" journalist melt before his eyes as she scanned his face, desperate not to find a trace of a lie.

Last year, he knew, she'd believed in him. But now ...?

"OK," she said at last, biting her lip. "I'll tell you."

Yes! Will's sense of victory reminded him of his brother whooping for joy when he'd bagged a deer. He thrust the thought from his mind.

"It must be soon," Will persisted. "And we must be careful."

"Yes," said Ruby Q. "But I'm sure my editor would jump at the chance of me interviewing you. That would give us a cover."

"I don't 'do' interviews," he said stiffly. "I never have."

"Then it's time to start," she said briskly. "I'll call you when ... Oh!"

Something had distracted her. He looked over his shoulder. At a distance, Lorenzo di'Abalo was talking to the President, who was ogling a woman in a scarlet dress standing between them, her face hidden by her bob of beautiful auburn hair.

Will turned back. Behind her glasses, Ruby Q's green eyes were the size of saucers and her cheeks were drained of colour.

"Are you OK, Miss Cooper?" he said. "You look as if you've seen a ghost."

She walked straight by him and ...

He caught her before she hit the floor.

Security guards rushed to the scene; the emergency services were called. Word spread among the crowd, and panic again fluttered in the air like a startled bird.

As he held her, Will remembered what Cage had told him about the hit-and-run incident which had left her in a coma for months. It was a miracle she'd survived. Cage had been in the street, had glimpsed the driver of the white van that had hit her. He was convinced that someone at Dekaydence thought she knew too much.

A furious thought came into Will's head that if Ruby Q Cooper died, without telling him everything she knew ...

And he realised then, more than ever, how much he'd changed.

9.5 'OID TO MENACE

"This needs fixin'," said the Black Tartan guard, depositing a large metal cage covered in a black and red tartan rug on a desk where only a pair of feet was visible.

"What's up with it?" said Bodkin from behind a copy of the Dekaydence *Daily Unigraph*. "Wrong tartan bothering it?"

"You tell me, sunshine," said the guard. "Call me when it's ready to collect."

Did their red-tartan sunglasses block humour from their miserable lives? Bodkin wondered.

He carried on reading, calling to Grout, who was working at the next desk.

"You better take care of it, Grout. The Professor's up to his eyes."

Grout sighed. He was busy, too. Luckily, Bodkin had no idea what with. He carried the cage through to the laboratory and slipped off the tartan rug.

The liz'oid flung itself at the sides of the cage, hissing and trying to bite though the metal bars, even though its jaw was already broken and blood and oil dripped from its jagged metal teeth.

Grout shook his head.

"Dear me, you are in a bad way. But not to worry, we'll

have you wearing this in no time." He held up a bright pink furry collar with a tinkling bell.

The liz'oid flung itself at the cage door, spitting and gobbing between yowls.

"Put a magnet in its mouth, for gawd's sake," Bodkin shouted.

"Mmm," murmured Grout, eyeing up the wounded liz'oid. "I'll get you better, don't you worry. And I'll tell you sommat else. I'm running a personal experiment; I'm going to turn you into a vegetarian. But you're not to tell. Promise?"

He presented the liz'oid with a dish full of tomato ketchup.

The liz'oid eyed the dish suspiciously, took a sniff, turned round and farted carbon monoxide in Grout's face.

"Strike a light! If that's one of yours, mate, I should call a doctor," Bodkin shouted, gasping and waving the paper about.

10 KITCHEN CABINET

The King hadn't left the party. Instead, he'd taken the party to his private apartment. To the kitchen, to be precise, where his one guest was the chubby little designer woman who required only an endless supply of cream crackers. He'd always had a fondness for cheap women, and this Petty Masters woman was fascinating. It was also a joy to escape being patronised at every turn by the oleaginous President.

"Marvellous stuff," the King spluttered through a mouthful of party food.

Really, if this was a taste of things to come, he was glad to have accepted Lord di'Abalo's suggestion that Dekaydence take over the Royal Palace's catering contract. It'd save the Crown a fortune in staff, wages and pensions. And he'd get his favourite steamed puddings, with double helpings of custard, delivered to his private apartment on a daily basis – without the Queen's knowledge.

"Marvellous, er ... costume," said the King, eyeing the designer woman's attire.

Petty was dressed in a Victorian gentleman's black-and-white striped bathing suit, a short layered skirt made of black bin liners, a luminous yellow lifeguard's jacket, and a pair of old, heavy metal diving boots. To crown it all, electric eels weaved in and out of her black tangled hair, through which he saw lighthouse-shaped earrings flashing every few seconds.

He'd been informed that this woman was respected worldwide, and worked closely with the Company of Dekaydence. So closely that she'd been given an office within Dekaydence HQ.

"You know the worst fing ...?" she was saying, chomping on cream crackers she kept pulling from various pockets.

Apart from her south London accent, which reminded him of loose knicker elastic, the King could think of nothing.

"Worse than havin' to design a costume for someone with six arms?" she continued, spattering the King's robes with crumbs, which were brushed from the royal personage by the bewigged footman standing behind him holding the crown.

"I cannot imagine," said the King, fascinated.

Petty Masters leant forward.

"That gory Doré, he never could keep 'is hands to 'imself. Even when he was normal. Imagine what he's like wiv six hands! I've got more bruises on my bum ..."

The King roared with laughter, wondering where the law stood on filling a Royal Zoo with people such as this woman. It could be a wonderful money-spinner. Dekaydence could film and televise it worldwide ...

The King saw the monarchy's profile rise. As for the

royalties ...

He mopped his mouth. He was salivating, badly. And this time it wasn't the food.

11 FINDER'S KEEPER

In the early hours before daybreak, the Phoenix, in dark hooded clothing, walked close to the hedgerows so as not to leave impressions in the fields of wet grass. He breathed in the sweet scent of hawthorn blossom and the richness of wild violets, listening all the while. A blackbird's chirrup alerted him that it, at least, knew he was there. He trod more carefully.

He arrived at a narrow track by a coppice of willow and hazel, beyond which was a wider track and dense woodland, and crawled deep into the gorse bushes, which sought all means to find his skin. Here, he waited for dawn.

"Keep your mouths shut and your wits about you," the big man barked at the dozen yawning, belching hung-over men who were piling unsteadily into two 4x4s as light filtered, like spilt milk, into the dark sky.

He enjoyed corralling townies that couldn't tell their buttocks from a blue tit. More, he enjoyed taking their money. He could make more in a night than his annual salary. On the circuit, his reputation had spread far and wide. Why, among this lot were a few from Japan. Or was it China? Whatever, they all looked the same to him.

"I said none of that," he snarled, snatching a bottle of hooch from a man who, sensing danger in the big man's voice, decided not to argue.

The big man, with his two muzzled thick-set dogs, drove off in his jeep, slowly and without turning on the vehicle's lights. The other jeep, driven by his son, followed for a mile or so before turning off to travel across country.

By the time both vehicles arrived at the coppice, the dawn light was smudging its way through the rain clouds.

The big man's son tied the dogs to a bumper and took off their muzzles, narrowly avoiding one sinking its slavering jaw into his arm.

"If anyone comes spying, remember this is the villain," the big man informed them all, as he threw on the ground the thawing body of a fox he'd taken out of the freezer. Then he checked his gun, savouring the fact that both actions were heightening the level of excitement and keen anticipation.

He threw a shovel to his son and another to one of the men, and walked the ground, this way and that, until the radio transmitter began to beep continuously.

"Get to it," he snapped at the diggers, who started shovelling as though their lives depended on it.

He was putting on a pair of thick, heavy gloves when one of the dogs slipped its leash and tore across the clearing, growling and pawing at the ground beneath some thorny bushes. It started to bark. The big man cursed and called the animal to heel, as loud as he dared. But the dog continued to bark. The big man picked up his gun and ran across to it.

"Shut it!" he snarled, grabbing hold of the dog's collar.

He squinted into the dark bushes and, seeing nothing, dragged the dog back to the clearing, on a choking hold.

"Dad!" said the man's son, urgently, indicating the ground.

The big man released the dog and ran to release the other. He threw down his gun and thrust both arms into the hole. He tugged at something, something struggling hard, which he sweated to drag to the surface and then threw at the dogs' feet.

A cheer went up from the men as the dogs lunged at the young badger as if it were a rag doll.

As was his taunting custom, the big man lifted a pickaxe high into the air, as though aiming for the badger's head, and the men cried for him to stay his hand. They wanted to drag out what they knew would be a desperate fight for life.

A shot rang out.

Then another.

A cry came from the big man's lips, the axe fell from his hands, and he sank to his knees, watching in stunned disbelief as blood poured from each dangling arm.

"Firkin' 'ell!" cried someone, as men shouted and screamed, and jostled one another in their determination to get a place in one of the 4x4s.

Two more shots rang out and first one dog, then the other, fell dead. The badger fled into the woods.

"It's a bleedin' lunatic!" screamed someone.

The big man's son crawling towards his father stopped and scurried back to the vehicles.

One had taken off at high speed but the engine of the other had stalled. The big man's son threw himself at the door, clinging on and shouting for help as the vehicle crashed through ancient complaining gears and lurched off and away, and his voice was lost in the dense foliage.

A quiet fell on the clearing, splintered only by the low moaning of the big man.

The Phoenix emerged from the bushes and moved swiftly into the clearing. He placed a long feather of red and gold into the man's top pocket, gently patted each of the dead dogs, and scrutinised the badger's fresh trail.

The big man watched him through eyes glazed with pain and hatred, realising his career, as well as his extra-curricular activities, were at an end. He sensed the younger man despised him for what he'd done to enrage his dogs sufficiently to fight, for killing the fox, which would've left defenceless cubs alone to die. And he read the body language of the younger man to interpret that the badger's trail was clear of blood, that it had escaped uninjured. And that he'd lost out in more ways than one.

As the Phoenix disappeared into the shadows of the

woods, a long, loud howl erupted from deep within the big man's belly, unsettling birds and wildlife in the near vicinity.

A tall, bearded young man in a long white galabiyya stood at the cottage door.

"*Ahalan was' ahalan*!" said the young man in Arabic, bowing his head, his hands palmed together in greeting. "Welcome of welcomes."

"*Memnon*," the Phoenix replied with a bow. "Thank you." He followed the young man inside.

12 CELL-BUY DATE

The early morning sound of farts, belches, curses and sluice buckets in use bounced off the walls of the prison like metal balls.

But in a cell where Tallis's "Spem in Alium" was playing softly, a youngish man in a loincloth was holding a yogic plank position before a makeshift shrine.

A guard, who'd been tapping gently on the bars for some moments, cleared his throat significantly. The prisoner's concentration returned to this world in fragments like falling leaves.

"Visitor for you, sir," the guard said politely.

Randall Candelskin sank his body to the floor. Then, slowly and fluidly, he arose, bowing low to the shrine before turning to the guard. As he did so he caught sight of his lean athletic frame in a wall mirror and sighed.

"Who is it at this time of morning?" said Candelskin, checking his one-legged standing tree pose in the mirror. "Not the Archbishop again?"

The guard chuckled.

"Guv'nor's thinking of offering him the cell next to yours on a time-share basis with the Cardinal, Chief Rabbi and the Grand Ayatollah."

"Heaven forefend," said Candelskin, his pose unsettled

briefly. "There are simply not enough hours in the day for them all."

The guard was unlocking the cell door.

"Who did you say it was?" said Candelskin, rolling his top torso towards his feet, his head hanging loosely between his legs.

"I didn't," said the guard. "They want to surprise you."

"How exciting," Candelskin said unenthusiastically. "Can't be the Presbyterians, then." He unrolled his torso to standing and made to get dressed.

"No time for that, sir," the guard urged.

"But I can't possibly ..." Candelskin looked aghast at his loincloth.

"Yes, you can, sir, and must," said the guard, authoritatively, thinking of the banknote in his pocket which he wanted to remain there. "Time's of the essence."

As Candelskin entered the reception room a tall elegantly attired man turned to him and smiled, the twinkling blue-green eyes looking deep into his.

"My Lord!" Candelskin said, shocked, and blushing at his own state of undress.

"Randall, I said I would not forsake you," said Lorenzo di'Abalo.

"Yes, I got the books, thank you," said Candelskin, tartly, tossing his head, painfully aware that the prison barber had effected a cut on his silken locks which could've been executed better by a blindfolded goat.

"But I didn't visit you and that has angered you, hasn't it, Randall?"

Candelskin pursed his lips.

"After all you did for me. My right-hand man, raising my profile worldwide. You feel I've abandoned you. That I should've fought the corruption charge against you? The second one, was it? No, the third."

Candelskin sniffed, but said nothing.

"I heard you brought with you the Bible I gave you at New Year," said di'Abalo. "And I understand that the other religious tracts I sent you have been, how shall I say, a godsend."

Candelskin went to adjust his shirt cuffs and realised, too late, they weren't there.

"Although you are legally no longer in my employ, you do know that money is paid regularly into your account," said di'Abalo. "And I have ensured that your old dog and your ageing mother receive only the best of attention. Why? Because, Randall, I believe passionately your time here has been time well spent."

"What *are* you talking about?" cried Candelskin, unable to hide his anger.

Lorenzo di'Abalo smiled.

"Your readings, Randall, your kindly dealings especially with needy young inmates, as well as your meetings with the clergy of all faiths. All of it will stand you in excellent stead when you become Archbishop of Canterbury."

Candelskin's speechless jaw dropped.

"Randall, my apologies," said di'Abalo. "I'm jumping to conclusions. Perhaps your newfound faith leads you elsewhere? Do you prefer to be Cardinal Candelskin? Or Chief Rabbi Candelskin? Or, perhaps, Ayatollah Candelskin? It matters little to me. Whatever faith you embrace, I ask only that you decide it quickly."

Candelskin stared at di'Abalo in amazement.

"We could have so much fun, Randall," said di'Abalo, his eyes alive with mischief. "Like we did before."

Candelskin swallowed hard. In the few months he'd been in prison, he'd seen the light, as well as a new career path, assisting religious leaders who eagerly sought his marketing advice. After all, as an acclaimed guru, he'd helped the Prime Minister become President of the Union and launched Lorenzo di'Abalo as the acceptable face of global consumerism, which had won di'Abalo a peerage for his community work in establishing the Sticky Rock Cafés. Lord di'Abalo of Croy Polloi.

But seeing di'Abalo reminded Candelskin of a former life, a life lived on the edge. The thrill of power; the joy of being at the centre of events; the ecstasy of being courted by the rich and famous. And he recalled how much he missed decent marmalade, exclusive Maccaroni suits, annual trips to Bayreuth for Wagner's Ring cycle. All of which, and more besides, could be bought with Dekaydence money. But there was a problem.

"This is a cruel tease," he said, indignantly. "I have ten years more to serve."

Di'Abalo shook his head sadly, but Candelskin saw the twinkle in his eyes.

"Bribery, where does it get you today? Did no one tell you, Randall, there was an appeal to the Union's Court of Justice? You'll be a free man in ten days' time."

Candelskin gasped. He felt his knees go weak. Thank goodness for exercise, he thought, managing — just — not to collapse in an embarrassing heap on the floor.

"We have some time to prepare," said di'Abalo.

"How much time?" Candelskin said, suspiciously.

Di'Abalo shrugged.

"A week. Maybe more, probably less."

Candelskin's knees trembled again. So did his stomach, recalling the terrifying roller-coaster life of last-minute deadlines in di'Abalo's world. He hesitated. The loincloth began again to cause him to itch and scratch. That settled it. He simply had to be back in his Maccaroni silk underpants.

13 ABOUT FACE

Piccolo enjoyed his new life in the country. Life at home in the Midlands or on the run in London with Will meant that he'd never before experienced such comfortable, dense peace and quiet.

He found that silence enhanced a sound, as a frame can a picture. Sounds such as the old hall clock ticking during the night, sparrows tap-dancing at dawn on the wooden ledge outside his bedroom window. Lady Catgut tending her plants or talking softly to her beloved goats. Catgut playing the piano. Best of all were the sounds he made himself, composing on proper manuscript paper with a fountain pen given to him by Lady Catgut to say thank you for giving her husband a new lease of life.

Whenever there was a break in the rain Piccolo sat up in a tree, playing his beloved wooden piccolo, which, like him, had survived much.

He thought of Ruby Q Cooper, the reporter who'd interviewed him, and Rallan, the musician he'd met underground in Dekaydence, who he'd realised only later was Ruby Q's father. In the months following the destruction of the old Dekaydence HQ, when he had been living and working with the GeeZers, it'd been impossible to contact anyone. And after the musicians' "miraculous

South American plane crash escape", he imagined Rallan and Ruby Q happily reunited. They'd have forgotten all about him.

And he thought of Will. It'd been a shock to discover that his friend was a royal. More shocking to see the passionate environmentalist had become a joined-up member of the partying establishment. What would a celebrity prince want with an impoverished musician? But the crux of the matter was that Piccolo had made a pact with God: if he kept away from Will, God would keep Will safe.

One evening, after days of incessant rain, Piccolo wandered into the study.

Catgut was staring out of the window.

"Fancy a walk?" said Piccolo.

"Bored, are you?" cried Catgut, rushing across the room so swiftly Piccolo had to dodge to avoid being knocked over.

Catgut sailed past, heading for the old record player.

"Get your milk teeth into this, Young Person!" Catgut snarled as a cacophony of saucepan lids, old mobile phones ringing and cars braking blasted out, followed by a chorus of women wailing and a flock of umbrellas opening and closing.

It was the third Rush Hour symphony, one of Catgut's early works, which the composer had played incessantly in the Dekaydence prison. Piccolo knew better than to say anything when Catgut was in this mood and prayed fervently that the kindly, reformed Catgut would return soon.

But what had happened to make Catgut regress? Piccolo wondered with a rising sense of unease.

14 EYE UP

"Will! Wiiiiill!" screamed the teenage girls standing under a sea of umbrellas in the pouring rain outside the 18th-century Hawksmoor church in Spitalfields. Small cliques vied to be loudest as they jostled the press photographers, while waiting impatiently for Will to emerge from his first official royal engagement, launching the latest Sticky Rock Café.

Inside, accompanied by the President of the Union and Lord di'Abalo, Will was touring the impressive English baroque church, refurbished to include a mini-hotel and café bar with TV, film, music and wi-fi areas. He chatted with young visitors about the free accommodation, drinks, fashion and music, and the alleged "environmental projects" they were working on.

"Hard work, small-talking with strangers," di'Abalo murmured to Will, with a twinkle in his eyes, "but if I might say so, sir, you appear born to the job."

Will muttered something incomprehensible.

He'd found the engagement disturbing and depressing: the young Café workers were unnervingly cheerful and incapable of free thought, the typical brainwashed products of the White Room.

The tour complete, the President and Lord di'Abalo

emerged from the building to polite applause.

A moment later, when Will emerged, the crowd cheered and there were loud, ecstatic shrieks from the young girls. His stomach tightened but he managed a wave and a grim smile. The photographers coaxed the three men to stand this way and that, while girls bayed for their hero and tried to grab at his clothing or anatomy.

Suddenly, the barrier ropes gave way. A roar went up as a wave of determined teenagers ran forward, overwhelming the security guards on duty.

Will felt a tight grip on his arm.

"This way, sir," a royal bodyguard urged.

Will didn't hesitate. He shrugged off the man, ducked down and forced a path through a mass of umbrellas, gumboots and legs, and sprinted away.

Twice he doubled back, pausing only to check that no one was following, before stopping in a dark doorway to slip on an anorak, an old misshapen ski hat and a pair of ancient spectacles.

He stepped back on to the pavement, intent on hurrying on, when he saw two girls running towards him, waving. He could outpace them easily but the commotion they'd create ... He decided to take a chance.

"Did you see him?" one girl said breathlessly.

"Who?" Will mumbled, trying to conceal his Highland accent.

They stared at him and, for a moment, he thought all was lost.

"The Prince, of course," they wailed, exasperated. "Will. He came this way."

Will looked puzzled.

"I wonder ..." he said, screwing up his face. "There was a chap in a terrible rush. Heading that way, towards St Paul's ..."

The girls squealed and ran off in the direction he was pointing.

He watched them turn a corner before heading in the opposite direction and jumping on a bus heading for Waterloo station. Having crossed Blackfriars Bridge, he got off and continued on foot, making his way to the London Eye, where a small crowd was gathering.

Checking his watch, he paced up and down, past County Hall, to and from the steps leading up to Westminster Bridge. When he saw several school-coach parties arriving, as well as an assortment of adults and children, he went to buy a ticket and edged his way into the queue shuffling towards the Eye.

As each cabin reached its quota, the doors slid shut and it took off into the air, the next one sliding into place.

A woman pushed in front of him, scolding her children who'd rushed ahead of others to get into a cabin.

"Hey ..." Will called out.

A uniformed attendant held out a restraining arm.

"Plenty of space in the next one, sir."

"But ..."

Will cursed. He had to be in the cabin. But it was too

late now. The doors were shutting and then the cabin shuddered and flew up into the air.

But then it stopped. As did all the others.

The flight attendant had a walkie-talkie conversation with the control tower before the cabin returned to earth.

What was going on? Will puzzled.

The doors slid open.

A young man about his own age, dressed in an anorak, bobble hat and spectacles, stepped out of the cabin, sneezing uncontrollably.

"Terribly sorry," he said with difficulty between sneezes. "Someone's wearing a perilously strong perfume. I must be allergic to it."

"That's OK, sir," said the attendant. "The office'll give you a refund."

"No need," the young man protested. "I'll get into the next cabin."

"But it might happen again, sir," the flight attendant said nervously.

"Not unless someone's wearing Dekaydence 321?" the young man enquired jovially of the few remaining in the queue.

"As if that's likely, at their prices," muttered one.

"Hurry up! Else we'll all be after a refund," shouted another.

The fight attendant looked anxious.

"If you're quite certain, sir?" he said to the young man.

"We'd prefer not to have any more, er, trouble, sir."

"Absolutely. Understand." The young man grinned, a dimple forming in his stubble-covered cheek as he saluted the flight attendant and waited for the next, empty cabin to land at his feet.

Low cloud and grey mists of rain restricted the view across London and the lands beyond but the children and adults, most new to the experience, went from side to side of the glass cabin, marvelling at what they could see.

"No more perfume problems?" said Will, casually loud, staring at the view as he wandered up to the young asthmatic man with cheap home-dyed dark hair, ill-fitting spectacles and the pallor of pavement.

"No," said Cage, casually loud, as he looked out of the window.

"Any news?" said Will, lowering his voice.

"The minister is in Intensive Care, unlikely to ..." Cage spoke equally softly.

"I know that," Will interrupted impatiently. "Anything else?

"The badger baiter is on the danger list and ..."

"Good."

Will walked across the cabin. After a few moments, Cage joined him.

"It's a bad business. If people find this badger stuff is connected with us ..."

"The bastard was a gamekeeper," said Will, through

gritted teeth.

"Yes, but we can't allow the Phoenix's beliefs in animal rights to get confused with our fight to save the planet," said Cage, softly.

"I'd say fighting for the well-being of farm animals ..."

"Precisely, farm animals, but a badger is not– "

Will walked off.

Cage sighed, waiting a moment before joining him.

"Look at it this way," said Cage, "the more the Phoenix does, the more he lays himself open to getting caught and we've lost our best – no, our only – operator."

"The Phoenix is no fool," Will retorted. "OK, he's got his own agenda but if that's the only way he'll do stuff for us, it's fine by me. If you can't handle that, Cage, best you go back to pussyfooting with the GeeZers!"

"I'm not quitting the Real GeeZers," said Cage, quietly. "But remember, this could be our last chance for every living thing on this planet. We can't afford to screw up. And while we're on the subject ..."

He held out a piece of paper as a child, running across the cabin, bumped into him, causing him to drop it on the floor.

Will went to pick it up but the child was there first.

"'S'not yours, it's his!" The child admonished Will, handing the paper to Cage.

"I think you'll find that it *is* mine," said Will, snatching hold of the paper.

The child glowered at Will and skittered off.

Will cursed under his breath.

Cage hesitated to say something about Will's increasingly short fuse – there was little time for business, let alone an argument.

"That's the contact details of GeeZers who've come over to our side," he said. "I know – I knew, them all ... North escaped the raid and will advise you who else did. I told him about you—"

"What?" Will was close to exploding.

"Listen," said Cage patiently. "He knows you only as the Highlander. He has no other information, no contact details, nothing. Only now, given my predicament, he knows to take orders from you."

They were on the descent when they were aware of a hum of excitement at one end of the cabin. They wandered across.

"Oh, no," Cage muttered, as they stared down at the police patrol cars.

"When we get off this thing, I'll head for the bridge," said Will. "You go whichever way suits."

Cage nodded.

"And take this," said Will, slipping him a package. "I should've given it to you long ago."

Cage felt the gun inside the wrapping, and shook his head.

"I don't want—"

"Keep it, goddam you!" Will commanded, thrusting the bag into Cage's hand. "If you are a Real GeeZer, you'll know to use it only when appropriate."

Cage said nothing, his face looking as though a smile hadn't visited it in years.

In the chaos to get through the police cordon and the crowds of people arriving, queuing and exiting the Eye, Will slipped away unnoticed. He was on Westminster Bridge, about to board a bus, when he heard someone shouting through a megaphone. There was a gunshot. A cry. Another shot. Another cry.

For a split second, he hesitated. If it had involved Cage he'd have to go back. But if he did there was a chance someone would say they'd seen him with Cage. And then what? And what of the future for the Real GeeZers?

He leapt on to the bus, ran up to the top deck and looked back. He saw the body of a young man lying still on the ground and a posse of police running towards the bridge. Will turned up his coat collar and looked straight ahead as the next set of traffic lights turned red.

15 A SMALL MATTER OF GREAT IMPORTANCE

"How can you be sure it was your mum? You haven't seen her in nine years," said the dark-haired girl with the deep blue eyes who was sitting on the hospital bed watching Ruby Q pack her belongings into a bag.

"She visited me here at Christmas, didn't she? When I was unconscious. And left me this," Ruby Q said, stubbornly, holding up a necklace with a glass heart that reflected the colours of the rainbow.

"I don't mean to be rude, Ruby Q, but it's a bit odd, turning up like that, not leaving a message and then never contacting you again."

I keep telling you, it wasn't your mother.

"OK, I can't be sure it was her last night but I did have this weird feeling."

That was something you'd eaten.

"You passed out, Ruby Q," said Taylor, "that's why they brought you here. It's not that long since the accident. And it's not the first time you've 'seen' things."

"I don't have a head injury, if that's what you're implying," said Ruby Q, fiercely. "That was months ago and I'm better. No, I'm not better, I've recovered."

Oh, yeah! So what are the pills for?

"So what are the pills for?" Taylor nodded at a bottle

on the bedside cabinet.

"I've no idea," said Ruby Q, stuffing the bottle into her bag. "Whatever they are, I'm not taking them, 'cos I don't need them. But I'm not telling the doctors that. OK? Let's get out of here. I detest hospitals."

I'm with you on that. People die in hospitals. More frequently than we're told.

"I've got to get back to work. And you've got to let me know how Jack, the Face and the other GeeZers are doing since the split."

"Don't forget this," said Taylor, taking a plant from the cabinet and reading the attached note. "Coo! It's from Will, Prince Drop Dead Gorgeous!"

"Bye, Ruby Q," a nurse called out. "Don't forget your next appointment."

Ruby Q waved to the nurse.

"And don't think I'm coming back for that, either," she muttered to Taylor.

You're being silly, Ruby Q Cooper. What's wrong with having a check-up?

"You're being silly, Ruby Q," Taylor said. "But it's up to you. All I want to know is, d'you prefer Will to my brother, Jack? I know I would, if I were you."

You're blushing, Ruby Q Cooper. Unnecessarily, and despite all protestations, as we all know you have eyes, and spectacles, only for Jack.

"If you won't tell me how you feel about Will," said Taylor, as they walked along the hospital corridor, "tell me how you're going to find out if it was your mum you saw."

"Dekaydence organised the event, I'll ask them," said Ruby Q.

"They're not going to tell you, even if you are their star reporter," said Taylor.

"I'll have to make them tell me ... Hang on, what's that noise?" said Ruby Q.

Someone was crying.

Someone behind a door marked *Private: No Admittance*.

"When has a notice like that ever stopped us?" said Taylor.

"Quite right," said Ruby Q, and tapped on the door.

The sobbing continued.

Ruby Q was reaching for the door handle when she heard a familiar voice.

"Why, Miss Cooper. Fancy meeting up wi' you again."

She spun round.

Standing before her was a short, dumpy man, dressed in the garb of a Dekaydence Red Tartan guard, holding tight the leash of a small metal dog, a haggoid, its teeth bared for action.

"Why, Mr MacMinor, how nice to see you. And, er ... Ross."

"It's been a time and the wee devils are hard to tell apart but it's Cromarty, actually, Miss Cooper," MacMinor said jovially. "But what are you doing here?"

"Oh, we were passing and heard someone crying," Ruby Q said airily.

"Och, it's a terrible sound, is it not? It's doin' ma head in," MacMinor tutted. "I've been on duty all day, standing in for a Black Tartan who went sick, allergic to the smell of disinfectant. Can you believe it? I cannae find a nurse and wee Cromarty had to go for a walk urgently, if you get ma meaning. He's already eaten two chairs."

"Meanwhile, someone needs help," said Taylor, her hand on the door.

"No, lassie, I've got ma orders," MacMinor said firmly, blocking her way.

"But ... Yikes!" said Taylor, finding the haggoid was chewing its way through her long scarf.

"Mr MacMinor, someone in there is in trouble," said Ruby Q.

"I've been told not to go in on any account," MacMinor said hesitantly.

"What if they die? Won't you get into more trouble?" said Taylor.

MacMinor looked startled.

"I think we ought to see what's wrong," Ruby Q said gently. "Just in case."

MacMinor chewed his lip.

The crying gave way to a prolonged moan.

"We could put our heads round the door," said Ruby Q.

"Och, I cannae bear the sound of someone in pain. OK,

go in. I'll stand here and keep watch. That way I'm still doing ma job. No more, no less. But be quick!"

MacMinor opened the door and the two girls stepped inside.

The door closed behind them and they found themselves in a small room, with blinds drawn over a window.

A low moaning was coming from a seven-foot incubator, attached to a bleeping monitor on a bedside cabinet.

For a moment, neither girl moved.

"Can we trust him?" whispered Taylor, nodding to the door.

"I think so," said Ruby Q. "Anyway, Red Tartan guards usually know next to nothing about what's really going on. Come on, let's see what's wrong."

They tiptoed towards the incubator and looked inside.

Oh, my goodness!

Ruby Q felt her legs go weak.

Taylor held back a scream with her hands.

"Ohmygod, ohmygod, ohmygod!" she said, repeatedly.

Ruby Q stared at a figure inside the incubator. A middle-aged man, wires attached to his body, stared back at her, his eyes full of terror. He was clutching a large violin, as a baby might hold an oversized teddy bear. Except the violin was a regular size, and the man wasn't. He was about the size of a doll.

The door swung open.

"Hurry out!" cried MacMinor. "Doctor alert!"

"We'll help you!" Ruby Q promised the man in the incubator, grabbing the plant from Taylor and putting it on the cabinet. "Here, take this as our promise."

"Come on, Ruby Q," urged Taylor.

"Och, too late, they're here!" MacMinor's panic infected the haggoid, which began yowling. The door was slammed shut.

"Now what?" said Ruby Q.

"Quick, in here," said Taylor, pushing her into a cupboard and squeezing in beside her.

They held their breath.

"Bit like old times," whispered Taylor, thinking of previous escapades.

Ruby Q didn't answer. She was trying not to think of Jack, and how much she missed him, and focus instead on the man in the incubator, a dwarf musician with a violin. Not for the first time she wondered what Dekaydence were up to. And why. She had a strong feeling it was connected to the IoU musicians who'd been locked away in Dekaydence. Musicians who included her dad.

16 A SHRINKING VIOLENT

"This is my son," Catgut had said in a gentler moment, showing Piccolo a photograph.

"He's got your eyes and Lady C's smile," said Piccolo, following Catgut's use of the present tense, knowing full well that the young teenager had died, breaking both parents' hearts and his father's mind.

"Such a good boy," Catgut had said, and started to cry.

He'd crumpled into a chair, the crying turning to sobbing.

Piccolo had stood there. He'd never felt so helpless. No, that wasn't true. He had felt that helpless when he'd been a child, and had witnessed the murder of his father. He wished he knew what to say to Catgut, but he didn't. Neither did he know what to say to the foul-tempered Catgut who'd returned to take centre stage, forcing Piccolo and Lady Catgut to listen, *ad nauseam*, to his traffic symphonies, played *fortissimo*.

The situation was made worse by the rains, which had turned local roads into rivers or quagmires, preventing traffic, human or mechanical, getting in or out. Lady Catgut and Piccolo each worried alone about Catgut's condition, while keeping a close but discreet eye on the fragile-tempered composer.

One day Piccolo found himself in an unfamiliar part of the house. He'd climbed a back staircase and was about to step into a small hallway when he saw a reflection in a mirror in a small box room: leaning against a door lintel, making pencil marks above his head, Catgut stood, trouserless and shoeless.

He then peered at the marks and kicked the door. Swearing and nursing his foot, he began hobbling towards a sewing table when something put him on the alert. He spun round, saw Piccolo and hop-stumbled towards him, panic and anger fighting for control of his mood.

"What's going on?" Catgut hissed, brandishing his trousers.

"You tell me!" said Piccolo, taken aback.

"Don't give me that! You know all about this. That's why you're here, isn't it? They sent you to spy on me, isn't that the truth? You traitorous Young Person!"

"If you believe that, you're madder than I thought," said Piccolo, steadily.

Catgut sank his head into his trousers and howled like a wounded animal.

"I've no idea what's going on," he cried, desperately. "I know that I must take my tablets but I can't because they haven't been delivered. And I know that if I don't take my tablets, I'm done for!"

"What do you mean, 'done for'?" said Piccolo, suspicious.

"I've no idea! I can't remember!" Catgut's voice was petulant.

"OK," said Piccolo, uneasy. "How are you feeling?"

Catgut stared at him with cold, steady eyes.

"For once, and ironically, Young Person, I am in perfect health," he said, icily. "Although I *am* shrinking."

A small whimper escaped his lips.

Piccolo stared at him.

"Catgut?" Lady Catgut called from the bottom of the stairs. "Is that you, dearest, making all that noise?"

"Don't tell her," Catgut pleaded, desperation in his eyes. "Please. She's had more than enough to cope with."

"OK," said Piccolo.

"What *are* you doing?' Lady Catgut was at the top of the stairs, staring in bewilderment at her husband's state of undress.

"Er, a bit of repair work, dearest," said Catgut, trying to sound casual.

"Don't be ridiculous, Catgut. You don't know one end of a needle from another. Hand me your trousers."

Meekly, Catgut handed them over and glanced anxiously at Piccolo.

Piccolo was thinking back. Imprisoned in Dekaydence, Randall Candelskin, di'Abalo's sidekick, had told him that, when released, IoU musicians would be given a drug to ensure they'd recall nothing of their time underground.

There was something else Piccolo had learnt. A musician had died trying to escape, and at some point had been reduced to the size of a doll.

He felt a wave of sick panic. He must get help. But from where? And from whom? One person only sprang to mind: the beautiful young man who'd flitted easily between the GeeZers and Dekaydence, working as a go-between or a double agent, no one was ever sure. The young man whose well-toned body shone like a dark bronze river, whose teeth gleamed like pearls in the dark and who smelt always of apple blossom. The young man who'd found Piccolo alone and in need and had promised to take him to the Promised Land. The young man who'd saved his life and then disappeared from it: Bianco.

The problem was that no one in the GeeZers, not even the Face, knew how to contact Bianco. He always came and went as he pleased.

There was no one else.

Or was there ...?

17 DISCONNECTIONS

In a gap between the door and its frame, Ruby Q and Taylor saw two men enter their field of vision. The older man began to examine the data on the computer; the younger man stood staring into the incubator.

"'Ello, little chap," said the younger man, cheerily, tapping on the glass lid. "You're lookin' a lot better. In't that right, Herr Professor?"

The Professor didn't answer.

"You got a good colour," the young man continued, encouragingly. "And I think you've grown a bit. I reckon it'll soon be goin' 'ome time for you."

The Professor looked up, irritated.

"Grout, you talk out of the back of your bottom."

"What?" said Grout, affronted.

"That's where your brain is," said a sharp-featured young man, sidling into view.

"Bodkin," said the Professor, addressing this second young man.

"Yes, Herr Professor?" said Bodkin, snapping his heels together.

"Disconnect the wires."

"*Jawohl*, Herr Professor!" Bodkin snapped his heels again.

"But, he'll die ..." Grout spluttered.

"He will anyway." Bodkin shrugged. "In't that so, Herr Professor?"

The Professor, focussed on the data, did not reply.

"And many more little musicians will, if they don't take their medicine like wot they're told. I'n't that so, Herr Professor?"

"Get on with your work, Bodkin," said the Professor, curtly.

Bodkin proceeded to disconnect the wires between the incubator and the life-support machine, whistling tunelessly.

Grout watched in stunned silence.

Taylor held fast to Ruby Q to stop her leaping out of the cupboard.

Ruby Q, you can't do anything. You really can't. And if you did, you'd be putting Taylor's life at risk. And your own. And mine.

"Put the body into the carrier bag, Grout, and get that tartan idiot outside to carry it to the car," said the Professor.

Taylor's grip on Ruby Q remained firm, as they watched and waited until the haggoid's yowling faded into the distance then quit the cupboard and went to stand by the empty incubator.

"I'm sorry, Ruby Q, I couldn't let you go," Taylor said, softly. "It's not only the GeeZers who couldn't manage without you."

Without thinking, she picked up the plant.

Ruby Q winced.

You mustn't feel guilty because you made him a promise.

I do feel guilty. I am guilty.

How were you to know what those Dekaydence madmen would do?

I should've guessed.

Don't be silly. How could you even begin to imagine what—?

"What should we do, Ruby Q?" said Taylor. "We've witnessed a murder. But who do we tell, who can we trust? Jack says there are Dekaydence agents in the police force."

Ruby Q was staring into space.

"Ruby Q, did you hear what I said?"

Ruby Q didn't move.

"Ruby Q ...?'

Ruby Q stared at Taylor.

"They said that other musicians will die if they don't take their tablets," she said, in a small voice. "I'm trying really hard not to imagine it, but what if this is happening to my dad?"

18 FIGURE THE FUTURE

"I am not paying people for not working," the King muttered to himself as he stood in the Armageddon Conservatory, watching men hired to upgrade the monarch's security system stand under the great oaks, sheltering from another heavy shower.

The King turned to see Will wandering about, aimlessly.

"And what are we going to do with you?" the King said tetchily.

Will frowned, equally irritated. He was under increasing surveillance (for his own security, he was told), which made it difficult to pursue his research, get news of Cage, or contact North. There was also something amiss with his ad'um, which kept re-routing him to a man called Bhupi in a call centre in India, who was charming but not what he wanted. To distract himself, he was checking out the spy-ware he'd installed secretly throughout the Palace.

"You need to be occupied, my boy," said the King. "It's not healthy at your age to mope about. But you don't hunt or shoot. Thank goodness, as far as I'm aware, you don't do drugs."

Will growled inwardly but said nothing.

"You must miss the Highlands," said the King. "Your

books, your mother ..."

Will felt an involuntary pang of homesickness, and more besides.

"And my brother," he said.

"Indeed," said the King, and moved on. "How about enrolling in the army?"

"Fighting, groups, discipline – not my scene, sir."

"No, didn't think so." The King sniffed, disparagingly. "Shame, we could've got a lot of good media coverage of you fighting hither and yon on our behalf."

"More so if I was killed?"

"There is that," the King conceded. "And the family isn't exactly flush with good-looking, intelligent young men who manage to keep out of the gossip columns."

Will said nothing. The silver-framed photographs on the old gramophone showed the King's son, the Crown Prince, astride his Harley-Davidson, swigging from a bottle of champagne, and his teenage grandson, comatose at his drum kit, a handful of pretty girls and boys draped all over him.

"Ever thought of ... social work?" The King tasted the words suspiciously, as he did most foreign food. "If it wasn't for you, I'm sure our granddaughter would be on the streets. Up to God knows what."

Will smiled.

"Indigo would make an excellent sovereign, sir. She has your determination."

The King guffawed.

"If, young man, you're trying to tell me that she's as stubborn as I am, then I'll grant you that. But, overall, you know a young woman different from the one I know."

Will shrugged.

"What d'you like doing?" said the King. "I confess you leave me guessing."

Will shrugged, worrying a frown this way and that.

"Managing the estate. Since my father, and Tommo, died, I've made a number of changes. Profits are healthy and growing ..."

"Aha!" said the King, triumphantly. "Then I know just the place for you!"

Will looked quizzical.

"CCM!" the King announced proudly. "Cataract, Cyclops and Mote."

"Are they ...?" said Will.

"City accountants, taken on the job of the Chancellor and the Exchequer," said the King. "Total madness, if you ask me. But happily the wife of the top man, Cataract, is a distant cousin by marriage of the Queen. So there'll be no problem getting you in there, my boy. That'll keep you busy."

"Sounds interesting," Will lied. "Thank you, sir."

He knew that CCM counted the Company of Dekaydence among its top clients, and that the job would free him from the stranglehold of the Royal Household. But, equally, a high-flying City job would rob him of his freedom to be an effective leader of the Real GeeZers.

He'd learn much but ...

Suddenly, he felt a keen need to talk to Cage.

18.5 'OID FOR SALE

Grout was in the laboratory, chatting happily to the liz'oid and spoon-feeding it tomato ketchup, when Bodkin flung open the door.

The liz'oid hissed, its eyes narrowing as it surveyed Bodkin. It wasn't often these days, thought Grout, that he saw Bodkin on his feet, but he said nothing.

"That thing mended?" said Bodkin.

Before Grout could answer, Bodkin had picked up the cage and was walking to the door.

Strange threatening noises began to emanate from the liz'oid's throat.

"You can't barge in 'ere and steal me liz'oid!" shouted Grout, pursuing Bodkin.

"What liz'oid?" said Bodkin, looking blankly round the room. "I don't see no liz'oid. You sure you ain't imagining things, Grout? You're good at that."

Grout stood in front of the door, blocking Bodkin's exit.

"It's sick! It's not mended. It's liable to do anything."

"It don't matter what state it's in, Grout," said Bodkin, lowering his voice, and stuffing several notes into Grout's coat pocket. "It's got a new owner."

"But I don't want ..." Grout threw the money into the air.

Bang! Bang! Someone was knocking loudly on the door before it was flung open, knocking Grout to the floor.

Bodkin stepped back quickly, colliding with a chair and dropping the cage.

The liz'oid shrieked, its tail battering the metal bars as it tried to find an escape route.

"Hello, lovelies. Is it party time?" said a large young man in a Cage mask, swaying perilously while attempting to drink Dekaydence champagne from a bottle.

He tipped the mask on to the top of his head, took a long, deep swig of champagne and beamed blearily at the floor.

"Coo, is this it? My present for my girlie?"

"No, that's Grout," said Bodkin, tight-lipped. "This is your present."

He pushed the cage containing the liz'oid across the floor until it lay within reach of the young man known as Innit.

19 BODY BLOWS

Cage staggered into the graveyard next to the abandoned, waterlogged allotments. His leg hurt like hell and his body moved between burning sweats and bitter shivers. All the while, he felt the cold, metal gun in his pocket like a snake ready to strike.

He slumped down against an old yew tree, wrapped his coat about him and closed his eyes, trying to block out the memory of what'd happened. The bullet had torn through his leg, but it felt as if something deadlier had ripped into his very soul.

The next he knew he couldn't breathe.

He was dragged down, on to his back, struggling against something, someone, pressing down heavily on his face, his mouth and chest.

"Keep still, Real GeeZer!" a voice snarled into his ear.

Struggle as he might he was no match for the powerful muscles of a hefty human body pinioning him to the ground. Amidst the pain and the confusion, a thought made its way into his head: If only he'd sorted things out with his brother Jack.

"Ja—!"

A strip of tape was pressed hard on to his mouth, something flooded his nasal passages, and he passed out.

20 CROSS LINES

Piccolo realised there was someone, other than Bianco, who might be able to help him save Catgut's life. He'd had their name all along, on a screwed-up ball of paper, deep in a pocket of his jacket. And because the home phone might be bugged ...

He found waterproofs and a pair of galoshes and, without a word, went out into the darkening night and driving rain. Head down, torch in hand, he waded along the garden path to the road, moving slowly through the swirling waters and mud.

It took about 30 minutes to reach the telephone box, which was on high ground, above the waters, and was neither flooded nor broken.

The phone rang at the other end. He counted the rings. One, two, three ...

"Hello, who is this?" said a cautious but curious voice.

He recognised the flute-like voice and an image appeared instantly in his mind's eye of the wild red hair and large green eyes.

"Ruby Q Cooper, it's Piccolo Smith," he said. "We met—"

"Piccolo!" Her voice relaxed and brightened. "Where've you been? How are you? Where are you? Are you OK?"

Questions. Always questions. He didn't need them. Not now, not ever. At home, in Dekaydence, with the GeeZers, always it was questions that demanded answers, which were always wrong, which always caused trouble or beatings. He would've hung up but he couldn't forget Catgut. Or Rallan, Ruby Q's father, who was probably suffering the same fate as Catgut.

"Listen, man," he begged. "Your dad ..."

"What about my dad?" she demanded.

"Listen, will you?" he commanded. "I'm at Catgut's. He's supposed to take these Dekaydence tablets but they've run out. And with this rain, there ain't no deliveries. So now Catgut's shrinking and ... Is this happening to your dad?"

There was a muffled sound at the other end.

"I don't know." Ruby Q's voice wavered. "My father didn't get out of Dekaydence with the others. I don't know where he is. I don't know even if he's alive."

"Oh, man," said Piccolo, "I'm sorry. I ..."

"Now, you listen, Piccolo Smith," said Ruby Q. "This morning I was in a cupboard in a hospital when I saw Dekaydence men switch off the life-support system of a man in a large incubator. The man was less than a metre in height and he was holding a full-sized violin."

"Oh, my god," said Piccolo, sinking to the floor. "What are we going to do?"

"I must think. Your number's showing. I'll call you back in a few minutes."

The line went dead. Piccolo sat on his heels, rocking backwards and forwards like a baby. He'd thought he'd escaped Dekaydence. He'd thought he'd found a perfect, peaceful life, living his dream – to play and compose. He realised, not for the first time, how naïve he was. Some things you could never escape, such as love, hunger, memories. And Dekaydence.

Another thought struck him. What was Ruby Q doing in a hospital cupboard? She was an investigative reporter, he reasoned, she probably got up to all sort of things he could never imagine.

21 CLOSET STUFF

"Will you check my geography homework, please?" Will's young cousin popped her head round the door to his room, late that night, after the King had accepted, grudgingly, his excuse that a mob of girls had rattled him and sent him running.

"You should be asleep." Will continued to scan his monitor for news of Cage and for the scientific evidence. But the incident at the Eye was not reported, and more websites were blocked inexplicably.

"Oh, I cannae do that," said his cousin, wide-eyed, mocking his accent. "I've got to wait up for my dollies and wee teddy bears to come home, and they'll be clubbing till late."

He shot her a withering look.

"Here," she said, putting a piece of paper on the keyboard.

"I'm busy, Indigo," he growled, and was handing it back when he read what was written: "You are not *that* busy. And this is important."

He sat back in his chair, a flicker of a smile playing about his face. Somehow, this feisty little slip of a girl always brought a ray of sunshine into his life.

"OK," he said. "It appears you're in dire need of help."

"Bizarre," she said, leading him from the room. "That's what Grandpapa says nearly every time he sees me."

"Why the cloak-and-dagger stuff?" he asked, as they walked along the corridor to her room. "The King about to invade another poor godforsaken land?"

"One has to be careful." She spoke softly, regarding him earnestly with her large dark eyes. "And the King no longer has such powers. He told me so himself."

She opened the door to her room.

"My homework's on the desk," she said, turning on the radio.

"Do we have to have that on?" he said, irritated. "I can't abide that Hunky Doré, with or without the Studs and Sluts."

"Tough. We're keeping it on," she said, firmly.

He assumed a sulky look and crossed to the desk, casually picked up a piece of paper covered in neatly drawn parallel lines and arrows. It was a childish drawing and he was about to discard it when he saw the compass mark showing north and realised it was a detailed map of tunnels and passages.

"I think it's the washer," she said more loudly than was necessary, then led him into her dressing room, and turned on the tap.

She opened the door to a wardrobe and pushed her clothes to one side.

"There's no fur coats, no snow," she said, softly, "but

there is this."

He stepped into the wardrobe, ran his hand along the wooden back wall, found and turned a handle and stepped into a small paved area with a spiral stone staircase leading downwards.

He felt like cheering: could this be his escape route out of the Palace?

Will reckoned the network of underground tunnels, which his cousin had discovered, had been built at the same time as the Palace by forebears, when foreign air had been thick with anti-royalist revolution and there had been fear it'd blow across the Channel. The old underground rail track, he assumed, had been laid for a speedy departure. To the coast, perhaps, and a ship set to sail to friendlier shores.

That night, after much argument with his cousin, he set off alone, following a route on the map that took him into an old derelict building in Terminus Place, directly opposite Victoria Station. He checked to ensure he hadn't been followed before crossing to the public telephones to make the call.

After three rings, the phone was picked up but no word was spoken.

"Everything in the garden ..." he began nervously.

"Is rosy," said North, calm and deliberate.

"The sun has ... "

"Got his hat on," came the reply.

"So, North," said Will. "Welcome aboard."

"So, Highlander," said North. "When do we meet?"

"Never," said Will. "What we don't know, we can't divulge, should one of us be unfortunate enough to be taken."

"OK," said North. "Any orders?"

"Go for high-profilers. Keep to your patch. Harm an innocent and you're dead meat. "

"Is that what's happened to Cage?"

Will hesitated. He desperately wanted to talk to someone about Cage and North sounded genuinely concerned, but ...

"I know no one of that name," he said sharply.

"OK," said North, slowly.

There was a pause.

"What if there's an emergency?" he asked.

"You deal with it," said Will.

"If I need to contact you?"

"You can't."

"But ...?"

"I'll contact you, North. From time to time. As-when."

"Right," said North. "One more thing."

"Yes?" Will was glancing over his shoulder, eager to be finished and away.

"Watch those southern folk, Highlander. There are some with more than two faces."

"Aye, I know, I've met them already," said Will, and put down the phone.

★ ★ ★

Will was no more than a few yards into the return journey, walking along the track in a long, dark tunnel, when he heard a deep, rumbling sound coming from afar.

The noise was coming closer, getting louder, the cool breeze becoming a rush of cold wind nearly blowing him off his feet. It was too late to turn back.

His fingers found an alcove in the brick wall and he was pressing himself tight into it.

The screaming stopped, the wind dropped.

The sound of hammering echoed along the tunnel. A few firm blows, metal against metal, punctuated by long pauses.

He stepped away from the wall and, using the thin light beam from his ad'um, moved quickly and quietly towards the noise, and a pinprick of light. The hammering grew louder, the light larger.

Then he saw it: a bullet-shaped train, standing on the track, purring softly. He saw movement and flicked off his light. Peering into the gloomy light, he saw someone on the track. And that someone – a short, stocky young man – looked up suddenly to peer questioningly into the darkness where he stood. A rat scuttled by. The young man threw something, which could've been a piece of cheese, on to the track. The rat had it in a moment and was off.

The young man looked familiar but ... Will realised and shuddered. It was one of the two thugs who'd kept him imprisoned secretly in the Palace of Dekaydence, lining him up for unknown experimentation. The thin spiteful one had been Bodkin. And this one? Will racked his brains. Yes. This one was Grout.

What was he up to? Other than no good?

Grout had packed up. He climbed back on to the train, which began to move, whispering gently past him like the ghost of an old Shire horse wending its way home from market. It had no lights, no driver, no markings and the windows were smoked but, as it passed, a light in the first carriage revealed stacks of metal vats and in the second carriage a number of similar vats, labelled "Private HRH (puddings)".

The third and final carriage was quite different.

There were young passengers. At the front, two dozen or more, dressed smartly in daffodil-yellow suits, a rainbow stud on one ear. Smiling. One appearing to grin at him. Vacant-eyed. Dekaydence Guides.

At the back, there were others, dressed in black T-shirts and trousers, a uniform he recognised only too well. He saw fear in their eyes. He saw, too, the rainbow ear-studs – flashing.

He wanted to scream. Bang on the windows to warn them. Though he guessed they knew already: the flashing ear-stud meant they were heading for the White Room, ready to be turned into Dekaydence Guides.

The train must be on its way to the Palace of Dekaydence, where the White Room was, deep underground, waiting to brainwash more youngsters. And still no one knew why.

He thought that if he got on this train he'd see for himself what Ruby Q Cooper had seen in the White Room. He might find out more. He wouldn't need her any longer. If he climbed on to the back ...

He went to move, to grab a handrail at the back, but, suddenly, the train took off at speed into the darkness, disappearing before he'd taken a second breath.

He checked the time on his ad'um. Another time, he thought. He'd catch the train another time.

22 BOXED IN

Piccolo considered the telephone box: it had a foldaway seat, several umbrellas, solar lamps, a plant, a framed picture on the wall, and books among the directories. Rush matting covered the floor and a scent of honeysuckle permeated the air. He was tucking into a tin of home-made biscuits and a flask of hot coffee, deciding Lady Catgut must be involved in this cosification, when the phone rang.

"We've got only one option," said Ruby Q.

"Which is?"

"I contact Signor di'Abalo."

"You're mad." Piccolo was appalled. "He's the madman behind all this!"

"He's also the only one who can help."

"He'll send people to get Catgut! And they'll ... "

"Piccolo, Dekaydence know where he lives, they deliver his tablets."

"But di'Abalo the freakin' enemy, man! Why should he help? He'd be admitting he's guilty."

"He won't want a story getting out about a bunch of shrinking musicians."

"It won't get out. He owns most every media outlet in the world!"

"There are the illegal websites."

Piccolo snorted.

"Yeah, the moment they start up, they're closed down."

"It's not that bad, and—"

"It is here! In the past few days, Catgut's shrunk another 90 millimetres!"

"OK, so what do you suggest we do?" Ruby Q retorted, crossly.

There was a pause before Piccolo spoke.

"I don't know. I just don't know," he said flatly.

"I'll think some more and get back to you," said Ruby Q.

The line went dead and he realised he hadn't given her the house phone number. Neither had he asked more about her dad.

He was distracted by lights outside, moving towards him through the dark. He heard an engine stop and footsteps slushing towards him, slowly and steadily.

The door of the telephone box opened.

"Hello there, laddie," said a tall, lanky Red Tartan guard.

Piccolo recognised him from his time in the Dekaydence prison: MacNoodle.

Behind him, Piccolo saw a powerful machine, built like a tank. Inside he glimpsed two snattering haggoids, their metals jaws bared, their infra-red eyes staring greedily into his.

23 COSTUME DRAMA

Rumours were rife in the prison that something was up. Speculation mounted when two wardens rolled along a corridor a full-length mirror and a tall "modesty" screen from the hospital wing. But no one knew what to think when a young man, in make-up and on rollerblades, sped past, overseeing numerous trunks and boxes labelled "PM".

Naturally, the dozen or so prisoners with affluence and influence learnt what was happening and persuaded the wardens that they must join in the fun. Which was how they came to be standing outside Candelskin's cell, devouring Dekaydence drinks and delicacies, which the doubtful bloke on rollerblades was handing out with gay abandon.

"I don't usually 'do' inside jobs, so you'd better behave," Petty Masters commanded the guests as she chewed on cream crackers.

"What is that?" one asked of another, eyeing up the chubby little fashion designer who'd dressed down for the occasion, in shocking pink and orange striped pyjamas splattered with arrows and the word "Alcatraz" in lime green; orange ribbons adorned newly dyed electrocuted bright yellow hair, with earrings shaped like handcuffs, and her feet encased in heavy metal diving boots.

"She's a celebrity fashion designer, you silly william. Don't you ever watch the *Dekaydence Diary*?"

The prisoners were too busy "relishing" so only one or two noticed Candelskin emerge from behind the hospital screen, dressed in a smart grey suit with a white dog-collar shirt. He surveyed himself in the mirror, while Petty Masters tweaked the clothes and chewed on.

Only when Candelskin reappeared, in an elegant dark frock coat, a wide-brimmed black hat and a long, dark and improbable beard, did several prisoners burst out laughing. The others turned and fell silent, looking at one another, questioningly.

"Is this for the prison pantomime?" enquired one, as Candelskin did a critical twirl in front of the mirror. "Or is it a modern-dress *Shawshank Redemption*?"

The others prisoners shrugged.

"Schneek!" shrieked Petty Masters, in a sudden panic.

A prisoner dropped a glass.

"Firkin' hell!" muttered another. "That's a nuclear fallout of a voice."

"Watch out!" shouted a third, as the youth rollerbladed at speed along the corridor to fetch and return with a large box.

"God, I hate these things," Petty snarled, ripping open a large pack of cream crackers and stuffing a handful into her mouth.

From behind the screen, Candelskin coughed before

emerging in a flowing grey-blue robe, with a high round collar and stiff embroidered panel on the chest.

A roar went up from the assembly.

"Where's your lipstick, Mrs Candelskin?"

"Show us your legs!"

"No, don't, for gawd's sake!"

"I wouldn't fancy me chances if I went clubbing in that."

"Shame on your ignorance," said a handsome dark-eyed young man with a gentle voice. "It's a *labbaadeh*, the attire of a Muslim cleric. In exquisite material."

Candelskin looked at Dark Eyes and smiled. He was having so much fun dressing up in this array of beautiful clothing. Really, the Masters woman might be an irritant in the *derrière* but she did use wondrous cloth, which she cut like a dream.

Someone in the crowd lit a cigarette.

Petty ignited.

"'Ere, put that out!" she shouted, rushing to prod the smoker in the ribs. "I don't use the most expensive fabrics in the firkin' world to have them poisoned by your filthy fag fume!"

The unnerved smoker, three times her size and inside for armed robbery and GBH, hurriedly put the stub in his pocket.

Petty glared at them all.

A few giggled nervously.

Candelskin withdrew behind the screen, humming

some Wagner. He did enjoy an audience, even if it was captive. But a fracas was another matter. He must not get involved, even for Dark Eyes, who could take care of himself. Whereas a person, such as himself, in his delicate position and with his sensitive physique ...

"Schneek, pack up. I've had enough," said Petty, turning on her heel.

A groan went up as Schneek whisked away trays of mouth-watering canapés.

"Oh, miss. Don't. Please. Carry on ..." The prisoners' cries came as one.

Petty Masters spun round.

Schneek's hands hovered above the packing cases.

"Take them back to their cells!" Petty ordered the warders.

"OK, fun's over, lads. Let's be having you," said the warders.

The prisoners began to bay and growl.

"A Petty criminal," said one. "That's what I want to be when I get out."

"You'll be pushing up daisies before that day arrives," retorted a warder.

The warders removed the prisoners back to their cells.

Candelskin gave a discreet cough.

Schneek mimicked a trumpet fanfare.

A rare shaft of sunshine fell through the window on to the shrine in the cell as Candelskin stepped from behind the screen, dressed in a well-tailored white suit with a deep purple silk shirt, deep purple suede shoes, a pearl and gold crucifix at his neck. It was a message, he decided, smiling at his good-looking, still boyish reflection in the long mirror.

Suddenly, his eyes widened, his hand shot to his mouth. He glanced at his watch. Hell's teeth, he was having so much fun, he hadn't realised the time. He looked at the guard, who nodded.

Petty Masters yawned.

"So you've settled on the lost leader?" she said. "The Church of England?"

"I'll have to get back to you on that," said Candelskin, running out of the cell.

"'Ere, where he's going in such a hurry? Stop him, he's got my clothes on!" cried Petty Masters, revealing a lava flow of chewed cream crackers.

She ran into the corridor.

"Stop, thief!" she shouted.

"Bit of a problem, miss," said the guard, recalling the wad of notes in his pocket which earlier Candelskin had kindly donated to him.

"Why's that?" She regarded him crossly.

He scratched his head.

"Well, it can get confusin' in 'ere, 'cos there's quite a few takers for that title."

"Right," said Petty Masters, in a tone Schneek recognised immediately and busied himself within the cell. "How much did that CandyCreep give you?"

"I don't know what you mean," said the guard, affronted.

"In which case," said Petty Masters, through her gritted, cracker-filled teeth, "this is the time when I say to you, 'Take me to your leader.' Or else!"

The guard struggled to resist her iron grip on his elbow but, from the sympathetic look on the face of the young rollerblader, he realised it was futile.

24 TARTAN TRAP

"You're out after curfew, laddie," said MacNoodle, leaning against the open door of the telephone box.

"I was waiting for a call," mumbled Piccolo, keeping his head down, hoping the guard didn't recognise him and that Ruby Q didn't call back immediately.

"Aha. A lady friend?"

Piccolo started.

MacNoodle laughed.

"Not much else would tempt a man out on a night such as this."

"Is that why you're out?" Piccolo shifted his collar to hide his face.

MacNoodle snorted.

"You're not from round these parts, laddie, are ye?" he suggested.

"No," said Piccolo. Was his accent or skin colour in question?

"Nevertheless, you might be able to help."

"I'll try," said Piccolo.

"We're looking for the home of Sir Harrison Catgut, the composer."

Piccolo nodded, noncommittal.

"Got an urgent delivery for him," said MacNoodle. He

lowered his voice. "So urgent that they ordered us to use the Black Tartans' brand-new Mostro Marino, which means in our lingo Sea Monster. Only trouble is, the sat-nav's dodgy."

Piccolo nodded, wondering what to do. Did they really have the drugs Catgut needed? Or could this be a ruse to kidnap the composer?

MacNoodle shone a torch into the darkness.

Piccolo stared at the Mostro Marino, glistening in the rain like a great whale. It was some beast: eight thick wheels stood high off the ground; the low-slung black metal body had narrow wraparound windows.

"If you know where he lives, I'll give you a lift," said MacNoodle, touching the ad'um on his wrist, triggering the vehicle's engine into a deep, growling life.

Piccolo watched a door unfold, like a bird's wing stretching into the sky, and heard the yowling haggoids, straining at their chains and throwing themselves against the side of the vehicle, metal against metal.

"Don't bother your head about yon wee beasties," said MacNoodle, who called out to the other guard. "They're pussycats, aren't they, MacMinor?"

"They can be, MacNoodle."

The voice of the unseen guard sounded strained, as he tried to control half a ton of chain and wild metal haggoid.

"I must wait for this call," said Piccolo.

"I understand. Young love. Been there. Got the T-shirt,

love bites and war wounds," said MacNoodle. "But it goes without saying, tho' I shall anyway, that if you do help us, we won't charge you for breaking the curfew."

"What?" said Piccolo.

"In fact, it's best I tell you now, Piccolo Smith, I've a warrant for your arrest."

"On what charge?" said Piccolo, indignant. "I haven't done anything."

"You broke your contract when you ran out on the Company of Dekaydence."

"Contract?" Piccolo exploded. "You kidnapped me, remember!"

"No, I don't. And even if I did, it's of no consequence," said MacNoodle. "But if you did agree to return with us tomorrow morning to your job as a composer, your friend Catgut will get his regular delivery of drugs. As will all other IoU musicians. Here, it's all in this wee letter. When you open it, read it quick – it'll self-destruct within three minutes. Now hop in and take us to your leader, there's a good man."

Piccolo steadied himself against the wall of the phone box as stark memories of prison life underground in Dekaydence ran amok in his head, and his legs and stomach felt as if they were filling with water.

25 NO ACCOUNTING FOR TASTE

The state-of-the-art glass and titanium CCM skyscraper on the Embankment was full of light, space, modernism, sparse metal music, bright young things, and a hinted scent of jasmine and orange. Yet the thirteenth floor to which Will was directed came from a more ancient century where old furniture and staff creaked comfortably together in a deep quiet. A Rembrandt darkness, rich with red, green and mahogany, gorged on any lighting source; a smell of leather, polish and dust pervaded the air.

Will was led by an elderly frock-coated servant into a large, gloomy room stacked floor to ceiling with books, box files, papers and folders.

By the window, an elderly man sat at an ancient wooden desk, scanning a state-of-the-art monitor, which gave off the only light in the room. Behind him an old grandfather clock ticked off the seconds with a stiff impatience.

Will stood waiting, his thoughts drifting to Cage, and how much he missed his steady mind, good counsel and equable nature.

It was too dangerous to contact the Martin family but there was Ruby Q Cooper. She'd left hospital. And with her media contacts, surely she'd know something ... All he had to do was agree to the wretched interview.

He sighed, cleared his throat, and adjusted his new, uncomfortable tie.

The old man continued to study the screen and make notes. Eventually, he printed off a document and rang a bell, at which point an elderly servant entered, blotted the document and carried it out of the room on a silver tray.

The old man regarded Will unfavourably.

"Accountancy comes before anything, including gods and royalty," he said, his tone as inflexible as a dead twig.

"I understand, Mr Cataract," said Will.

"Sit," said Cataract, gesturing to a chair by the desk.

"Thank you, sir," said Will.

"Why did your great-uncle, the King, send you to us?" said Cataract. "Putting aside our tenuous family connection."

"His Majesty is keen for me to have a career."

"Army turn you down?" Cataract sneered.

Will shrugged.

"I'm not interested in playing soldiers."

"Not even for GeeZers, Real or otherwise?"

"For no one," said Will, returning the old man's steady gaze.

Cataract raised a quizzical eyebrow.

"Seems only yesterday 'most every youngster wanted to fight to save the planet. But fashion is fickle, I hear, so here you are, not interested in playing soldiers or terrorists, wanting to play at accountancy instead."

"I don't *play* at anything ... sir," Will replied, coolly.

"Good, because neither do I," Cataract lashed back, quick as a whip. "And what makes you think you'd be any good for accountancy?"

Will thought for a moment.

"I enjoy creating order from chaos."

Cataract leant forward, regarding Will intently.

"How are you at taking orders?"

"Not good."

"How about giving them?"

"Better."

Cataract tapped together his long bony fingers, reminding Will of the deadly traps poachers set on the estate.

"You know that this firm now acts as the Chancellor of the Exchequer?"

"Aye, I do." Will nodded.

"The President of the Union is a busy man, not much interested in figures. Thus, Cataract, Cyclops and Moat decide and implement all monetary and fiscal policy. For example, on tonight's news you'll learn that all police stations in London are to be sold off and all policemen, uniformed and plain clothes, are to be sacked."

Will looked startled.

"Police will be replaced by Tartan guards, contracted from the Company of Dekaydence. Should this project work, which it will regardless, as have trials in Slough,

Swindon and Sussex, it'll be introduced nationwide."

For a moment, Will did not know what to say.

"What happens to the sacked policemen and policewomen?" he blurted out.

"They retrain as Dekaydence guards. Or lose their pension rights," Cataract replied. "There is no symmetry in waste."

He mumbled something to himself, before addressing Will again.

"We shall launch the scheme throughout the Union. As and when we attain sufficient numbers, and can boast a Tartan Guard Army, we go global."

Will nodded slowly, unsure how to respond.

Cataract leant forward.

"It gets better," he said, with a dry laugh. "In phase two, we sack nurses and teachers, Union-wide, and replace them with Dekaydence operatives and cheap labour from outside the Union."

Cataract sat back in his chair, all but purring with satisfaction,

"In the right hands, accountancy is a thing of exquisite simplicity and beauty."

Will attempted a smile.

"I have a dream," pronounced Cataract. "A Museum to Accountancy. Funded by taxpayers. I envisage vast canvasses of spreadsheets and ancient bought ledgers. Rooms dedicated to Archimedes, Gauss, Newton and Riemann. Interactive VAT returns, and shrines to Piero della Francesca, Manucci and Pacioli, the fathers of double-entry bookkeeping ..."

For a moment, Cataract sat lost in his own enchantment. Then, abruptly, he snapped at Will.

"You'll have a three-month trial as my research assistant, starting Friday at six a.m. You are to think of new ways of taxing young people, who have more money than sense and are too busy to think or argue.

"Also, I want new taxes for the middle class, who have mortgages, school fees, health insurance, house extensions to pay for and can't afford the time or the money to fight us. The poor will fall by the wayside, as they do always, while the rich will pay us heavily for using our offshore facilities to enable them to ... how shall we say, cheat fairly."

Will was speechless with confusion and anger.

Cataract leant across the table, yellow teeth showing in a rictus.

"I'd work for the devil himself if he paid handsomely enough."

Will gave a quick, tight smile.

Cataract sat back.

"My grandfather's great-grandfather, Cedric Cataract, known as the Great Extractor, founded this firm with his cousins, Charles Edmund Cyclops and Morpeth Mote. My role is to maintain the firm's robust health. If you prove detrimental to that ideal, you will be dismissed instantly, no matter what your connections. Do I make myself clear?"

"Aye. Perfectly," said Will, wondering how on earth he could work for this man and come up with ideas he'd like.

26 SPORRAN AND GOMORRAH

"D'you think he recognised us as the ones who locked him up last year?" said MacMinor, anxiously.

"No," MacNoodle replied, confidently. "People his age think people our age all look alike. And what if he did recognise us? Stop fretting and strap on your water wings, MacMinor! Here we go!"

MacNoodle flicked a switch. The Mostro Marino roared into life. So did the haggoids.

"Awch, I feel seasick already," said MacMinor. "Do be careful, MacNoodle. We mustn't damage the machine."

"I've no intention of damaging it," MacNoodle retorted, touching a button, which caused the Mostro Marino to turn away from Catgut's house and head across the waterlogged fields. "Which button d'you think starts the web-wheels?"

He squinted at the control panel.

"You want to play around wi' it, don't you? That's why you told the lad we'd pick him up tomorrow instead of taking him back tonight like we were ordered."

"MacMinor, man, no one's going to argue wi' us about the terrible weather conditions."

"But I don't want to sleep in this thing. Imagine what it might do to us."

"Who said anything about sleep? No, no. I've heard there's some great wee pubs around here. We'll put on our macs, so no one will know us. And let me do all the talking, d'you hear, MacMinor?"

"Drinking and driving? That's not on." MacMinor tutted. "You'll lose your licence and your job. If nothing else, think of wee Cromarty and Ross, they depend on you."

"They're having a whale of a time. It's you spoiling things, as usual, MacMoaner. Och, I'm tryin' this button."

Instantly, both men shuddered in their seats as, with a mighty roar and a deep rumble, the Mostro's wheels transformed into powerful amphibian legs and began pacing over the waterlogged land.

"It's like it's alive," MacMinor whispered, as the yattering haggoids jumped up to look out of the windows.

"Wouldn't surprise me, given the Professor designed it. Think of those liz'oids, I don't know which is scarier — them or the Black Tartans," said MacNoodle.

"D'you know, I think this thing knows where it's going," said MacMinor.

"'Course it does, you haggis head," said MacNoodle. "I've programmed it to find a pub."

"Aye, and mebbe it's listening to everything we say," MacMinor whispered.

"You've been putting sugar instead of salt on your porridge again, haven't you, you daft oatcake?"

"Mebbe I have but you never know what goes on at Dekaydence," said MacMinor, darkly.

"Aye, that's true, and it reminds me," said MacNoodle. "MacGluten told me that there's container-loads of these Mostros down at the docks."

"Ah! Still enough people on this planet with more money than sense." MacMinor sniffed. "Mind, if we could agree a bonus for any sale we made ..."

MacNoodle feigned banging his head on the steering-wheel.

"How many times do I have to tell ye, MacMinor? Dekaydence don't do pay increases. Dekaydence make dead Aberdonian misers appear generous."

27 MOTOR MOUTH IN GEAR

It had been a long day for the presenter and film crew of the popular TV programme *Faaast Cars*, involving far more travel and retakes than was usual because of the cold, relentlessly wet weather. One by one the crew had drifted off to bed but in the bar of the small, remote inn, deep in the countryside where they were filming, the mouth of the TV presenter had many miles more to motor.

As he warmed his large corduroyed bottom at the log fire in the grate, the TV presenter fanned his great ego before an appreciative audience of drinkers.

Over the hours, even the bleary-eyed audience dwindled until eventually the publican and a couple of drenched latecomers forced themselves to stir and leave the cosy, warm hearth of the inn.

"I'll bid goodnight to you, old man, and the young'un," said the publican. "No need to lock up, we're safe here in the country."

"Old? *Moi?*" said the TV presenter, eyeing the young man sitting opposite: Mediterranean colouring; an ancient cap and half-moon glasses; and a nose that'd seen better days. "I'm scarcely out of swaddling clothes."

The barman and young man exchanged a smile.

The TV presenter, on his sixth beer and in his element, nodded encouragingly at the young man, who obviously knew his motors and much more besides.

"D'you know," the TV presenter confided, "I've driven over and destroyed more of the world's natural habitats than anyone else?"

"Really?" said the Phoenix, sounding quietly impressed.

The TV presenter nodded, smugly. He leant forward and spoke softly.

"I've heard talk that a rare hawk has moved into town. Not even the twitchers know about it."

"I heard that, too," said the Phoenix, with a knowing smile.

"The barmaid?" The TV presenter grinned broadly and made a fighting fist.

The Phoenix gave a shy shrug.

"Aha!" said the TV presenter triumphantly, with one of his honed-for-TV wicked but winning smiles. "So, will it be your car or mine?"

The Phoenix was about to say that he had no car when the TV presenter answered himself.

"Tell you what, let's make it mine. It's built for murder."

Stepping out of the pub, the TV presenter steadied himself against the pub sign he was peeing on, and then threw his keys to the Phoenix.

"You drive, ol' man," said the TV presenter.

"OK," said the Phoenix. "And don't worry, I come fully insured."

"As if I'm worried," said the TV presenter, farting. "It's a loan car."

They climbed into a brand new 4x4, and the Phoenix drove off along the road for a few miles, before turning into a field and driving across country.

The TV presenter turned on the radio and began to sing along with a song.

Welcome to Dekaydence, and its world of splendificence,
Fighting green pestilence in the youth of today.

He faltered on a note; the music carried on without him.

"This is the life," said the TV presenter, swigging from a bottle of Scotch he'd pulled from the glove compartment. "Jolly early morning japes. Reminds me of when I was a student. Shame there's no women. Want a drop?"

He offered the bottle to the Phoenix, who was slowing the car to a halt.

The TV presenter peered out of the window.

"God! I don't fancy this. Suddenly it's tipping it down."

"Get out," said the Phoenix, quiet but firm.

"Look, I know you're dead keen, old boy," said the TV presenter, slouching further into his seat. "And so am I, believe me. But let's come back tomorrow. When the weather's eased. Whaddyasay? We'll bring booze. Maybe women. My treat."

The Phoenix took a gun from his jacket.

The TV presenter was distracted.

"Hey! A Baldwin Defender Mark 3. That's a fine, rare beast. Haven't see one of those since—"

"Take off your jacket and trousers," ordered the Phoenix.

"Oh, come off it, sonny," said the TV presenter, taking a long swig from the bottle. "I'm not that way inclined. And no gun's going to persuade me otherwise."

"Take off your jacket and trousers," the Phoenix repeated. "And get out."

"Is this some Gay Pride stunt?" said the TV presenter, yawning. "Because I refused to perform at your ... God, you people are vindictive."

The TV presenter was taking another swig of Scotch when ...

A steel partition slammed into place, separating the two men and isolating the TV presenter in a box, through which poked the barrel of the Baldwin Defender.

A shot rang out.

The bottle of Scotch exploded, showering the TV presenter in thousands of glass shards.

He screamed with his eyes and mouth shut tight, aware from the warm, stinging sensation that his entire face was awash with blood, glass and alcohol. With a free hand, he felt round the box but there was no escape.

He saw the gun barrel appear again through the hole in the partition. This time aimed at his groin, an asset of which he was known to be especially proud. He was mumbling, his eyes widened in terror, as he fumbled with bloodied, shaking hands to get out of his clothes. Sweat and blood dripped from his face as the old song continued to play on the radio.

"A car will follow you and indicate, with its lights, in which direction you're to travel." The Phoenix's voice came through speakers hidden within the steel box. "Do anything foolish and you'll be shot by a marksman."

The steel plate over the passenger door lifted. The TV presenter stumbled from the car, his socks sinking into mud and the cold rain seeping through his shirt and underwear and biting into his open wounds.

"I don't understand," he managed to cry out from a corner of his mouth.

"Your children and, if we're lucky, your grandchildren will ask you the same question," said the Phoenix. "What did you do to save the planet? What did you do to ensure their future? The answer is you did nothing – except work to destroy it!"

The Phoenix drove off, skidding the tyres close to the TV presenter who was forced to throw himself out of the way. He sobbed as pain attacked almost every part of his body. The lights of a vehicle drew closer, and began flashing him.

"Get up and walk," came the command from a voice in the vehicle.

Film of the TV presenter stumbling drunk, half-naked and bloodied along a busy motorway was short but of such excellent technical quality, and amusement, that it made it on to the illegal websites that night.

Secretly, the long-time producer of *Faaast Cars* was delighted. Viewing figures were averagely good but he'd long wearied of the TV presenter's demands for outrageous pay increases, and fretted about the increasing costs, and relevance, of producing a petrol-based programme in a time of severe oil shortages. Unofficially, he'd been offered another job and he hoped the short film would persuade some TV mug looking for ratings to buy out the programme and its presenter.

As for the TV presenter himself, from his hospital bed, he tried to brag-lad his way out of the situation, saying he'd worn a pair of old holey pants on purpose to provide air-conditioning on a motorway marathon he was doing for charity, but declined to name the charity. Most fans laughed it off but a good few couldn't because the TV presenter's pants had been tainted with shit, which they realised was much like him.

The Phoenix abandoned the car and put the gloves, cap, spectacles and prosthetic nose into a brown envelope, which went into a letterbox.

He checked out the new safe house, before knocking at the back door.

"*Shalom*," said the young woman who opened the door. "Welcome to my house."

"*Shalom*," replied the Phoenix, and followed the woman into the kitchen, where a young man wearing a *yermulke*, a skull cap, sat at a table, cradling in his arms a sleeping baby.

27.5 MONEY WALKS

Bodkin was at the bar of the Tartan Brawl, a public house close to Dekaydence HQ, ordering a pineapple juice, when Innit strode in.

"I'll have champagne, mate." He slapped Bodkin on the back. "A bottle of the Dekaydence. That'll do for starters."

Bodkin's face muscles tightened.

Innit yawned, stretched and looked the other way.

Moments passed.

Finally, Bodkin dug his hand in his pocket.

"How'd the present go down?" Bodkin said, after Innit had had several glasses of champagne.

Innit snorted.

"That liz'oid is a ruddy psychopath. Doesn't know what it's doing. And it's a fussy eater. But she likes it."

"That's alright, then," said Bodkin primly. "So, what else is new?"

"MacCavity's promoted me. Put me on surveillance duty, keeping an eye on dodgy stuff."

"Inside or out of Dekaydence?"

"That'd be telling." Innit winked, and took a swig from the bottle.

Bodkin sniffed.

"What I must not tell you but I will 'cos you're me mate and you probably know already ..." Innit leant forward, lowering his voice. "I'm also trialling an Ashcan."

"An Ashcan?" said Bodkin, frowning. "You picking up old cigarette butts?"

"Sort of," Innit said with a lopsided sneer. "But it's old people I'm collecting. Taking them to and from the shops or the hospital or bingo."

Bodkin gave a derisive laugh.

"Well, it ain't promotion you got."

"'Cept we don't take 'em home," Innit continued, slowly.

"What d'you mean?" said Bodkin.

"Don't you know?" said Innit. "It's one of your Professor's ideas. And some bloke at CCM."

"No, I don't know," said Bodkin defensively. "But the Professor has been in and out of meetings with them for months. That's why me and Grout do all his work."

Bodkin hesitated.

"So, what do you do with these old people?"

"We check their new ID cards ..."

"The ones me and Grout done? Which show how much each and every one of us cost the state, and how much we pay in? We did a good job on that one."

"You sure did, Bods," said Innit.

"So what's it all about?"

"Can't you guess?" Innit said teasingly.

Bodkin looked puzzled.

"I'm driving an Ashcan, Bods. It burns the rubbish you feed into it. The stuff that's not worth anything. That's too costly to keep or maintain. Stuff that puts a financial burden on the rest of society, which includes you and me. Taxpayers. Well, you are. We can't be having that, can we, Bods?"

"Firkin' hell!" said Bodkin, and swallowed his pineapple juice in one go. "That's what must've happened to my gran."

28 IN THE SOUP

The pain in his leg hadn't woken Cage, though it was bad enough. What woke him in the early hours was guilt. For taking the gun, for using it. Guilt. And a smell of cooking that made him realise how long it'd been since he'd eaten.

He had to think and then remembered the attack in the graveyard and realised, instead of wet grass and mud, he was lying on bare boards, under a thin blanket, staring at the flickering shadows on a wall of peeling wallpaper.

He moved, and realised his hands and feet were not bound. He checked his pocket – the gun had gone.

He hauled himself up on to one elbow.

The room was small and bare, at its centre was a brazier, with a cooking pot. Beyond, slightly to one side, a hooded figure sat cross-legged, facing him.

"I owe you for taking out the bullet, Face," said Cage.

The hooded figure didn't stir.

"Mind if I have some soup?" said Cage. "It was always your speciality."

The figure sat silent and motionless.

Cage hesitated and then dragged his body across the floor, clumsily dunking a mug into the cauldron of broth. Half sitting, half lying, he sipped at the hot broth.

The hooded figure didn't move.

"So, Face, am I free to go, or what?" he said.

Abruptly, the hooded figure stood up and walked to the door.

"Ask her yourself, traitor," the figure said with undisguised disgust.

"Jack!" cried Cage, but his youngest brother had already left the room.

29 BREAKING NEWS

So, this open-plan mess of desks, terminals, people and paper is Mission Control?

Yes.

It's quiet, isn't it, above and under the hum of computers?

It's early but what did you expect?

People in green visors running about shouting, 'Hold the Front Page!'

That happens only in movies.

And we're here because we've failed to get an audience with di'Abalo about the shrinking man.

Yes. We're trying for an interview with Candelskin, to get him to ask di'Abalo. About shrinking men and much else besides.

"Why should she get to interview Randall Candelskin?" said a young man, clutching a clipboard.

"What's your problem?" said Spiky Hair, the editor of the *Daily Unigraph*.

I do think her purple hair looks great with that green leather trouser suit.

Sshh!

"She's no more than a child. With zilch experience,"

said the Clipboard.

He's got a point.

"She delivers exceedingly good copy," said a man in a smart suit.

Coo, and coming from such an eminence!

"And I don't?" snapped the Clipboard.

"And he knows Miss Cooper," said the Suit, in a measured tone.

The Clipboard snorted.

"Great! So the interview will be totally unbiased!"

"We are a Dekaydence newspaper," said the Suit.

"I don't need reminding," snorted the Clipboard.

"Anyone else got any thoughts?" Spiky Hair interrupted.

"If I might interject," said a bespectacled man in an old-fashioned suit and accent.

"Yes, Milton," said Spiky Hair.

"Rumour has it that Mr Candelskin is taking up the cloth. Perhaps Miss Cooper and I could do an interview together?"

A murmur of approval went round the room.

You and the religious affairs correspondent. What a whizz idea.

I think not. How can I discuss getting a supply of drugs urgently to Catgut with Milton present? Lovely though he is.

Point taken.

But I'll call Piccolo, tell him I'm on the case. Maybe

stop him worrying

"That's settled, then," said Spiky Hair.

The door to the editor's office was flung open and a handsome youth rushed in, waving a sheet of paper. "What is it, Jarvis?"

"It's Randall Candelskin, ma'am," said Jarvis, excitedly. "He's broken out."

"What in? Spots?" sneered the Clipboard.

"He's escaped!" Jarvis persisted. "Run away! Done a bunk!"

"How can they tell?" said Spiky Hair. "Isn't he in an open prison?"

"Sure is. En-suite facilities and a front-door key for all," said the Clipboard.

"The deputy prison governor's put out a red alert," said Jarvis, breathlessly. "The police are on to it and ..."

"And Dekaydence...?" queried Spiky Hair.

"Refusing to comment," said Jarvis.

Murmurs erupted all round the room.

"That's put paid to the interview, then," said the Clipboard, smugly. "Even if Candy is an ex-employee of Dekaydence, they won't want us touching their ex-man."

"Oh, dear," said Jarvis, crestfallen.

"Rubbish!" shouted Spiky Hair, and all eyes were on her.

"Jarvis!" she barked, rolling up her shirtsleeves. "Get the low-down from our police contact. Milton and Ruby

Q, follow whatever lead we get. Oh, and, Jarvis, just in case ..."

"Yes, ma'am?" said Jarvis, breathlessly.

"Hold the front page!"

The journalists cheered.

Yes!

30 BREAKFAST SERIAL

"He's in bed, listening to Elgar," said Lady Catgut cheerfully, as she entered the breakfast room. "Such a relief. Would you like to take him his tray?"

"Yeah," said Piccolo, staring out of the window.

"So kind of those Scottish gentlemen to deliver Catgut's tablets last night, and in such dreadful weather," said Lady Catgut, noting that Piccolo hadn't eaten a thing.

"I do wish one of you would tell me what the tablets are for," she said.

Piccolo said nothing.

"He's made you promise not to tell me, hasn't he?" said Lady Catgut.

He turned to see her departing back going into the kitchen. He hesitated to follow her. What did he know about comforting people? In fact, what did he know about people? He'd lost his only two friends, Will and Bianco. No, he was better off without people, and they without him.

The trouble was, where to go? Where to hide? The letter the Red Tartan had given him made it clear. He had to work for Dekaydence or else Catgut and the other musicians would die. Suddenly, the feeling of helplessness was replaced by one of rage. All he wanted was music, peace and quiet. All he wanted ...

Lady Catgut popped her head round the door.

"I forgot to tell you," she said, in a voice brighter than her eyes could manage. "Two of my ladies rang. They were tidying up in the phone box when the telephone rang. It was a young lady, a journalist, wanting you. Turns out they'd given her a job on their gardening magazine. Anyway, they gave her this number but she was in a hurry, off on some story. She said she'd call you later."

Hell's teeth, thought Piccolo crossly. She was probably already hammering at Lorenzo di'Abalo's door. He couldn't be bothered to phone her. It was pointless trying to stop her and, anyway, she couldn't do anything. Everything rested on *his* shoulders. And his alone.

How had he imagined he could escape Dekaydence by running away? It might've worked last year when he was only a kid but as he'd grown, the world had somehow got a lot smaller.

31 DRESSED TO KILL, OR COUNT

"You look about as happy as an old haggis," said Indigo, who was sitting beside Will in the locked but marked royal 4x4.

Will grunted. He was watching the street scenes beyond the armed but discreet outriders. An expensively dressed man walked swiftly along the street, dodging the previous night's vomit, rubbish, broken glass and torn-up paving stones, to head into a busy delicatessen, saluted by an obligatory armed guard on the doorstep. Limousines were double-parked illegally, waiting for owners to emerge from exclusive boutiques, thus avoiding any beggar or emaciated dog that hadn't yet been swept away from the doorway.

He glanced up at the stormy sky. The Eye-Spies overhead would alert Dekaydence HQ to clear the streets of the unwanted, and the next heavy downpour would wash away all trace of them. Shelter, food, water and healthcare were available for some, on ration; though naturally, only after the rich, those with official passes or right connections had had their pick.

"Don't worry, you won't feel a thing. The executioner is skilled in his work," said Indigo, reassuringly. "Trust me. Remember, I'm your cousin."

The 4x4 stopped outside a smart smoked glass-fronted store. Will and his cousin got out. A large armed man in a blue and gold frock coat saluted as he opened the door. His young cousin marched in before him as though she owned the place.

Will ran his fingers through his long, dark locks, took a deep breath, and followed her inside.

"Oh, my!" cried Indigo, as Will emerged from the changing room.

In place of his jeans and T-shirt, he was wearing a dark designer suit, a crisp white shirt and tartan tie, while the shaggy locks had been exquisitely sculpted into a tidy-wild haircut.

"What's wrong?" he said, regarding her with the dark moody eyes, which matched hers.

"Nothing," she said, clapping her hands together. "Quite the contrary. You look fantastic. I guarantee you'll be made a partner within a week."

Will grunted. He was glad that this city-slickering-up business had given his restless young cousin something to organise. As for himself, he understood that if he was to play the part, he had to look it, too. The next stage would not be so easy. He had to survive at CCM. He had to be seen as a keen, mean, cost-cutting accountant, not a rabid eco-warrior, not even a researcher for off-message facts.

He heard shouting coming from outside the store. Then sirens.

Clients in the hairdressing salon looked up in alarm. Surely to goodness their oasis wasn't under threat? Surely someone was being paid to see to that? Will went to the door but found his path blocked by the guard.

"Small fracas, sir," said the guard. "Better wait inside for a while."

Will glanced through the window.

A Black Tartan guard was hauling a handcuffed man into the back of a Dekaydence security van.

He heard a familiar voice shouting in protest and recognised the man, despite the dazzling white suit and purple shirt.

"I tell you, this is all a frightful mistake. I am a man of the cloth. Almost," the exasperated voice of Randall Candelskin boomed out.

A posse of Black Tartan guards were bundling three other people into the van – a serious-looking bespectacled elderly man carrying a notebook, a photographer and a wild, red-haired ... Ruby Q Cooper!

Will pushed the guard to one side and ran into the street.

"Stop!" he cried, as the Black Tartans slammed shut the van doors. "Where are you taking them? They're journalists, doing their job!"

Ignoring him, the Black Tartans jumped into the van and drove off at speed.

Will ran after them, shouting, until he was left standing at the side of the road.

"They were breaking the law, sir," said a voice beside him.

He turned to see his own Royal Guard, smoking, and leaning casually on the bonnet of the unmarked royal 4x4.

"What are you talking about?" Will demanded.

The guard drew a last gasp on his cigarette before discarding it.

"As of today, five people or three journalists constitute an unlawful assembly. It's a new law from your new employers, Cataract, Cyclops and Mote. It's been rushed through the courts to protect civilians' privacy throughout the Union in their everyday life. I'm surprised you didn't know about it, sir."

Will shut his eyes. What was happening in the Union? Why this obsession to control and stifle freedom of action, let alone information and thought? Was it fear? If so, wasn't everyone working together for the good of everyone on the planet? If not, shouldn't they be?

Will urged a wish to fly like an invisible arrow through the air until it reached its destination: Cage, wherever you are, contact me, for god's sake.

In the meantime, he must call Lord di'Abalo to get Ruby Q released: he'd say he'd witnessed some terrible blunder. Truth was, he needed her, free and available, at all times – to give or to extract information.

32 CAGE'D

The young woman with dark eyes and almond-coloured skin tended his wound, morning and evening. Her name was Waat and, in the better world they both desired, she told him she wanted to be a nurse. She washed him, helped him stagger outside to the bog pit, brought him food and newspapers, but was guarded in her conversations with him.

He watched her, finding balm in her gentle manner. Usually a listener, with her he found himself prattling on, trying to coax from her a smile which, when it did appear, made his heart soar.

One evening, she was changing the dressing on his leg when the door opened and a short, stocky figure in dark, well-worn trousers and grubby T-shirt marched in.

"Hello, Face, long time no see," said Cage. "Sorry, I can't get up. I—"

"You'd better get up, if you want to stay alive," said the Face, looking at him through narrowed eyes. "We're leaving. This place isn't safe any more."

Cage tried and failed to get to his feet.

Waat went to help him.

"Leave him," said the Face, quiet and but firm. "He's on his own now."

"What do you mean?" Waat demanded.

"What I said," said the Face. "We're off. He has to manage on his own."

"But ..." Waat began.

"Thanks, Face, you've done more than enough," said Cage.

"Yeah, I know. So don't think we're stopping for a traitor," the Face retorted.

"But you can't just leave him," said Waat, looking desperately between Cage and the Face. "What if—?"

"Wait downstairs," said the Face. "And remember you're not in the GeeZers to be a permanent nursemaid to traitors."

Waat hesitated, before scooping up her medical supplies.

"Here," she said to Cage, pressing a small envelope into his hand.

"What's that?" demanded The Face.

"Painkillers," said Waat, and then to Cage, "Be careful, they're very strong."

Had he imagined it, or had she given his hand a slight squeeze as she'd given him the tablets? And was there more than concern in her eyes?

She was gone, and he had to stifle an urge to call after her.

He turned to the Face, who was watching him with disdain.

"Try not to kill another policeman, GeeZer traitor," she

said, flinging on the ground his gun, a few bullets and his ad'um, which skittered across the floor.

And she was gone.

He lay back on the floor in a pool of cold sweat.

So, his worst nightmare had come true. He had killed someone: a man who was someone's son, maybe someone's father, a husband, a son, an uncle or a friend. In a moment of madness or self-preservation, he'd pulled a trigger and shattered irreparably the lives of countless people. Because of his action, children would never again play with their dad, never know him, never groan at his bad jokes. Because of him, a woman would never again feel the warmth of her man's embrace.

Maybe his victim had been a bachelor, alone in the world yet committed to his job. Prepared to give his life, as he and as Will were prepared to give their lives, but ...

He'd never once imagined that it'd come to this: that he'd fire a gun and kill. He was the go-between, the practical organiser between an ideas man and a practitioner. He was simply a bureaucrat, a listening ear, a manager. But now ...?

Suddenly, he couldn't bear to be alone with himself. Somehow, he had to get on the move. Not just to evade a police raid but more to escape the torturous thoughts creating havoc in his head.

He dragged himself to the wall, using it to lever himself upright.

He could see through the window on to the back garden.

The windows were filthy, yet he could distinguish them as they left, following a few hooded younger GeeZers – the Face, Waat and Jack. He saw Waat glance up at the window. He saw Jack take hold of her hand. He saw the looks they exchanged.

It was then Cage felt an altogether different pain from that in his body. This pain cut deeper. He'd never experienced anything like it, but he understood what it was: jealousy.

33 TATE CANDY

"Here we are, Miss Cooper," said MacMinor, bringing the Mostro Marino to a halt. "Good luck wi' your interview."

"Hang on," said Ruby Q Cooper, peering out of the window. "This can't be right. This isn't a prison, it's the Tate Modern."

"Aye, I know," said MacMinor. "But until the roads clear – and they're terrible, Miss Cooper, terrible – we can't return Mr Candelskin to Sussex. So, he has to be held here in a London prison."

"But Mr MacMinor," Ruby Q Cooper persisted, "this isn't a prison, this is the Tate Modern and it's an art gallery."

"I know that, Miss Cooper, even if I don't get out much. But they've assured us they have secure facilities. Now, reassure me you've got your special pass and then I'd best be on my way."

The beaming young guard at the Tate Modern's visitors' entrance gave Ruby Q's pass a cursory glance and waved her through.

"Where do I go?" Ruby Q enquired.

"Straight ahead. First display," the guard said brightly.

"Hang on ..." Ruby Q frowned, but the young woman had moved on to deal with a large party of visitors, with an even larger smile.

Are you thinking what I'm thinking?

Another Dekaydence Guide, in a job beyond Dekaydence?

Yes, spooky, but for the moment we've got other things to worry about.

Ruby Q looked the length of the vast Turbine Hall. In place of the old engine was a long, tall rectangular-shaped edifice. As she drew closer, she saw above the entrance seven gold and silver snakes, intertwined, and in giant letters the words: "The Seven Deadly Sins". Underneath, in slightly smaller letters, were the words: *Sponsored by Dekaydence*. She joined a small, moving queue.

Ooeer. I'm not sure I want to go in, Ruby Q.

Pull yourself together.

I've done that: it doesn't work.

Here we go. Oh, it is dark, isn't it? Ah, we go through this door and here is ... a metal cage, about 27 metres square.

Inside, lights are flashing and pretty underwear hangs from the bars. Nude, life-like mannequins, men and women, are strutting their stuff.

Yes, thank you, I can see that for myself. Just look at the TV screens showing boys and girls trafficked around the world. And see the sign by the coiled snake.

LUST, the first deadly sin. I want to move on, and it's not only 'cos we both know your underwear is falling to bits. But what's this got to do with Candelskin?

I don't know but I have a feeling we'll find out soon enough.

Look at all that! Carcasses of meat, piles of half-eaten cakes, huge cheeses, crates of beer, bottles of everything, crisps, caviar ... all rotting. And the sounds of chomping, gurgling, swilling, belching.

GLUTTONY. Look at the film clips: children worldwide starving and dying; the ill-treatment of thousands of animals bred for slaughter and the seas depleted of fish ...

Wow, this cell looks like a palace, full of gold, silver and jewels. Everything shimmers and glisters. And there's a fat banker. So, this is GREED ...

Yes, and see the film clips of poverty, even here in London, where people are robbed of their livelihoods, forced to see their families die in impoverished and incompetent hospitals. All because of the greed of others.

All the ringing phones in this "office" are unanswered. The mannequins are too busy gossiping, painting their nails or talking about last night's football or TV soap.

Meanwhile, people are dying of neglect or carelessness. This is SLOTH.

★ ★ ★

This red light is so bright. But I can see the fury on those men's faces. Agh! Blood is dripping from their mouths. What kind of creatures are they?

They're politicians, can't you tell? Watch the screens and see what their anger or pension greed bring about: war, devastation, destruction, death, financial ruin ... See how the tears of real people are red with blood. This is WRATH in tooth and claw.

Aha! Green-eyed models watching each other eagle-eyed. I know this one: it's ENVY.

Yes. Even the light in here is sour and mouldy. And now I know where Mr Candelskin will be.

This cell is full of mirrors and applause. Oh no, and Wagner. And here's Candelskin. He appears to be praying to a mirror. He hasn't seen us, or anyone else. Hardly surprising, we've reached PRIDE. Yes. Look at the screens. Politicians, prelates, today's celebrity, and captains of industry crowing their importance.

While we mere mortals queue for food, jobs and healthcare. Come on, we've got to work to do, every minute could be a millimetre lost for Cataract and the others.

"Lack of communication, that's what got me in here," Candelskin said suddenly, the interview at an end. "Countless organisations are let down by it. That, and their ghastly vending-machine tea."

And as for the coffee ...

"I don't follow," said Ruby Q.

"It's obvious," said Candelskin. "Your paper forgot about the new public disorder law: three journalists gathered together, etcetera. "

"Or the paper wasn't informed," Ruby Q interrupted.

"Granted, but still my point," said Candelskin. "Thus, in my case, the prison governor had issued me with a pass to visit this exhibition of religious art, but his office didn't log it. It's happening in every organisation, big or small."

"Even Dekaydence?" said Ruby Q, quietly.

Ouch.

Candelskin's mouth twitched.

"Out of interest," he said, "how did you get you out of prison so quickly?"

Ruby Q blushed.

"I was told it was Signor di'Abalo."

Candelskin nodded knowingly.

"So, your editor leant on him?" he asked.

"I suppose so." Ruby Q shrugged.

"Print the truth about this escapade, like the good little star reporter you are."

Ruby Q face flushed scarlet.

Don't get rattled, Ruby Q.

"Would that be the Dekaydence truth that says the IoU musicians escaped a plane crash in South America?" Ruby Q demanded. "Or the plain truth that knows the musicians were all imprisoned inside Dekaydence HQ?"

Hell's teeth, Ruby Q.

Candelskin regarded her with narrowed eyes.

"If journalists knew otherwise, why didn't they write about it?" he said, icily.

"Putting to one side the fact that most media is Dekaydence-owned," Ruby Q retorted, "you know as well as I not all journalists can be bothered with the truth."

"You surprise me," said Candelskin, sardonically.

"I doubt I can," said Ruby Q. "But try this: Sir Harrison Catgut is shrinking."

Ruddy hell!

Candelskin's eyelid flickered uncontrollably.

"Bad weather has prevented his Dekaydence medication getting through," she continued, noting Candelskin's other eyelid had begun to flicker. "He's losing height fast. I've heard you're in contact with Signor di'Abalo. Perhaps … You can't allow Catgut to shrink to death, can you, Mr Candelskin?"

Candelskin fiddled with the sleeves of his prison jacket.

"And if he's affected, there must be other musicians, too," Ruby Q continued.

Candelskin pursed his lips.

Ruby Q leant across the table.

"One of them could be my father, Mr Candelskin. Unless, of course, someone at Dekaydence has murdered him already."

Double ruddy hell! What have you gone and done?

Candelskin caught the eye of the guard, who looked away.

"My father, Rallan Cooper, is a musician," Ruby Q continued. "He was working freelance with the IoU musicians. But he didn't 'come home' with the others. Is he alive or dead? Try as I might, I can't find out. Can you, please, Mr Candelskin?"

"I'm not sure why you think I ..." Candelskin tried to rearrange his neck within his collar. "However, because it's you, I shall ... make some enquiries."

"Thank you. I'd appreciate that."

There was another long silence.

Ruby Q drew a deep breath.

"Mr Candelskin ..."

For heaven's sake, now what?

"I have one more question ..."

"Oh, dear, I'm not sure I'm up to—"

"Do you know a woman by the name of Angelica Nera?"

Ruby Q!

"No, I can honestly say I don't believe I do."

He's lying. I can tell.

"Are you sure, Mr Candelskin?" Ruby Q passed held out a photograph.

"Not allowed," said the guard, snatching it through the bars.

"Don't be silly, Jeffrey," said Candelskin, snatching it

back and studying it.

He's not saying anything but he's still lying. I can tell.

"She was at the Royal Garden Party a few days ago. With the President of the Union and Signor di'Abalo," said Ruby Q.

"Really?" said Candelskin. "And she is?"

"Someone who went missing ten years ago and hasn't been heard of since."

"Intriguing," said Candelskin, returning the photo. "But I'm sorry, I can't help on this one."

34 FAREWELL TO ALMS

Piccolo ignored Ruby Q's several calls, and warned Lady Catgut not to intervene.

He was too angry – with Dekaydence, with Catgut, with the whole wide world, including Ruby Q Cooper. They were all to blame, he'd decided. They all prevented him from composing. So, once again, he was to be harnessed to Dekaydence, composing for them. For how long this time? A lifetime? Or the lifetime of Catgut and the IoU musicians? And when they tired of him, would they shrink and kill him?

The only thing in this sorry mess that made him smile, albeit grimly, was the letter, given to him by the Red Tartans, which should've crumbled to dust and hadn't. Even the mighty Dekaydence had employees as incompetent as everywhere else in the land. And it gave him hope: a previous time, such incompetence had enabled him, and Will, to escape Dekaydence. Perhaps ...

There was a gentle knock at the bedroom door.

"Yeah," he called, unenthusiastically.

The door opened and the Catguts entered cautiously.

"I ... We were worried. You haven't eaten all morning," said Lady Catgut.

"Knowing how much you like your grub," said Catgut,

attempting humour.

"Sorry," said Piccolo. "Had a few things on my mind."

"You do look somewhat peaky, dear, are you alright?" said Lady Catgut.

"Yeah, I'm fine," Piccolo said dully. "I've got a job."

"That's wonderful!" Catgut exclaimed.

Lady Catgut looked wary.

"Yeah. " Piccolo shrugged. "But it means living in."

Lady Catgut's face crumpled.

"But you'll come and see us, won't you, old chap?" said Catgut. He went to put a reassuring arm round Lady Catgut's shoulder, and, in the circumstances, decided on her waist.

"Yeah," said Piccolo, putting his piccolo in his inside jacket pocket and reaching for a small duffel bag.

"Anyway, I'd better be going," he said awkwardly.

"You can't be off now, in this weather? And no transport?" said Catgut.

"They're waiting for me."

"Who ...?" Catgut strode to the window and squinted through the rain.

"You cannot go!" he commanded, so loudly that Lady Catgut started.

"Try and stop me!" said Piccolo, softly, staring fixedly at Catgut.

"I forbid it!" shrieked Catgut. "I will not have you do this for me."

"What are you talking about, Catgut?" cried Lady

Catgut, fearful of what she knew not. "What has Piccolo's job got to do with you?"

Piccolo's look challenged Catgut to tell the truth.

Catgut opened his mouth but no words came. He collapsed on to the bed, head in hands.

"What is it? What is going on?" said Lady Catgut. "One of you must tell me."

"I have to go," said Piccolo, slinging his bag over his shoulder.

"S'long, bossman," he said to Catgut, trying to sound upbeat. "Keep workin', and keep away from them traffic-noise pieces. They is seriously bad for yous health."

Catgut could not, would not look up.

Piccolo went up to Lady Catgut.

You's a good cook, Lady C," he said, gruffly. "And a mighty fine lady."

He reached clumsily for her hand and held it gently for a moment, and then he was gone. Out into the gale of wind and the rain.

He climbed into the Mostro Marino, the gull-winged door folding down, tucking him back into the world of Dekaydence. He shut his eyes, trying to erase the last picture he had of Catgut and his wife, at the window, clinging to one another, like abandoned children, their eyes full of tears and fear.

35 RELATIVITY

Look at this, Ruby Q! The name of the artist who created the "The Seven Deadly Sins".

I don't believe it! How can it ...?

My thoughts exactly, but let's read the name together, slowly to make sure: Lily Nera. The artist otherwise known as your aunt. And your mother's older sister.

It's amazing! Why, how didn't I know? I've been searching for her for months and here she is, right under my nose, with an exhibition at the Tate Modern.

As they say, you don't come here often.

No, but there must've been stories in the papers ...

You don't read everything that's printed. Anyway, we've work to do.

What do you mean?

I mean Auntie Lily might be staying here in London.

Wow, d'you think so?

There's a good chance. The official opening was only a few days ago.

I'll get on to the press office.

The smartly dressed young woman with bright blue eyes and neatly bobbed blonde hair approached Ruby Q, a broad beam showing a set of perfect white teeth.

"Hello, Miss Cooper, I'm from the press office. How can I help you?"

Yikes, Ruby Q. It's another Dekaydence Guide.

I know, I know.

"Hello," said Ruby Q, handing across her card. "I'm from the Dekaydence *Daily Unigraph*. I've been interviewing Mr Candelskin. I want to contact Lily Nera."

"Doesn't everyone?" The girl giggled. "The press reaction to her show has been phenomenal. But, alas, she doesn't give interviews."

"No, I don't want an interview. I want to talk to her. You see, I'm her niece."

"Gosh, how weird is that? 'Most every journalist I talk to is related to her."

"No, I really am her niece," Ruby Q insisted. "Call her. Tell her my name."

The girl smiled.

"Even if I could, I can't. She's probably at Gatwick Airport, probably boarding the plane home to Italy at this very moment. But is there anything else I can help you with?"

Where are we going in such a hurry? We'll never make the airport in time.

I know, but I need to get better reception to make a call.

There's the announcement. It's saying "A matter of urgency" ... I wonder if it'll work ... Ooer, I can hear high-

heeled footsteps approaching fast."

"Who is this?" demanded a deep, Italian-accented voice, suspiciously.

"Is this Lily Nera?" Ruby Q felt her heart attempting to exit via her throat.

"Who wants to know, and what's this matter of life and death?" The voice demanded.

It's her! It's her! It's her! Isn't it?

"I'm sorry about that," Ruby Q faltered. "I couldn't think of any other way ... You see, I'm your niece ... Your sister's daughter, your sister, Angeli—"

"Anyone can research that information. And, believe me, many have. If I had time I'd demand the police charge you for harassment. But, young lady, as I'm being called to my plane ... You should count yourself lucky."

Do something, Ruby Q, quick. You must convince her who you are before ...

"At my parents' wedding," Ruby Q interrupted, words tumbling out fast. "You bought a dreadful hat from a charity shop to cover the disaster the hairdresser ..."

There was a silence from the other end of the phone before Lily Nera spoke.

"Who are you?" she commanded.

"I'm the daughter of the musician Rallan Cooper and the actuary Angelica Nera. I am your niece, and my name is Ruby Q Cooper."

"Oh," said Lily Nera, and it crossed Ruby Q's mind that Lily Nera sounded disappointed.

"I must go," said Lily Nera. "Your number is on this screen; I'll call you when I get home."

"Please ..." said Ruby Q.

But the line had gone dead.

Oh, my, Ruby Q Cooper! You have an aunt! Well done, congratulations for remembering what Mrs Wedding Guest told you! I'd forgotten completely.

She didn't sound very pleased to hear from me, did she?

Might be a bit of a shock for her, discovering she's got a niece.

Maybe.

She'll come round. Trust me.

36 CANDY'S CRISIS

Oblivious to the late-night visitors, some recognising him and taunting him mercilessly, Candelskin was engrossed in weighing up his allegiance to his boss on earth and his boss in heaven.

He was puzzled and not a little irritated that he couldn't get a straight answer from God. So eventually he called di'Abalo to tell him of his visitor.

"Miss Cooper is indeed a troublemaker," said di'Abalo. "But troublemakers make life such fun, such a challenge, Randall."

"What about the ... er, shrinking problem? It's not going to go away."

"Being attended to."

"And the girl's father?"

"Being attended to."

"And you are happy with my religious decision?"

"Oh, yes," said di'Abalo.

"And there is time to make the necessary adjustments?"

"Indeed."

"And complete them?" Candelskin's anxiety was palpable.

"Trust me, dear boy."

Candelskin sighed. A thought occurred to him.

"The girl was also enquiring about Miss Nera."

"Randall, at the next Olympic Games, I shall enter you for the worry marathon."

The line went dead.

He sat on the edge of his bed.

What was this interest in Angelica Nera? What could she do that he couldn't? Apart from add up. Oh, and speak with an accent that had grown men such as di'Abalo and the President drooling at her feet?

He peered through the mock cell window, looking angrily towards a mock sky. It was infuriating. For some reason God was refusing to make Himself apparent unto him. What was His problem? Modern art?

Candelskin scratched furiously at the rash on his groin, caused by the constant chafing of the rough fabric of his prison trousers. He imagined himself back in his exclusive Maccaroni silk underpants. Not long to go, thank God. No, he corrected himself, thank di'Abalo.

36.5 FAREWELL TO ALL THAT

"There's one of those new free taxis for us golden oldies," shouted one of the four elderly folk on the pavement outside the Bridge Club in Chelsea where they'd all been playing. "We have to try it, darlings – we can't possibly walk home in this weather."

From under their umbrellas, the other three senior citizens squinted in the direction she was waving.

"Botheration," said one old gent. "Call of nature. Don't wait for me."

"Are you sure, Cedric?" said his female bridge companion. "We could wait."

"'Course we can wait, mate," Innit shouted as he pulled to a halt the large claret-red taxi-coach, with its flamboyant gold letter D on the sides, which matched his gold-braided claret suit, tie and hat.

"No, no," said Cataract, coughing embarrassedly. "I might be some time."

His companions nodded sympathetically. They understood that problem only too well.

Cataract waved and hurried to the door of the club.

"Come along, girls," said the other old gent, patting them on the behind. "Move your tail ends."

The two ladies hooted with laughter.

"Oh, Whitstable, you are sooo naughty," said one.

"ID cards, please, ladies and sir," said Innit.

"Is it true you take each of us to our doorstep?" asked one lady, as the driver passed a wand over her card.

"Yes, and if you're really good, we carry you indoors." Innit guffawed as he wanded the cards of the other two. "Wait by the door and when the light above it flashes, step inside and you'll find I've put you in first class with a few others."

"Ooo, what delicious fun!" the woman chirruped, as she stared at the light.

Slipping a mask over his mouth, Innit started the engine.

The taxi-coach purred into life and set off down the road.

Cataract stepped out of the doorway of the club and watched the taxi-coach travel along the road towards Sloane Square as a huge plume of black smoke shot out of the exhaust in the roof. He turned up his collar against the rain, and walked off in the opposite direction.

It was a shame about the girls, though, given their recent dire financial circumstances, probably for the best, he thought. But Whitstable had it coming. The bounder had persuaded lots of people, the girls included, to invest in his Tumbleweed Trust Fund and lots of people, including the girls, had lost their entire savings. Cataract hadn't lost a cent. But he wasn't one to forget, let alone forgive, someone who cheated him out of anything, or

GREEN FIRE

made an attempt to do so. Happily, Signor di'Abalo had
understood fully and introduced him to Professor Zola,
head of Dekaydence's research and development.

166

37 NAKED TRUTHS

Two paparazzi stood on the balcony in the pouring rain at Bern Airport, watching a plane taxi into a bay. They'd been tipped off by an impeccable source that the chief executive of 24/7, the world's biggest supermarket chain, was arriving on a late-night flight from London on a private trip.

The two photographers had raced through the night from different parts of the Union to the tiny Swiss airport. They weren't there to photograph the chief executive for her beauty, or because she was seen rarely in public. Not because 24/7 megamarkets were going global, or because 24/7 mini-stores were springing up in every high street — despite a worldwide recession.

No, no. Rumour had it that the happily married woman had an insatiable appetite for young men. As yet, there was no photographic evidence: the tip-off implied there soon could be. And in these hard times, freelance photographers hungered for such a lucrative tip-off.

But the woman didn't appear, neither did anyone vaguely resembling her. Eventually, a few passengers left the plane. Then the crew. Then nothing happened.

The photographers waited for an hour or so, just in case, pacing up and down to keep warm and awake. But no other plane arrived, left or was expected.

"To hell with this," one photographer said abruptly, packing away his cameras as baggage handlers, ending a wildcat strike for overtime payments, came out to unload the hold. "I haven't come to film suitcases and mailboxes."

The other shrugged.

"It was a long shot. She's always changing her plans. That's probably why we're the only two here. That and the weather."

"Yeah," said the first, swinging a heavy kitbag on to his shoulder. "I'm going to have words with my contact. It was a duff lead. More fool us."

The other shrugged, noncommittal.

"You not coming?" said the first, suddenly suspicious that the other knew something he didn't.

"I've got a job later, a couple of hours from here. I thought I'd use my time getting some nice, arty, atmospheric dawn-sky shots for my library."

"Yeah, well, mind you don't shrink in the rain," said the first, realising how damp his clothes were and that, in any event, he was too tired to change his mind.

The other chuckled.

"See you around," said the first photographer, walking off into the dark, wet night, uneasy to leave but overwhelmed with a longing for a hot bath and a warm bed.

"See you around," muttered the second, already

distracted by shots demanding to be captured instantly.

He was absorbed by how the rain teased light, dark and drama into the dreary scene. He was focussing the camera on the baggage handlers when he heard one of them, then another, cry out. He panned the scene, then zoomed out.

Men were running across the tarmac towards the plane. He zoomed in. They were staring into the hold. He found the subject – a large metal cage. Nothing unusual, but as he zoomed in further he saw attached to the bars of the cage was a placard with the 24/7 logo. He allowed the lens to probe further.

Inside the cage, sitting on top of a pile of vegetation, was an unclothed plastic mannequin. A split second later, he realised it wasn't a mannequin, it was a real, live woman who was screaming orders as she tried to cover her body with handfuls of lettuce, asparagus and purple sprouting broccoli.

The photographer's camera caught the fury in the woman's eyes. As he panned out, he came close to dropping the camera. He steadied his hands, ignored the tirade of questions in his head, and pressed the button over and over again. He grabbed another camera as the woman banged on the bars, shrieking at the baggage handlers. No one moved towards her. She was one wild woman.

It was disappointing that there was no man at her side. And certainly she didn't look her best, despite the trademark heavy golden chain round her neck. But she was naked. And he soothed himself that the nude shots of her *in radicchio* might make him a bob or two on the illegal websites.

It was only later, much later that he realised the significance of the words on the placard: "Must every vegetable travel 600 miles ... or more?"

That night "Naked Truth 24/7" pictures were splashed over all the illegal websites, with the news that the naked chief executive of 24/7 had flown some 966 km, or 600 miles – the same distance as the flight of an average vegetable within the UK alone before ever it reached a consumer's plate. And for years, added the blogs, she'd had the naked nerve to be economical with the truth about that fact, as well as many others.

The story made it into the nationals, most blatantly the Dekaydence media. TV, print and radio. Some blogs hinted that was because there was no love lost between the woman from 24/7 and Lorenzo di'Abalo. Though no one knew why.

The Phoenix returned to the unoccupied safe flat in London. He threw off his dinner jacket, undid his shirt, which he threw in the bin, and had a long shower to rid himself of the woman's lipstick and singular perfume.

Emerging with a towel around him, he took an apple from a bowl, poured himself a drink, slumped into a large leather chair, and sent several coded texts from his ad'um.

He'd heard nothing from Cage. Or Will. Or anyone.

Not that he cared.

He walked to the window, watching the city lights flicker in the driving rain.

For the moment, he was content with the way things were working. He had free rein. And with research it was easy to combine his agenda with that of the Real GeeZers. Very soon, though, it'd be time to quit. He had a score to settle. Two deaths to avenge, which he wanted to do in kind ...

He felt a sharp sting in his neck.

His mind ordered his hand to rip out the dart he knew it to be. He also knew it was too late, that within the next few seconds his body and his brain would have no strength. He wondered if it was the end as he tried to turn to confront his attacker and saw instead the ceiling of the room slide about his head as he collapsed on to the floor.

38 WILL WONDERS

Will had begun to sleep badly. Dreaming of familiar faces he couldn't name. Of scaly creatures leaping from ledgers to consume wallets and purses, and computer bugs devouring savings from people's bank accounts.

He'd get up in the night, exhausted, to trawl through the few remaining illegal ISPs. What was going on? he wondered. He was searching for scientists who spoke out against global warming. Those who condemned the alarmists who proclaimed that the end of the world was nigh, which they said wasn't true. Their research showed that climate change was an inevitable product of the sun's cycle of heating and cooling, that man's production of CO_2 was negligible in itself and, in any event, that carbon emissions had no significant influence on global warming. Their research argued that the focus should be on man's damaging impact on the environment, and that saving the rain forests was among the top priorities.

Why were these voices being blocked? Why were these eminent scientists being sidelined, their research funds cut dramatically? Why did people want them silenced? Who were these people frightened of free speech? And why?

Yet again it must involve money, he concluded. Power

and money. Maybe CCM was the best place to find out more.

That evening he left the Royal Palace and walked to the underground to Holborn, savouring the fact that once again he'd given his security guard the slip.

He studied his fellow travellers on the busy train, most semi-comatose with tiredness, work and/or alcohol. He sensed their irritation, their anger and frustration with their lot. It'd take but a match to incite them to ... well, anything. Protest on the streets? Become Real GeeZers, to fight, to surrender their lives to save the planet? Or to work for other causes – to stop child abuse, to put an end to famine, to command governments to intervene where genocide was taking place ... If only he knew what he must do to light that match.

On his way through the main doors at CCM he tore up his notes and decided to go for broke.

"My, but you *have* smartened up," said Cataract, as Will sat down opposite him. "I deem your appearance justifies an additional 25 per cent our clients' bills."

Will kept his smile at shallow, realising the old man wasn't joking.

"We might get away with 33 per cent."

"Suffer the clients, Cedric. Do remember us poor wretches."

Will froze, recognising the voice coming from the shadows of the room.

"That goes without saying, My Lord," said Cataract, his yellow teeth showing in a rictus. "Shall we proceed?"

A tall, languid figure came into vision. Lorenzo di'Abalo! Did that mean he was under suspicion already? thought Will.

"If His Royal Highness has no objection?" said di'Abalo, his voice reflecting the music of Eire and Italy. "I had a meeting here with Cedric and he mentioned you'd be coming with a view to working here."

"No problem," Will said, curt but polite.

He cleared his throat and stood up.

"Whether or not you believe in climate change or sunspots or a new Ice Age, there's no doubt that our world is changing, in many ways, on many levels. What matters is how CCM rides these changes, which may or may not come to nought, and how CCM can benefit financially from not one but all sides."

Cataract sat impassive. Di'Abalo listened with a wry smile.

"The basic law in accountancy is balancing the books," Will continued. "In practice, this means achieving a balance in favour of CCM, which, I believe, is best achieved, for now, by hitching a lift on the climate change bandwagon."

"Really?" said Cataract, noncommittal.

"Aye," Will replied quickly. "In fact, I think CCM should act more like Dekaydence."

"Bravo!" cried di'Abalo, with a roar of laughter.

Cataract frowned

"I thought of a conference, funded jointly perhaps by Dekaydence and CCM, a conference entitled 'Carbon: the new Cash Cow' ...

"It's aimed at investors, investment bankers and compliance buyers. And it shows how to profit from the growing number of carbon-related investment opportunities, which market research shows grew from $10 billion to $34 billion in one year, a few years back, and which is reckoned to soon be worth well in excess of $100,000 billion.

"So, I think CCM must agitate for laws that form, govern and regulate a carbon market. If we cap greenhouse gas emissions, the right to emit these gases becomes a commodity, which can be traded. We pacify the green lobby, and as law-maker, enforcer and collector of taxes, we – that is CCM – make money at every turn."

A silence engulfed the room.

Will saw di'Abalo glance at Cataract with an amused air.

Cataract pursed his lips, and regarded Will suspiciously.

"Oddly enough, Lord di'Abalo and I had exactly the same thoughts. A conference is planned for a few months hence, though nothing has yet been announced. Our title, however, is slightly less amusing: 'Carbon – the Essential Financial Future' ... If you wouldn't mind, please take your telephone call outside ..."

Will was scrambling for his ad'um, convinced he'd switched off already.

"Apologies," he said, as he silenced it. "However, if I may add—"

"No, sir, that's enough, thank you," said Cataract. "Please, wait outside."

Will left the room.

He was anxious. He felt he'd been dismissed like a naughty child. Had he gone too far?

He slumped into a chair outside Cataract's office. Edgy and distracted, he checked his ad'um. It was ...

He felt someone was watching him, and he looked up.

A young girl, sitting behind a desk where a few days before an older woman had sat, was regarding him coyly from under her eyelashes.

He frowned. She looked familiar. Where had he met her, and when?

He knew the answer the moment she pushed her hair from her face and he saw the rainbow stud in her ear. She was a mindless Dekaydence Guide from the Palace of Dekaydence, programmed to smile, even when there was nothing to smile about.

What was she doing here?

She pushed a box of Dekaydence chocolates towards him across the desk.

He held up his hand to decline.

"It'd be rude not to take one." She smiled. "Tommo would be so disappointed."

He felt his blood go cold, and then hot, hearing his brother's name.

"What are you talking about? What do you know about Tommo?" he demanded, grabbing tight hold of her wrist, his eyes fierce and close to hers.

She squealed as the door opened and Lorenzo di'Abalo walked in.

Will released the girl's arm and stood up.

"Excuse me, sir," said di'Abalo, an eyebrow raised at the scene before him. "Knowing your campaigns against violence, I thought you'd be most anxious to hear some news breaking on the wires. The young man who calls himself the Phoenix has been taken."

Will held himself tight.

"Alive or dead?" he asked, as calmly as he could.

"D'you know, it really wasn't clear," said di'Abalo, reflecting.

39 MUSICAL DISHARMONY

Grout was good at fixing things, long before he realised he couldn't fix his parents' relationship with one another, let alone with him. He fixed TV sets, fridges and washing machines. When he went to school and discovered computers, it felt like Christmas. Or, rather, how he imagined a family Christmas could be.

He was 15 when he decided he'd had enough of his parents' arguments. The night he walked out, they were too busy arguing to notice. And he felt no need to tell them.

He'd intended calling on a boy he knew vaguely who lived nearby to ask for a bed for the night. He'd have been disappointed but, before that could happen, he was picked up by the Black Tartans and taken to Dekaydence HQ. When he mended the mainframe computer in Reception, which no one else was able to do, he was extracted from the night's bunch of kidnapped kids and put to work with the Professor and his assistant, Bodkin.

The work absorbed and tantalised him and, at first, the Professor's icy manner and Bodkin's spiteful jibes didn't bother him. Then, when the plug was pulled on the musician ... Until that moment, Grout hadn't understood the difference between right and wrong. And when he did, he didn't know what to do. He immersed himself in work but found bits of his mind fretting and questioning the other bits.

Grout was thrilled when the Professor told him he was to work on a new music project, but when he was introduced to the man he was to help, he recalled how he'd treated him when he'd been imprisoned underground in the old Dekaydence HQ with the other musicians. And he felt ashamed.

The man never made mention of it. He worked diligently and in silence, and would grin and give a thumbs-up sign for Grout to start work.

There was a problem: Grout loved his music but the noise this man created ... Well, it wasn't Shed Music, which the previous year had set alight not only Grout but people all over the world. This stuff, thought Grout, would be lucky to raise a yawn. But he kept quiet. That's what you did in Dekaydence, lest you got yourself into trouble. Grout knew that saying anything would get this man into trouble.

The situation worried him: what would be the man's fate when the bosses heard this dreadful music? And what could he do to help him?

After Piccolo's medical tests, MacMinor went to the Professor's office where Bodkin sat, feet on the desk, head behind a newspaper. MacMinor tried to explain Piccolo's deep depression.

"Just take him to the Music Lab." Bodkin yawned from behind the paper.

"But he ain't quite right in the head, Mr Bodkin," said MacMinor, anxiously.

"What d'you expect? He's a musician," said Bodkin.

"Aye, I know, but he's so out of it. He's ..."

Bodkin lowered the newspaper.

"Are you asking to be out of your job and your pension?" he said, coldly.

"No, sir!" MacMinor saluted, unnecessarily, and quit the room.

When he entered the Music Lab and saw Grout at the control panel, Piccolo's spirits sank further. His memories of Grout were not good.

Someone coughed. Piccolo looked to the far end of the room and saw a large bear-like figure seated at a desk, head bent over his work.

"Rallan!"

Piccolo could scarcely believe it. This was the man who'd saved his sanity, if not his very life, when they'd been holed up together underground. This was Ruby Q Cooper's missing dad.

The man carried on working.

"RALLAN!" Piccolo shouted, and couldn't understand why the man didn't respond.

He moved to cross the room. Grout grabbed his arm.

"He can't hear you!" said Grout.

"What are you talking about?" said Piccolo, shrugging him off, and then, suspicions mounting, "What have you done to him?"

"Nothing, honestly," said Grout, blushing. "It happened after you escaped."

"What are you talking about? What's happened? Is he shrinking, too?"

Piccolo imagined Rallan, like Catgut, dependent for ever on Dekaydence drugs to keep him alive and the right size.

"No, he ain't shrinking," said Grout, nervously. "Thing is, he was hiding when they came to take everyone out of the old Dekaydence HQ. They found him later, unconscious. But in the explosion ..."

"What is wrong with him?" Piccolo repeated angrily.

"It must've been the noise," Grout trembled. "Of the explosion. The thing is, he's gone deaf."

Piccolo tried to imagine life without hearing music, and knew he'd rather be dead.

At that moment, Rallan turned and saw him.

"Piccolo!" The big, bearded musician stood up abruptly, sending his chair flying, and ran across the room to engulf Piccolo in an embrace.

"Thank God you're safe!" he said, beaming, as tears clouded his spectacles.

"You too, man!" Piccolo mumbled into Rallan's old ill-fitting tweed jacket.

Grout retreated quietly to the control room.

"Can you hear me?" Piccolo mouthed the words and touched his own ear.

"Yes, yes." Rallan shrugged dismissively. "Just speak clearly and loudly."

They sat down at the desk and pumped one another for news. Piccolo explained about Catgut, his shrinking and the drugs crisis. Rallan told his story.

"The night the old Dekaydence HQ was blown up, I saw Bodkin adding something to the water. I didn't touch it. I tried to stop the others but ... It all happened so fast. The guards were on edge and in a rush. I managed to slip away and hide in a tunnel. A big one, of course." He stared ruefully at his large stomach.

"Everyone was hustled out. I thought I'd be safer staying put. But I was knocked unconscious in the explosion. A policeman found me in the rubble, called the guards who brought me here. And what do you do with such a large bit of evidence? Then this project came up."

He shook his head.

Grout watched them from behind the glass. He could hear them, too, in a conversation that was quite unlike anything that passed between him and Bodkin, or him and the Professor, or indeed anyone he'd known. He frowned. He'd think about it later. For now, time was running out.

He tapped the microphone and gave an indiscreet cough.

Rallan turned and waved.

"Apologies, Mr Grout," he spoke into the mike, and

turned to Piccolo. "Best we crack on. Like the old days, we've got less than a week to produce the first album for Hunky Doré and the Studs and Sluts."

Rallan leant closer to Piccolo.

"I must get a message to my daughter, Ruby Q Cooper," he said. "I must tell her I'm alive and well. Even if they never release me, I can't bear her living without knowing that I'm here and OK."

Piccolo nodded but said nothing. He hadn't wanted to upset Rallan by talking about his daughter. And he was feeling guilty at not responding to her calls.

He also knew there was no chance of getting a message to her when neither of them were allowed out, or permitted to make or receive calls.

Grout was thinking the same thing.

BREAKING NEWS

Years ago, when I was very young, some youths captured our cat. They put a firework up its backside and lit the touch-paper. The cat was found, clinging to life but so horribly injured that it was put to sleep. The police could do nothing. Not enough evidence. Even though we all knew who did it.

Time passed. I'm not tall but I'm strong. I work out regularly in the gym. As do my mates. I've known them since schooldays, like the cat murderers.

The cat murderers drank themselves into a stupor routinely on a Friday night, at the home of one or another. That Friday, there were six of us watching and waiting. No one else was in the house, just the three of them. They didn't have many friends. Not surprising. We waited some more and went in, masked and ready.

Somehow, better not ask how, we separated them. Put them in three separate rooms and turned up the music. We blindfolded them and trussed them up so they were lying face down. We rolled down their trousers and said we were sticking fireworks up their arses. Threatened to set light to them. Oh, did they holler. Struggle. Beg. Offered us money. Anything. One called out for his mum. We gagged them and before we left we set fire to the stuff

LIVE FROM AN ILLEGAL INTERNET SERVICE PROVIDER

in the rear ends. They certainly had sore bums but they didn't explode into pieces.

No one came after us. Lack of evidence.

But when the police discovered what was stuck in their bums, word got out pretty quick. Three red and gold feathers.

The Phoenix lives

40 CAGE DREAMS

Cage had found a boarded-up store, with a supply of water and a few tins of food. The ad'um still refused to work and, not for the first time, he cursed the Face's temper.

He was flicking through a pile of newspapers under the letterbox when he discovered the "Naked Truth 24/7" story. He was sweating and shivering with fever but, for the first time in weeks, he laughed, deepening the dimple in his left cheek.

He'd no idea how the Phoenix had pulled it off but he revelled in the news that the story had gone global within 48 hours. It wouldn't win the war. Neither would it change everyone's behaviour towards the planet, animals or one another. But if it made people think, a few influential people ... to take responsibility for their lifestyle, to rein in their greed... . And if governments and business did likewise, maybe climate change could be halted, the planet could be saved.

It'd be too late for many, including Will's brother Tommo. But there were millions more, people and species, that could still be saved. If only ...

Cage allowed himself a daydream.

It was a summer's day. He was back at home. Mum

was in the kitchen; Dad was plying everyone with Mum's home-made fruit punch. Meryl, his elder sister, had driven up from Brighton with her two dogs in her hydrogen-operated lorry-home and was setting up her latest metal sculpture in the garden. Like old times, middle brother Kane, on leave from New York, was sunning himself in a deckchair. Taylor was organising him and Jack to carry trays of Mum's home-made food into the garden, both young men having settled their differences, because now there was no need for conflict.

A noise outside the room alerted Cage to reality.

He cursed himself. Was he getting lazy or simply tired of living alone and on the run? Whatever, he prepared himself once more for fight or flight.

Cautiously, he slid along the wall towards the broken window and found himself breathing in an unseasonable scent of apple blossom.

He scanned the small balcony. It was empty but for an exceptionally large black bird perched on the balustrade. Such a bird, he recalled hazily, had hovered near Piccolo's unconscious body when they'd discovered him close to the GeeZer camp.

"Sorry, old chap, he's with Catgut," Cage murmured, for a reason he couldn't fathom, before he sank slowly to the floor, into a deep fever of pain.

Cage dreamt he was wrapped in soft yet powerful warmth. That he was lifted up with immense care and carried effortlessly out of the room and across London. He heard the rain, but felt only warm sun on his body. Eventually, he dreamt he was laid gently on a wooden floor. He heard creaking sounds and felt a rocking movement, and imagined he was on a boat sailing home.

41 HOME TRUTHS

Who's making that dreadful noise?

Don't be pompous. It's Hunky Doré.

The barmy one with six black and tan arms, who's rather delicious?

Depends on your taste. He's done this great track. The album with the Studs and Sluts is out next week, to coincide with the launch of the Dekaydence mall.

But despite the music, you seem depressed.

You've noticed how much I sigh and stare out of the window.

Yes, but why? You've got an auntie.

Who sounded as though she wished I didn't exist.

It's early days.

Maybe, but there's no news of my dad or my mum. And neither Will nor Piccolo is talking to me ...

Could it be the bright pink dress? The lime-green tights? Your hair ...?

There's nothing wrong with my hair! I like the way it does its own thing, OK? And this charity-shop clothing is the only stuff I can afford. And it's different.

You can say that again. But on the bright side, the editor likes your interview.

Not sure Mr Candelskin will.

He'll be too busy admiring his own photograph to notice.

Thank goodness the great Lars Sparks agreed to do the photo-shoot. I do hope the *Unigraph* photographer is OK, and Milton. But why did the Black Tartans have to beat up two elderly journalists who couldn't fight back?

Because they're not allowed to beat up the Red Tartans? I dunno. What else can the poor lambs do for fun when they've got brains below sea level?

Sounds like my new contact at Cataract, Cyclops and Moat. Her favourite expression is 'No problem!' But nudge her, she panics, and she's relieved when I say goodbye.

Like the Guides at the Palace of Dekaydence. Hang on, who's that running up the stairs?

Your faith in me is touching but, as yet, I cannot see through doors.

Taylor burst in, her violet eyes bright with excitement.

"I had to come and tell you straight away: Mum has heard from Jack."

What's that fluttering in your chest, Ruby Q? Aha! It's the ol' love machine. You've still got a soft spot for Jack, haven't you?

"He said Cage is OK."

"Great!" said Ruby Q. "But hang on, how does he know? Cage is missing. And Jack's off with the GeeZers, swearing he'll never speak to Cage again."

"I don't know, I'm only repeating what Mum said," said Taylor, unsettled.

"Sorry," said Ruby Q. "It's good you've heard. It must be a relief."

"Yes, it is," said Taylor. "It was unbearable not knowing if Cage was …"

"I understand," Ruby Q said. "It's good you have a large family."

"What do you mean?" Taylor said. "I never see Meryl. She lives miles away; Kane's in America; Cage and Jack are too busy fighting to get home. So it's just me and Baghilde, and she's too independent, even for a cat."

"You've got your mum and dad," Ruby Q persisted.

"Look," said Taylor. "I know you yearn for a family and sometimes I think you envy us. But the bottom line is, Ruby Q, I envy you."

Blimey! There's a turn-up on your trousers.

"Me?" said Ruby Q, surprised. "Why on earth should you envy me?"

"You've got a purpose in your life. You dreamt of being a journalist. Now you are one, and doing really well. I won't ever get to be an actress. Not with the way the world is today." She hesitated. "Perhaps one reason you've done well, Ruby Q, is that you're on your own. You don't have family distractions. You can focus."

"Focus? *Me?*" said Ruby Q.

She's got a point, Ruby Q. You forget families can have a downside. Fewer Christmas presents, less food and attention, squabbling, petty jealousies …

Much like the GeeZers.

Yes, exactly like the GeeZers. They need their heads knocked together.

That's it!

What?

The GeeZers need their heads knocked together.

Er, Ruby Q, you don't do violence, remember?

I know. But you've made me think.

"What are you thinking, Ruby Q?" said Taylor.

"We must contact Jack, urgently. Can you do that, Taylor?"

Taylor shrugged.

She's fidgeting. She doesn't want to lie to you but ...

"Taylor, this is serious," said Ruby Q. "The GeeZers and Real GeeZers need to meet. Need to talk. This split is stupid. We've all got to work together if we're serious about saving the planet."

Taylor said nothing.

"Taylor, are you listening?"

"Yes, but it'll never happen."

"Why not?" said Ruby Q.

"Well, for a start ..." Taylor hesitated. "Will is the leader of the Real GeeZers."

"That ... He swore to me that he didn't have anything to do with them!"

"He's lying."

I knew it.

"Why?"

Taylor shrugged.

"I s'pose he has to be careful, and you are a journalist."

Ruby Q took a long, deep breath.

"OK, accepting Will is a liar, why can't this meeting take place?"

"There's bad blood between the Face and Will – and it's not only a row over peace and violence."

"What d'you mean?"

"It's about lurve, Ruby Q. Unrequited lurve. And sex, I s'pose. "

"What *are* you talking about?"

"Cage told me in confidence but I think you ought to know. When Tommo was killed, Will took his place in the GeeZers, working undercover for the Face. Seems she fancied him. But he didn't fancy her. He also thought she was losing the plot so he quit the GeeZers. She couldn't forgive him. When Piccolo arrived on her doorstep, she made his life a misery. She was jealous of his friendship with Will."

"How totally and utterly ridiculous!" Ruby Q exploded suddenly. "The whole world is in crisis and meltdown. And its survival and the future of millions of people and animals depend on a couple of emotionally crippled idiots! What hope is there?"

"Put like that, Ruby Quby ..." Taylor said, and giggled.

"It's no laughing matter!" snapped Ruby Q.

"You're quite right," said Taylor, trying to frown away her laughter.

Ruby Q sighed.

"Sorry, I am a pompous prig from time to time."

"Someone has to be," said Taylor.

"But you have to admit—"

Ruby Q's ad'um bleeped. She read the text message and sat bolt upright.

"What is it?" said Taylor.

"It's Will. He's agreed to do the interview."

"That's great. You can confront the lying toe-rag about being the leader of the Real GeeZers and ... Hang on, he told you he didn't do interviews?"

"Yes," said Ruby Q. "Something's happened to change his mind."

"Like what?"

"No idea." Ruby Q shrugged. "But it must be something big. He says he must meet me later tonight. He'll let me know where and when."

"How exciting! Text me when you get home and tell me what's happening."

42 A VISION OF VENOM

Deep underground, below the White Room, Grout had found empty chambers and, lower still, abandoned cells. He could tell by the depth of dust that no one had used, let alone visited, the cells in years. After researching their access and installing security measures, he took over a few of the cells for his private projects. Here he could work peacefully, away from Bodkin's prying eyes.

After finishing work, producing some pretty catchy songs, courtesy of Piccolo's arrival on the scene, and after a brief visit to his cells, Grout was climbing the steps of a hidden staircase when he heard voices. Knowing there were no cameras, he checked to see there was no one about before emerging cautiously into the corridor.

"I think that's enough, sir."

He froze.

But the voice was coming from the room opposite. He sensed it was a Tartan guard, and an unusually anxious one by the sound of it.

"Enough?" said a second croaky voice in a tone serrated with venom. "Oh, no, it's not nearly enough. And if you fellows could take off those idiotic sunglasses, you might see why. George!"

There was a dull thud, a groan, an odd squeaking noise

and a horribly long, throttled laugh.

"Get a bucket of water!" the Voice of Venom commanded, hoarse but authoritative. "And make sure it's freezing cold."

Grout sped across the corridor and slipped into the neighbouring room, as footsteps fast approached the door.

He went to the wall and knelt down. If he remembered aright ...

He found the spy-holes. The light was bright, though the view was restricted. Immediately, he saw the cause of the squeaking: a wheelchair. The occupant had his crumpled back to Grout; by his side stood a dark-suited attendant, visible only from the waist down, who appeared to be in charge of a stand of drips and tubes leading to and from the wheelchair user's body.

There was a long silence broken only by a bout of wheezing and choking from the wheelchair user, who snatched hungrily at the oxygen mask offered by the attendant.

The door to the room opened. Someone entered, with a bucket.

"Throw it, man!" shouted the Voice of Venom, dropping the oxygen mask in order to manoeuvre the wheelchair to one side, enabling Grout to see the man's broken torso. And his face.

Grout stared, transfixed.

Beneath a shock of expertly coiffed chestnut locks,

beneath the high Roman forehead covered in scars, were bloodshot blue eyes wild with a distemper of madness, and a jagged nose, half flesh, half metal.

Suddenly, the man appeared to stare intently at the spy-hole, seeming to fix Grout with a gaze, and a half-sneer of a smile, which exposed teeth fashioned in the shape of small human skulls.

Grout started back from the wall.

When he looked again, he saw water all over the floor and heard a low moan. He shifted his position and saw the water had been thrown on to a figure lying prostrate in a small pool of blood. He pushed his eye closer into the spy-hole. The figure stirred, and he saw the face and body of a young man judder with pain. He saw also, scattered about the young man, for a reason he didn't understand, a pile of white feathers and a smattering of feathers of red and gold.

43 BREAKING-IN NEWS

Ruby Q waited in her room for Will to contact her. She was furious that he'd lied to her about his connection to the Real GeeZers. She grew more furious as the hours passed and there was no call, no text, nothing. Then she grew worried. Where was he? What had happened to him?

Ruby Q, stop fretting. You've got plenty to do.

OK, OK.

She had a list of nine women who'd worked for CCM, with the major projects they'd worked on outside the office. But all leads had taken her nowhere.

What now?

Look ... Anjelica, Farishta, Malak, Mal'ach, Angelina, Ingelosi, Angelita, Angelo and Angela. In translation, each name means Angel.

A weird coincidence. Maybe they were all spies and that was their codename.

Yes, and I'm the Jacqueline of Knaves.

Only trying to help. But it must mean something. Hang on, what's that noise?

I've told you, I'm not clairvoyant but it does sound like someone on the stairs.

Yes, but who? Elsa's in her study, typing. The Treasures

have gone home.

It must be Will! At long last! Am I going to give him a piece of my mind ...

"Aagh! Who are you? If you're a burglar or something, you ought to know my grandmother is downstairs talking to the Chief of Police himself. In her room!"

I never knew that ... Ah, I get it. Good move.

The small stocky nervous-looking figure appeared terrified.

"Please, don't call the police, Miss Cooper. I rang the doorbell and when no one came, the front door was open so ..."

"Who are you? What do you want? Has Will had an accident?"

"I don't know who Will is. My name is Grout. And I wanted to tell you your dad is alive and well."

"What?"

"He has gone deaf but at least he's not shrinking like all the other musicians."

"What? How do you know all this? And why should I believe you?"

"I work with your dad."

"What? Where?"

"At Dekaydence."

"WHAT?"

"Please, they mustn't know that I'm here. Otherwise ..." Grout paled beyond his usual pallor.

So, your dad never escaped. How did he survive?

Where—?

"Why on earth is he still in that damnable place?"

"They've got him composing music for the launch of the Dekaydence mall. With Piccolo Smith."

"Piccolo! So, that's why ... OK, Grout, take me to my dad now, please! This moment!"

Grout stared at her. He hadn't counted on this. Truth was, he hadn't given a thought to any reaction. Plan was, deliver the news, make the girl happy. Return to Dekaydence, make Rallan happy. End of story. People! They made things so messy.

What about Will?

I can't wait for ever. He's got my number. He can call.

"Er ..." said Grout. "I'm really not sure about this. You see ..."

At that moment, there was an almighty crash as the bedroom door was kicked open and three masked figures burst in, one brandishing a gun.

BREAKING NEWS

I'm hiding in the bushes outside the London home of our MP, who's also the Minister for Truth. I've heard that, without permission, she's sneaked out of Parliament, where all MPs are held under the new Politician Internment Hot Air/Electricity law.

I have a camera.

Here she is! Getting out of a taxi, nervously looking around as she walks up the garden path. I'm behind her but she hasn't heard me because of the noise from the house. She's angry. She opens the front door; the noise gets louder. Teenagers and pensioners fill the hallway. As you can hear, our MP is shouting but she can't be heard above the chat and the music.

She tries to enter but is blocked by an elderly lady, holding a cup of tea.

"This house is no longer yours, dearie," the elderly lady tells the MP. "As taxpayers for many years, my husband and I provided you with the funds to buy it. We went short of everyday necessities, including food and heating, so that you could claim off us for this place, even though your main home and parliament are but a few miles away. We've paid for your new kitchen, a state-of-the-art TV, a lavatory brush, and heaven knows what else. We've had enough.

LIVE FROM AN ILLEGAL INTERNET SERVICE PROVIDER

The system may have changed but you still have this house so we're reclaiming it to get back our money to meet our needs, and the needs of your other constituents."

A loud cheer goes up.

"What?" Our MP, who is also the Minister for Truth, close to imploding, slumps into a chair. Luckily, the existing teenage occupant sleeps on.

A police siren sounds. The MP pales. The siren approaches fast. The MP pales further. She barges a way through the proletariat to the front door and bolts down the street.

Immediately, according to our plan, all lights in all houses in the street go on, illuminating the MP's departing figure, and the police van follows and apprehends her.

Another cheer goes up in the street. We've heard that penalties imposed on absconding MPs include a drastic cut in pension, expenses and holidays, as well as six months' community service. As in a real service to the community.

Of course, our MP has friends in high places. But at least you, and many more besides you, will have seen what was fixed into her heavily backcombed, hair-sprayed coiffure as she scuttled down the road: a red and gold feather. This ISP may well be closed down but don't ever doubt, we shall rise again.

The Phoenix lives

LIVE FROM AN ILLEGAL INTERNET SERVICE PROVIDER

44  KIDNAPPED!

"Keep quiet and you won't get 'urt," cried the gunman, as the other two hooded youths searched Ruby Q and Grout to see if they were armed.

Grout squinted at the unusual gun with a Baldwin logo on it.

"Don't you try nothing. Comprendo?" the gunman snapped at Grout, cocking the gun's hammer.

"I'll have you know downstairs a senior police officer is talking to my grandmother. And there's this huge hound that ..." cried Ruby Q.

Attagirl, Ruby Q! Good idea, adding the hound.

"Then they won't miss you, will they?" sneered the gunman.

"Who are you? And what do you—?"

A piece of tape was slammed across Ruby Q's mouth. Grout's too.

"We'll all step outside, nice'n'easy, 'cos I can get a bit jittery. Comprendo?" the gunman commanded.

"We were told to get the girl," whispered the second thug. "There was nothing about a bloke."

"Yeah, well, we can't leave him here to spill the beans, can we?" said the gunman.

"We could tie 'im to a chair?" the first thug suggested.

"We got no more rope. Nor time to go poncin' around tryin' to find some," said the leader. "We could kill 'im but that'd be messy. So we'll take him. Comprendo?"

The two unarmed thugs led the way down the stairs, the gunman bringing up the rear, constantly nudging Ruby Q and Grout with the gun, to move and keep quiet.

The gun and the presence of Grout stopped Ruby Q making a run for it. The Treasures would've gone home but she fretted about the fate of her grandmother until she heard the faint tapping of typewriter keys. She hoped the thugs hadn't heard it.

They were led through the back gate, which opened on to a deserted cul-de-sac. A small van, with its lights off, crept slowly towards them. They were bundled into it, the thugs clambering in beside them. The van set off, as Grout concluded the gun was a fake and Ruby Q puzzled over the presence of two Red Tartan guards.

Meanwhile, in the unlit street, having arrived at the house and seen some of the action, Will decided that whatever was going on, he'd best follow and fast.

45 THE BEGINNING OF THE END?

The ivory room at the top of the Palace of Dekaydence, which overlooked the river Thames, was sparsely yet stylishly furnished and lit only by the flames gushing out of a great stone Fountain of Fire in the corner. A scent of jasmine wafted on the breeze fluttering through the open window and tweaking the ears of the two sleeping cats – one black, one white – lying on the back of an ivory settle.

An elderly man in butler's attire stood on the balcony, savouring a cigarette while watching the rain-soaked grey sky. He was growing tired of the cold and damp, which resided deep within his body.

Two large dark birds sped by, so close and fast the old man felt the rushing air from their wings. The birds soared into the sky, then dived to earth, heading for the new Dekaydence building, flying a hair's breadth above the construction, close enough to frighten the builders working through the night, before they turned and flew back towards him.

The old man drew deep on his cigarette before stubbing it out on his hand and pocketing the stub. He sprayed a tad of Dekaydence 3-2-1 into the air, waved a hand to disperse it into the tell-tale aroma, and went back into the room.

It'd be over soon, he thought. Lord di'Abalo had assured him. He'd be glad. He was getting too old for games. And this one had lasted ages. He shivered, hungry for the warmth of home.

The man on the balcony was dressed from head to toe in black. His forehead was beaded in sweat, his blue-green eyes sparkled like jewels and on his gloved left hand was a large black bird.

"Come, let's settle you for the night," said di'Abalo, stepping into the room and gently securing the bird to a golden perch.

The bird beat its wings and tried to take off but was restrained by the heavy chain on its legs.

The cats awoke and eyed the bird intently. Was it the black cat, or the white, that stretched out its paws, and flexed its claws?

"You have news, Phlegm?" di'Abalo enquired.

"The private secretaries of the King and the President continue to press for the launch date of the Dekaydence Mall. Mr Candelskin is anxious to know it, too, sir."

Di'Abalo chuckled.

"Advise them it'll be very soon, Phlegm. And tell Mr Candelskin I promise to give him at least five minutes' notice."

Phlegm bowed and held out his butler's silver tray on which stood a goblet filled from the Fountain of Fire.

"Thank you, Phlegm," said di'Abalo, taking the goblet and raising it in salute to the bird. "Here's to our beautiful friend, Bianco, who, from time to time, needs his wings clipped."

As he took a long drink from the goblet, a flash of lightning shot a jagged arrow across the sky, the rains beat down heavier and harder, and a moment later a thunderclap rent the air. And the deep blue-green eyes of the noble lord, staring with amusement as the cats crept towards the bird's perch, appeared to take on the colours of the flames erupting from the Fountain of Fire, red and orange with the pupils a thin black slice of jet.

45.5 'OID DEVOID

"Innit! Come quick!"

"Hang on, Bods," said Innit, and called down the stairs. "What is it, my sweet? Shops run out of ketchup again?"

"Fog the shops! It's Colin! I found him on the floor in the kitchen. He's collapsed! It's like he's dead!"

"He's alright, luv. Honest. We just had to ... borrow a bit from inside him, that's all."

"WHAT? Innit, you come down 'ere and you fix him."

"Down in a minute, Jezza."

"No, Innit. NOW! D'you hear me? NOW. Or else there'll be trouble."

"Right-ho, dearest."

"It's alright," said Bodkin, wishing he had Grout's skills. "I've cracked it. Here, have his brainbox back. And don't forget to ask her if she's got my stamps."

"At this juncture, Bods, given that my experience of women is a tad superior to yours, I don't think now is the best moment to ask about stamps."

"INNIT!"

BREAKING NEWS

Our photographs show houses in China and India with rivers of smouldering ash pouring out of them into the streets. Here we are inside one house. See the pregnant woman at work by the fireplace, burning laptop adaptors to recover lead. In a corner, her sister is using acid to burn off bits of gold from a circuit board.

Both women are smiling, happily. We can see that because neither is wearing protective clothing. Perhaps they do not know that their town has the highest level of cancer-causing dioxins in the world, as well as unusually high rates of miscarriage? Perhaps they can't afford to do anything else to earn a living?

We suspect the man in the other corner of the room, gagged and strapped to the chair, with a red and gold feather tied to his head, does know this because he is the chief executive of one of his country's largest waste disposal companies. But to make sure, we've made him our on-the-spot reporter. See how excited he is to be here for an indefinite period. You can see that from his twitching eyebrows.

What this man will know is that one 15-in (38-cm) monitor can contain 7 lb (3 kg) of lead, and as Americans alone discard 350,000 cellphones and 130,000 computers

LIVE FROM AN ILLEGAL INTERNET SERVICE PROVIDER

on a daily basis ... there's a lot of lucrative work for a recycling toxic e-waste business such as his.

He'll know also that many electronic recyclers send e-waste abroad, that authorities rarely stop the export of such waste, and that enforcement of any rules is often "lacking".

We brought him here to reflect on these matters.

The Phoenix lives

46 ALL AT SEA

Lady Catgut sat in the boathouse loft, listening to the river pound against the wooden walls and the rain thunder down on the roof. There was something about water ...

Years before, when her son had died and she had been too numb to weep, she had taken to walking the Seven Sisters, a series of physically demanding hills overlooking the English Channel. She preferred the weather to be bleak and raw, the waves thrashing against the shore and cliffs, and a driving cold wind biting relentlessly into her skin. She found comfort in the raging elements screaming their anger, frustration and pain in ways she couldn't.

She wore a brave face, for Catgut's sake. He had wept. Oh, how he had wept for the loss of his son. He blamed himself. Tortured himself with recriminations. She couldn't soothe his wounds, and didn't try. He was to blame, although she never said it. She would not wound him further with words or tears. Instead, she went walking, to grind away at her own pain.

Strangely, losing Piccolo, a boy she scarcely knew, had made the tears come. Suddenly. Unannounced. In free-fall. She quit the house, leaving Catgut to attempt escape from his own unhappiness through composing, day and night.

But walking the Downs was impossible now. And the

relentless rains made the roads mostly unusable. Locally, houses were flooded out or isolated by the waters. The Catguts' house, built on higher ground, was safe, for the time being, though the lawn and the lower level of the boathouse were underwater. A few days before, the neighbouring two elderly "girls", who worked on a gardening magazine, had reached them by donning long wading boots. But the weather had worsened.

So instead, every day after breakfast, Lady Catgut went to the boathouse, climbing the ladder to the upper level, which Piccolo had made his own.

Sitting alone, she imagined herself drifting in a boat, at dead of night, dead like Ophelia. Unlike Ophelia, she took with her a flask of fresh tea or soup and a pack of cheese and bread – and remained alive, just in case. Just in case Piccolo should return.

It was late into the night and in the boathouse, by the light of a torch, Lady Catgut was pouring soup into a mug and breaking chunks off a loaf of home-made bread, while singing softly a childhood lullaby she'd sung to her son when he'd been a baby.

The young man lying on the bed stirred. His eyelids flickered and opened. He stared warily at her, and then quickly scanned his surroundings.

"Mushroom soup," she said, offering him the mug and bread.

She saw his hesitation.

"You don't have to tell me anything and no one need ever know you're here," she said, briskly. "If it helps you, I live in the house across the lawn with my husband who lives mostly in his own world. I have basic nursing skills and can care for you until you're better. I've already taken the liberty of cleaning your wound."

The young man said nothing.

"We must all do our bit," said Lady Catgut, matter-of-factly.

The young man stared at her, curiously.

"I mean, we must all help one another," said Lady Catgut.

The young man remained silent.

Again, she offered him the mug and bread.

He took it, devouring it all hungrily before flopping back on to the bed.

She took a cloth from the table and went to mop his brow.

Instantly, his hand was tight on her wrist. They held one another's gaze for a moment and she saw the sadness seep into his eyes at the fact that he'd misinterpreted her action. She wondered what he must have been through.

Gently, he released her arm.

"It's not only you young people who care passionately about the evils being done to the world," she blurted out.

He looked at her.

"A few of us decrepits are right behind you, and

sometimes ahead of you," she said, more forcefully than she'd intended.

He smiled briefly, a dimple appearing in his cheek, which reminded her of her son.

She swallowed hard, before continuing.

"Certainly, the Phoenix, whoever he is, appears to have started something."

She saw the immediate interest in his eyes, and the way he tried to mask it.

"Here," she said, taking papers from a bag. "I thought you'd be interested. They're stories from the web. All over the world, young people are fighting to save the planet and using a red and gold feather to show solidarity with the Phoenix."

She saw his face light up as he took the papers, and she hesitated.

"There is something you may not know," she ventured.

He looked at her, on the alert again.

"The Phoenix has been captured," she said. "That's all I know. No one knows for sure whether he's dead or alive. You'll see that's why every story on an IW, blog and the cheep-cheeps ends with the words *The Phoenix lives.*"

He was staring into the distance, seeing things way beyond her field of vision. She waited, silently, for him to return.

They heard it at the same time: the sound of an engine approaching.

He stumbled to his feet, unsteady as a newborn deer, grabbing the torch to douse the light. From his look, she could tell that he didn't know whether or not she'd betrayed him.

"I've told no one you're here," she said, firmly. "You must believe me."

He was staring out of the window. Had he heard her?

The noise drew closer. She followed his gaze. Something was emerging from the darkness. It was a big old vehicle, built like a tank, spluttering across the lawn on its way towards the boathouse. Somewhere a bird cried out in alarm.

What on earth was it? More to the point, who was it?

She saw the young man touch his pocket and froze. She'd found the unloaded gun while tending his wound, and taken away the bullets. But were there more? She'd read about Cage Martin and dismissed it as propaganda. But now she was doubtful. What if he was a murderer? What if he'd hidden the ammunition before she'd found him?

She thought of Catgut, her foolish, forgetful, exasperating husband, and felt a wave of warmth and fondness wash over her. She would protect him at all costs.

47 TROUBLE BUBBLES

Innit opened another bottle of Dekaydence champagne, took a long lingering drink, belched and yawned, and went back upstairs.

"When you coming to bed, Innit?" a woman's voice called, enticingly, from a back bedroom. "I got bags of those big fat self-heatin' Dek-o-dyno-chips you like and there's a new Dek-o-Dynamighter film on."

"In a bit, girl. If you're lucky," he called. "Got some work to do."

"Oh, you're always workin' now. Workin'. Workin'."

"Gets you nice presents though, dunnit?"

"Yeah, can I have another?"

He heard her giggle and paused.

He took another long swig from the bottle. He did enjoy his new jobs. He liked spying and he enjoyed the waste disposal; and he got good money, and time to do stuff on the side.

He popped his head into the front room. That idiot, Grout, had done the business with the listening devices. Not that he'd ever tell him. Surely it'd operate for a while without his managerial presence, wouldn't it?

His brief was to record the goings-on in the "safe" house across the road, known to be used by the GeeZers. It'd been a piece of cake. And he'd already hit the jackpot: he'd got the Face.

He was distracted by a crunching noise coming from the corner of the room. A trickle of fresh blood was flowing slowly across the floor.

"Good boy, back on the live stuff!" He raised the bottle to the caged liz'oid, which had found its supper. "I'll be back in bit."

"I'm coming to get you, girl," he cried, running along the corridor to the back bedroom, screeching like the engine of a racing car taking a hairpin bend.

He grinned as he heard her utter a squeal of delight.

48 COMPRENDO?

Before they were blindfolded, Ruby Q and Grout caught a glimpse of the Red Tartan guards sitting in the front of the van. Ruby Q felt she knew one but as neither acknowledged her nor spoke ... Grout didn't recognise either of them, but it didn't stop him trembling in his trainers.

The van progressed slowly and with difficulty through roads awash with floodwater. There was no way of knowing where they were going and the thugs' monosyllabic grunts gave away nothing as to their identity or intent.

Ruby Q wondered who would want to kidnap her. Or why. Grout fretted about being returned "officially" to Dekaydence and the consequences.

Eventually, the vehicle stopped. They were bundled out, and down a flight of stairs. Footsteps surrounded them all the way. They were shoved forward, the bonds removed, the tapes ripped off. The thugs marched off; the door was slammed. A key turned in a lock. Ruby Q felt the damp chill of the room. Grout began to shiver, more through nerves than cold.

The dim light from a small bulb in the ceiling revealed they were in a small room with a bed and several buckets collecting rainwater leaking through the ceiling.

They heard shouting on the other side of the door.

"I gave a simple command: 'Get the girl!'" a voice like thunder shouted. "So you decide to bring her love life as well!"

Ruby Q pressed her ear to the door.

"He was in her room," she heard Comprendo reply, sulkily. "What we supposed to do? Leave 'im there to shop us?"

"And what did I tell you about weapons?"

Something hit the wall outside the room and cascaded off it.

"It's only plastic," Comprendo pleaded.

"I don't care if it's made out of marmalade – you don't carry this stuff."

"What if we need to defend ourselves ...?" Comprendo said, aggrieved.

"You use your brain. Here's your first lesson: open this door!" said Voice of Thunder.

A key was in the lock so fast that Ruby Q had only a moment to jump clear before the door swung open.

In the doorway stood a shaven-headed, solid-built figure, in well-worn combat trousers and aged trainers, arms akimbo.

"I apologise for the morons with plastic toy weapons and matching brains. The invitation to come here should have been conducted in a polite manner. However, it is good to meet you at long last, Miss Cooper. And if you haven't guessed already, I am the Face."

219

The Union Jack and the hanging baskets proclaimed to Lady Catgut that the occupants of the approaching vehicle were friendly.

"That'll be the 'girls'," she informed Cage. "Miss Edwina Gardening-Fork (pronounced Spade) and her friend, Young Miss Burgess."

Cage said nothing but he knew of both women. His father worked with them on *Shed Monthly*, a gardening magazine, and they'd given Ruby Q Cooper her first job in journalism. He puzzled at the coincidence, and who exactly this woman was who was caring for him. And how on earth he got to be there, wherever 'there' was.

A klaxon sounded as the vehicle nudged the boathouse's veranda.

"Lady C!" roared a cultured, commanding voice.

"What shall I say?" whispered Lady Catgut, looking anxiously at Cage. "They could ferry you to the house. It's warmer and drier there and ..."

"No one must know I'm here," Cage said.

"Lady C?" roared the voice below. "I know you're in there, dear. The smell of home-made bread gives you away."

"Be with you in a sec, Edwina," Lady Catgut called, her

hand on the ladder rails. She looked pleadingly at Cage.

"Say nothing," he said, firmly.

"Right-ho," she said, deflated. A thought occurred to her suddenly and she took something from her coat pocket. "I found this on the floor beside you. Do be careful – they're exceedingly strong."

Cage took the envelope, which contained the tablets Waat had given him.

"Shall I pop in later with some supper?" she ventured.

She wasn't sure he'd heard her. He was staring at the envelope and when he did look up, he stared out of the window, at something she couldn't see but which made him smile. The dimple in his cheek hastened her on her way; away from her memories.

Cage sat on the bed, switched on the torch and emptied the contents of the envelope on to the blanket. There were some 20-odd yellow tablets, in a drift of powder. It was kind of Waat but he'd never "done" tablets, not even medicine. He abhorred dependency of any kind. He'd seen the effects of alcohol on his father. And, thus, on his mother.

Now he was tempted. Not because of the pain in his leg. Raw, draining and frustrating though it was. No, it was the heavy grey mist residing inside him, weighing him down. Seducing him endlessly towards sleep from which he never awoke refreshed. It robbed him of energy. It took the light out of the sky, and his life.

He'd never felt like this before. Was it guilt? he wondered. Was this what becoming a murderer did to you? Would he never be able to shake off this desperate lethargy? Was this his life sentence?

And all this when he was working for the Real GeeZers. When he was needed by Will and by the Phoenix. He'd put his life on hold, given up on college and fulfilling a dream of becoming a farmer, because he knew he must. What was more important than fighting to save the planet?

Except ... He imagined the woman who'd cared for him, inside the house, preparing supper for her husband, children and friends. He imagined fresh food, warming drinks, conversation, maybe music and laughter. However bleak the world outside, inside, for them, there was warmth, laughter. And occasions to look forward to. But for him ...?

He felt as if he were on a long, hard sandy track, with flat, bleak moors on either side. A faint light showed the track running through the dark landscape like a pale, golden river. There was no sign of life but he had a feeling that something, somewhere, was watching him, waiting for him. And he'd no idea whether it was good, bad or indifferent.

The moon slipped in and out of the clouds.

He shifted his aching leg and began returning the tablets to the envelope. Something caught his skin. He looked inside. It was the width of a hair. A tiny, flat piece of metal.

He held it in the palm of his hand. It wasn't scrap but ... Every time he tried to follow a thought of what it might be, the heavy mist demanded he sleep. Struggling with the feeling, he stood up and looked out of the window to the lights in the house. Why not one day? he wondered, thinking of Waat.

And then it came to him. Maybe the piece of metal was a security device for the ad'um. Long before their rift, he remembered Jack had been working on making an ad'um safe from monitoring and bugging. If he was right ...

The only problem was the ad'um. It neither received nor sent messages. It simply stared back at him, blankly. He opened it up and slipped inside the thin metal piece, switched it back on, and prayed for a miracle. If he could make only one call ...

"I recognise you, Miss Cooper, from the photo in the paper alongside your byline. But you'll understand, for security reasons, I need to know the identity of this gentleman." said the Face, nodding at Grout.

"How dare you?" Ruby Q's face was fiery red.

Steady on, Ruby Q.

"And how do I know you are the Face? There's no picture of you that I've ever seen. The only thing I know is that the Face is a peace-nik. Well, let me tell you, whoever you are, your thugs didn't give a peaceful impression when they barged in to my bedroom with a gun, tied us up, and kidnapped us."

"I am sorry, truly. They were not acting under my orders."

"You think that makes it OK, then? Well, it doesn't! Now, if you'll excuse me, my friend and I are leaving. Come on," she said to Grout, as she made for the door.

"I can't let you go. Not yet," said the Face, blocking her path. "I need to talk with you."

"Tough!" said Ruby Q. "I've got a pressing engagement elsewhere. Come on, Grout."

The three thugs stood blocking in the doorway.

"Grout?" said Comprendo. "Aren't you a Dekaydence

boy? Work in the lab?"

Ruby Q saw the look of terror on Grout's face.

"So what if he does?" she snapped. "I work for a Dekaydence newspaper. Does that make me a thug or a murderer? Come on, Grout. I've had enough of this."

"Take him out," the Face ordered the thug, nodding at Grout.

Comprendo's face lit up.

"What?" said Ruby.

"As in take him out?" asked Comprendo, excitedly.

"No, moron," the Face said. "I mean take him outside, while I have a chat with Miss Cooper. Keep a close eye on him. Think you can manage that?"

Comprendo put his arm around Grout's shoulders.

"I've got questions for you, mate," he said.

Grout swallowed hard.

"Keep your mouth shut, and if you touch or bully him, I'll ..." said the Face, crunching her knuckles.

Comprendo's cocky look fled from his face, his arm shot back to his side.

"I'll be with you in a moment, Grout, don't you worry," said Ruby Q.

"Right-ho," said Grout, sounding far brighter than he felt.

"OK, so what's this about?" said Ruby Q.

"The GeeZers are on the march," said the Face.

"Jolly good," said Ruby Q, unimpressed. "But given

your reduced numbers, who's going to notice?"

"More than a few," said the Face. "This gathering isn't only about GeeZers."

"You mean, you're finally getting together with Real GeeZers?" said Ruby Q.

"No, they're not invited," said the Face, dismissively. "GeeZers are peaceable, remember."

Ruby Q looked at her, questioningly.

"OK, granted, there are a few who need reminding," said the Face. "I apologise but we're few in numbers. But we have worked on contacts in other peaceable organisations. And we're holding a party – a Power to the People party, a peaceable rally of people from campaigning groups – environmentalists, anti-war groups, student groups, children's charities, animal welfare organisations, trades unionists, pension groups. I wanted to tell you this, in person, so that you can be on the case to cover the story."

"It sounds interesting," said Ruby Q. "When's it happening, and where?"

The Face scanned the room, even though it was obviously empty.

"The day after tomorrow."

Ruby Q looked aghast.

"We meet up early in Hyde Park," the Face continued. "We hold talks, lectures and demonstrations. In the evening, there's a rally in Trafalgar Square with speakers from all the major groups."

"OK," said Ruby Q, thinking out loud. "I must tell the editor, and get it put in the diary."

"No," said the Face, defiantly. "I don't want it broadcast. Not yet. Not till the day. Just in case the authorities make a move on us."

"OK, I understand, but it is cutting it close."

Yes, and it'll be a bummer trying to get your hair done in time.

For heaven's sake!

"It has to be that way, Miss Cooper," said the Face.

"OK, I'll say nothing. I'll just book myself a day's holiday and see you on the day."

"Excellent," said the Face. "It seems we've got the timing right, the weather forecast promises an unusually hot and dry day. The first this summer. Couldn't be better, could it?"

51 COLIN ON THE LOOSE!

Innit snored himself awake. He reached for the girl and was surprised she wasn't there. Suddenly, he remembered where he was. Back in the front room overlooking the street. He sat up with a start. He'd nodded off while on duty. He was supposed to be overseeing the recording of activities in the GeeZers' "safe" house. He glanced at his watch: he must've been out of it for a good 40 minutes.

"Firkin' 'ell!"

He realised his feet were soaking wet. Oh, no, he thought, not another personal accident. He looked down: a bottle of Dekaydence champagne was on its side, drooling its remnants on to his socks.

"Firkin' 'ell!"

He kicked the bottle across the floor to join its empty compatriots. It'd been the last bottle. He'd have to filch some more.

It dawned on him that it was very quiet. Too quiet. He looked at the sound equipment. The light wasn't on. Could he have switched it off in his sleep? Had he, or the recording equipment, missed anything?

"Firkin' 'ell!"

He swore as he kicked the equipment. Of course, he'd blame it on Grout. And Grout, being Grout, would gibber,

228

believing it *was* his fault. Some people were born to be scapegoats. Grout was one of them.

He ran to the window and peered along the street at the "safe" house. Hang on, was he imagining it? He squinted harder. No, he wasn't! It was Grout, talking to a young lad on the doorstep of the "safe" house. Grout with the GeeZers? Who'd have thought that miserable stick of nerd and panic would be a traitor to Dekaydence? Innit knew he'd hit another jackpot.

"Firkin' 'ell!"

He'd better call the boss. Immediately.

Innit reached for his ad'um, which was when he saw the gaping hole in the empty cage, the metal bars reduced to serrated stumps.

"FIRKIN' 'ELL!"

He ran from the room, along the corridor, hesitating as he reached the back bedroom. Gently, he pushed open the door and went in.

There was blood all over the bedclothes, scattered across the bed and the floor. But there was no sign of her. Of Jezza. His woman. Or the liz'oid.

"FIRKIN' 'ELL!"

He crept down the stairs, aware of the smattering of blood on the carpet and the wall. He heard music coming from the kitchen and felt in his pocket for the liz'oid's remote control. Trouble was, he remembered, it didn't always work on this reject 'oid. He snatched an ancient cricket bat from the umbrella stand and raising it in one hand, kicked open the door and stepped inside.

The voices of Hunky Doré and the Studs and Sluts grew louder.

He crept into the dark room, his socks squelching on the floor, and squinted into the darkness. He couldn't see a body, or anything much, but what he did see was a large irregular hole in the back door. He walked slowly towards it.

"'ERE!" A harsh voice behind him startled him.

He spun round, swinging the bat.

"Wot you doin'?" she shrieked.

He blinked, the bat stopping in mid-air.

She wasn't dead. Far from it. But her hands and face were covered in blood.

He was relieved but, gawd, he could've killed her, there on the spot, she'd frightened him so. He'd have got off, he knew, pleading provocation and/or self-defence.

"What are you doing, 'smore to the point?" he shouted, in his relief. "Skulking about in the kitchen in the dark? And where the bleedin' hell is Colin?"

"Where d'you think?" she shouted back, nodding at the door.

"What ...?"

"He couldn't wait for me to open the door to let him out to do his business."

"I told you, Colin don't do business. We have to do it for him."

"What you talkin' about? He has to do business. Like

us. How else ...?"

"Alright, alright. Just clean yourself up, there's a good girl," said Innit, squeezing his soaking feet into a pair of strong boots parked by the door. He stopped suddenly, standing on one foot, scanning her. "'Ere, you ain't badly injured, are you, Jezza?"

She gave a dark laugh.

"Nah! It's Colin. You know he's a playful little sod. And well greedy for tomato ketchup with his chips. He had two big bottles of the stuff. I brought 'im down 'ere to clean us both up. The next I know, he's run straight through the firkin' door. You better go after 'im. I don't want 'im coming to no harm, d'you hear me?"

Innit blinked at her in disbelief, struggled to get into his boots and then was gone, through the back door, across the paving stones, following the ketchup trail up the side alley on to the main road. He looked up and down the road, but there was no sign of the liz'oid. Or ketchup.

He decided he'd contact MacCavity, after he'd captured Colin.

He started to run, feeling panic at the devastation the liz'oid could wreak. Grout, too, most importantly, in his own life.

At the back of his mind a thought kept returning: why did women name everything that came into their home? Even if it didn't have fur. Even if it was a machine. One day, he must ask Jezza why she'd chosen to name a firkin' reject killer liz'oid after her dad.

BREAKING NEWS

The Museum of Contemporary Art, Tokyo, has a new exhibit in its main entrance hall, which is attracting enormous attention. But hurry — the exhibit, which arrived in the building some time during the night, will be ending soon. Or as soon as someone can release the fulminating man from the quick-drying cement.

As you can see, the gentleman's bare feet are firmly set in the ground, on a small concrete island in the centre of a huge tank filled with water and blood. And he is being circled by a baby whale, intent on feeding.

This gentleman does not look happy, even though the whale is electronic. Certainly, the whale has had nips out of his legs, arms and nose. And each leap is taking the whale closer to his throat. And we believe the man is aware that the exhibit is secured by a gadget from his own factory, which permits one key holder only to switch it off.

This gentleman is the head of a multinational electronics company and is on the board of one of the country's largest whaling companies. Oh, and he has a huge collection of modern art. But not to worry, his son, who holds the key, is with us, though he is taking rather a long time before he steps in to stop the event.

The Phoenix lives

LIVE FROM AN ILLEGAL INTERNET SERVICE PROVIDER

52 GROUT FLOORED

Will had followed the slow-moving van containing Ruby Q and Grout and, soaked to the skin, had clambered on to the roof of the abandoned 'safe' house.

He'd heard most of the conversation between the Face and Ruby Q, including the date of the rally, and thought the Face was on to something: the power of the people. But he himself was beginning to doubt the cause: climate change was happening, no doubt. But it was due to natural, not manmade, actions. Sunspots, he believed. The world was in a constant natural cycle of heating and cooling, and currently it was not, as many advocated, in a time of heat and droughts but rather a cooling phase which would in time lead to another Ice Age. He concluded that man's energies would be better employed facing up to that fact, as well as dealing with man's destruction of the world's ecology, the issues of sustainability and the depletion of the earth's natural resources.

He yearned to talk over the matter with Cage. And the Phoenix. The fate of them both nagged at him day and night. And now he'd met a Dekaydence Guide who talked about his brother, Tommo.

Who was there to turn to? He'd thought of Ruby Q Cooper. But he'd arrived at her house a moment too late,

233

to see her being bundled into a van with that spook Grout. What had he been doing at her house? Could he be her type? Or was he supplying her with secret information? Both seemed unlikely. And then this kidnapping, with a gun. It wouldn't do the Face's reputation any good if the story came out. And Ruby Q was obviously not happy about it.

One of the Face's sidekicks came out of the "safe" house, with Grout.

Will ducked down.

"What happened wasn't personal, matey," said Comprendo. "Wanna ciggie?"

"No thanks," said Grout, who hovered nervously by the door while Comprendo smoked, paced up and down, and talked softly into his ad'um.

When Comprendo had finished his conversation, Grout asked him a question.

"How do you know I work for Dekaydence?"

Comprendo took a long drag on the cigarette, before throwing it to the ground.

"We got mutual friends," he said, and winked. "Close mutual friends."

Grout was about to ask who when something sprang at him out of the bushes, knocking him off his feet.

"Bloody 'ell! It's a firkin' liz'oid!" Comprendo screamed, pushing past Grout to run into the house and slam the door behind him.

Will heard pandemonium inside the house. He

reckoned, from experience, that any moment the Face and her sidekicks would leave by the back door and head for another "safe" house. The van would drive off. Ruby Q would be on her own. Grout would be, too.

He hesitated to go to Grout's aid, remembering the man had been happy to see his demise, then he heard footsteps coming from either end of the street. In the next instant he saw someone he loathed as much as Grout. Innit. The bully who'd tried to intimidate him and Ruby Q Cooper. And then came two Red Tartan guards. Where had they all come from? And what was going on?

"Colin!" shrieked Innit, rushing at the liz'oid and trying to grab hold of it by the pink collar round its metal throat.

"I wouldna try that, sir," the first Red Tartan advised.

Will frowned; the guard's voice sounded familiar.

"Tomato ketchup!" Grout gasped.

"He's starting to hallucinate," said the second guard.

"No, no, he's not. Honest!" cried Innit. "Get some firkin' ketchup, quick!"

The second Red Tartan sped off.

"Don't 'urt 'im," Grout pleaded. "He's friendly ... over-excited but—"

"Stand aside," the first Red Tartan ordered Innit, and knelt beside Grout.

He pressed his ad'um and the liz'oid collapsed, slithering off Grout's body.

"Good morning, and how are we today?" a bright

Indian voice cried out from the ad'um. "The weather today is—"

"Bhupi, I'll call you later," said the Red Tartan, zapping the off switch.

"You've killed Colin!" Innit cried, accusingly, shaking the liz'oid's lifeless metal frame.

"No!" Grout sat up sharply, concern overriding any injury he'd incurred, and began examining the liz'oid and cajoling it gently to open its eyes.

At that moment, Will saw Ruby Q come out of the front door.

"What is going ...? Jack!" she said, staring at the Red Tartan guard, who shook his head for her to be quiet.

The others were too busy with the liz'oid to hear but Will heard, and stared, perplexed, at the guard.

The second Tartan guard returned with a bottle of ketchup, and Grout began squirting large globules into the liz'oid's jaw.

Will saw the two guards exchange glances, and saw that Ruby Q had seen it, too. He saw shock register on her face, then disappointment. Cage had told him of Ruby Q's feelings for his kid brother. Once, he might've felt a pang of pity for her. Once, but not now.

The liz'oid was reviving.

"Home time for you, Colin," said Innit, holding the liz'oid tight in his arms.

"Could I buy him back from you, Mr Innit?" Grout begged. "Please."

"No," said Innit. "Anyways, where you'll be going, they don't allow pets."

"Where am I going?" said Grout, fearfully.

"These guards will tell you." Innit sneered. "Officers, arrest this man for consorting secretly with the enemy, the GeeZers; likewise, this carrot-topped bint here who also works for Dekaydence. I've got it all on tape. See you back at HQ."

He marched off.

"But ..." Ruby Q began, and caught Jack's eye.

"Don't worry, he's got nothing on tape," he said, and looked from Ruby Q to Grout. "We erased it all when we picked up the signal coming from his house along the way. And I don't think he'll be able to figure out why the Red Tartan guards didn't arrest you and your boyfriend."

"Grout is not my boyfriend," said Ruby Q. "He's taking me to my dad."

"Ruby Q! That's wonderful. I'm so happy for you," said Jack, giving her a pat on the back. "Oh, let me introduce you to Waat. You remember Waat, don't you, Ruby Q?"

"Yes," said Ruby Q. "You're Innit's sister, aren't you? And he didn't recognise you."

Waat nodded, and smiled shyly.

"I kept my head down. We've gone our separate ways. He's no idea what I do and if he found out ... Not that it matters, now I've got Jack."

Oh, no. Does that mean what I think it means?

"Yes," said Ruby Q. "Now you've got Jack."

"We'd better get going, Ruby Q," said Jack. "This commotion may well have unsettled the neighbours. We could be inundated with real Red and Black Tartans, liz'oids and Eye-Spies. We're off to another 'safe' house. Do you two want to come with us?"

"No, thanks," said Ruby Q, quickly. "Grout and I have stuff to do."

"If you're sure," said Jack. "We'll catch you at the rally. It should be a great, great day for the GeeZers and for the planet!"

He waved. Waat waved. And they hurried off together hand in hand.

Ruby Q waved to an empty space.

She heard the van drive off and, after a moment, sat down beside Grout who was slumped on the ground, crying, silently. She handed him a handkerchief.

"Are you hurt, Grout?" she asked.

No," sobbed Grout. "Well, yes. I love that crazy beast. I really do."

"I know what you mean," she said. "I know exactly what you mean."

Up on the roof, Will sat watching, and waiting. Once, he could've joined them in their tears. Once, but not now.

53 MALL HORREURS!

"So we'll launch the day after tomorrow, my lord?"

Yes, Mr MacCavity. Can you manage the time frame?"

"It is a tight one. But we're used to that, aren't we, m'lord? And we've a good team."

"Indeed. Do congratulate your three boys. They did well."

"They did, sir."

"I heard Comprendo is from a Young Hoodlums' Training Scheme?"

"Aye, sir."

"He does know not to cause any unnecessary disturbance on Saturday?"

"Aye, m'lord."

"I want a party atmosphere to reign supreme, Mr MacCavity. Peace and harmony."

"Peace and harmony it shall be, m'lord."

"Excellent. And remember, if you have any problems, and can't reach me, you can contact Miss Nera."

"The date of the Dekaydence Mall launch has been announced, Mr President. It's the day after tomorrow."

"Drat. I was rather looking forward to my meeting with god."

"It's the Pope, sir."

"Same difference. Better send apologies to Rome as well as flowers, holy water, whatever you deem necessary. Lash out, boy. Oh, and give the air ticket to someone in the office. They can enjoy their stay at the delicious Hotel Aleph, and owe me a favour. Even if it was bought on taxpayers' money."

"Yes, sir."

"I'll wear a dark navy suit, gold tie, cufflinks. Oh, and the best ceremonial chain of office. The one with the diamonds. Book the hairdresser, and ... "

"Will your children be attending, sir?"

"I imagine Maria will be too busy, as usual. And who to goodness knows where Jesus is."

"Quick, get off the ad'um, Petty. This is urgent!"

"Gotta go, I'll call you back. What is it, Schneek? If it's that six-armed sex maniac ..."

"No, but you're not going to like this either."

"What? Spit it out, Schneek!"

"The launch is the day after tomorrow."

"Oh, my giddy aunt ..."

"Ooh, that was a record! You had nine cream crackers in your mouth. Shame they're all over Mr Candelskin's new silk ..."

"Mr Candelskin, sir. I know you're resting but you did say, as soon as ..."

"Oh, god, when is it?"

"The day after tomorrow."

"Oh, god ... "

"Stanley, quick! Fetch the prison doctor."

"By the look on your face, Sinus, this is not good news."

"No, Your Majesty, I fear it is not."

"Very well. I'm sitting down. Tell me."

"The Mall launch is the day after tomorrow."

"Oh, teacups! Not the treacle sponge and custard day.
Really, it's too much."

"Mr Doré?"

"Could be, for someone with such a beautiful husky
voice, Miss ...?"

"Er ... it's Phlegm, Mr Doré. Signor di'Abalo's butler."

"Aha, Phlegm. You got news of the launch?"

"Yes, sir."

"Hit me, Phlegm. I got 30 fingers to count with. Sixty,
if you like, 'cos I could go back the other way as I've had
my multi-vitamin injection."

"It's the day after tomorrow, sir."

"The day after tomorrow?"

"Yes, sir."

"That's two fingers, Phlegm."

"I believe so, sir."

"Maybe one and a half?"

"Most likely, sir. Yes."

"Phlegm, do you know how long it takes me to get into my new outfit?"

"No, sir."

"Three days, Phlegm. Three days. I'd better go, Phlegm. I need help. And fast. Hey, Rudi, call me a manicurist. No, make it three. After that ..."

"Rallan!"

"What's the matter, Piccolo? You look worried."

"I am. I've just heard: the launch is the day after tomorrow."

"Yikes! And still no news of Grout's whereabouts?"

"No. All my calls keep re-routing to Bhupi, a newsagent in India."

"It's out of character. Grout's a conscientious young man and he loves his music. Something must've happened to him."

"That's what worries me. In this place, anything can happen and often does."

"Randall? Ah, good, you've heard the news. Yes, well, I'm sorry, too. Dratted nuisance. Only got the necessary information a few moments ago. That's why I'm calling you. I know you're busy with religious matters but I want you to take on the marketing of the launch of the Mall.

"Randall? Randall? Ah, good. For a moment I thought I'd lost you. Of course, you're up to it. Silly boy. Yes, yes, loads of help. Whatever, whomsoever you need. Oh, I forgot to say, Mr Maccaroni is making you three suits. Yes, I know. That's half his output for the entire year. Lucky you, Randall, eh?

"Now, there is one other small thing. A big rally is taking place on the same day. Yes, bizarre, isn't it? GeeZers, climate campaigners, child and animal welfare organisations, anarchists, environmentalists, anti-war, anti-drug and ante-natal bodies, transport and elderly action groups. I don't want anything spoiling the launch of the Mall, I want peace and happiness to reign. So, for a guarantee of good behaviour from those on the rally, I'm offering an amnesty. Free overnight accommodation in Hyde Park and unlimited Dek-o-dynamic chips and burgers, etcetera, etcetera, etcetera.

"Randall? You've gone awful quiet again. Of course you can do it. I have every faith in you. Talking of faith, I nearly forgot to tell you. I fixed for you to have a private dinner with the Pope Thursday week in your new penthouse in Rome. Oh, begorrah, did I not tell you that either? I bought it for you from Monsieur Canapé. It's the one that's been in all the papers. His dream home. He was planning to return there when he's finished refurbishing California. So it was kind of him to agree to sell it to me, don't you think?"

54 AN EMPTY CAGE

"Cage? I've got you supper and news. I had to wait until everyone was in bed. But the girls told me that the Dekaydence Mall is opening ...

"Cage, where are you? Are you alright? My god, you're not ill or ...

"Ah, no. You've made the bed and you've gone. You've left nothing. No trace. To protect yourself, and maybe me? I understand but I wonder why? What's happened? Have you heard something? What is it that's taken you away? Or has something driven you away? There's no note. There should be a note, Cage, telling me why. Telling me why and telling me that you'll come back.

"I don't need a date. But I do need to know that you'll come back. That I'll see you again. I can't lose three boys and never see them again. I know you're in some kind of prison, some kind of hell. I know it because I've been there. I know what it's like and I want to help you, Cage. I so want to help you."

BREAKING NEWS

HOME NEWS MUSIC VIDEOS DIARY BLOG

"You had another good day at the office, Pa?"

"Yep! Some big juicy company's gone down, so I kindly stepped in. Bit of asset stripping never hurt no one. And there's real estate going begging, son. Looks like I can buy you Vegas, France or Kentucky for Thanksgiving. Any preferences?"

"I'm fine with my room here, thanks, Pa."

"Howsabout a little business to play with? IBM? Starbucks? Dreamworks?"

"That's kind, Pa, but I've got a fair bit to do on my studies."

"You still wanna be a teacher? My son, the loser. Head in the clouds or in his books. You want to be like Eddy's dad, the butcher?"

"He was doin' good, Pa, until the Dekaydence supermarket moved into town, undercutting his prices. His meat was better, too. And then the Dekaydence bank you're involved in demanded his loan back."

"No savings, no pension, what kind of a family man is that?"

"He had a happy family, Pa. And not everyone can beat a bully."

"That's why you gotta *be* a bully, son. I keep tellin' you

LIVE FROM AN ILLEGAL INTERNET SERVICE PROVIDER

this. I dunno. Did Eddy tell you what his father's doin'
now? Sweeping streets, I heard."

"He ain't doin' nothing, Pa."

"That lazy, no good son of a—"

"He's dead, Pa."

"What?"

"He hanged himself. He left a note. Said he couldn't fight
the supermarket no more. Nor the bank. D'you know, Pa,
he'd gone after some 300 jobs and gotten nowhere? He
wrote his family saying he was worth more to them dead
than alive."

"He was right there, son. Stupid coward. Hey, will you
stop foolin' around with that old feather? It's disgusting.
Where d'you get it from, a circus? And what are you
doing with it?"

"I got plans for it, Pa. Great plans. And you wanna
know something? They include you. And this little guy. I
bought him off an illegal ISP. Apparently, he's a clone of
some crazy British creature called Colin. Let me just set it
to active/attack and press the 'on' button."

"Chrissake, son, get it off me, before it ... Aaagh!"

The Phoenix lives

55 GROUT RISING

"Come on, Grout, I want to see my father," said Ruby Q, briskly, trying to push from her head thoughts of Jack and Waat. "We need to move quickly before any Tartans or Eye-Spies are on our case."

Grout nodded as he blew his nose.

"I am worried about getting you into Dekaydence." he said. "And then getting you out."

"Let me worry about that and if we're caught, I'll tell them I kidnapped you or something," said Ruby Q.

Grout nodded, unconvinced. But he'd decided she wasn't as bad as Bodkin had said. She had stood up for him against the Face. Like he was a friend. It had made him feel good. Like he felt with the liz'oid. He squeezed his nails into his hands. No, he mustn't cry again. He really mustn't.

They walked quickly along the unlit roads, each deep into their own thoughts.

Grout puzzled over friendship. Ruby Q thought of her father: his big warm embrace, which would swallow her up. His prickly beard. His big laugh. And his deafness. Surely there was someone who could help with that? When he came home. After all, he'd have to come home with her, wouldn't he?

She had a sudden thought.

"Do you know where we are, Grout?"

Grout stopped.

"Er ... no."

They were looking around at the unfamiliar surroundings when a tall lean figure emerged from the shadows.

"I know where we are," the figure announced quietly.

"Will!" said Ruby Q. "How on earth—?"

"I'll tell you on the way to Dekaydence. Let's get going."

"Um, excuse me," said Grout. "But I don't think I can get you in as well as her, whoever you are."

"You can try, though, can't you?" Will said coldly.

"It might be difficult," Ruby Q intervened. "This gentleman's taking me in only because I've bullied him into it."

Will raised an eyebrow.

"You've bullied this 'gentleman'? That's novel," said Will, with a sarcastic laugh. "This is the gentleman who was happy to see me go to the White Room. Or worse. Isn't that so, Grout?"

Grout paled as recognition sank in.

"Selling out, Grout?" said Will. "I hope he's not costly, Miss Cooper?"

"I'm not paying him a cent," Ruby Q said, crossly. "He came to tell me my father's in Dekaydence and he kindly agreed to take me to him. Now, if you don't mind, we'll make our own way. Tell me what you want to say another time. Come on, Grout."

She turned on her heel and walked off, but soon realised Grout was not following. She turned round. He was standing on one foot, then another, running his hands through his sparse hair, a pitiable wreck as Will berated him quietly but fiercely.

"What is it, Grout?" she said, walking back to him. "What's the matter?"

"He's right. I've done wrong, I know that," said Grout, sweat mixing with the rain on his forehead. "I don't know nothing about anyone called Tommo. Honest. But there is something I must tell you."

"Black Tartans on the way?" Will said snidely. "The White Room being prepared for us, as we speak?"

"Now who's the bully?" said Ruby Q. "Let him speak."

"I'm not quick at working things out," said Grout, wretchedly. "I'm good with machines but not people. I've been carrying this around in my head, puzzling. Then I realised ... I can't do death things no more. It's not right. But I ain't got no one to tell 'cept you."

"OK, Grout, OK, but before you say anything, maybe you need to know you're talking to a GeeZer and a Real GeeZer."

"You stupid ...!" Will spat out at her.

"He must know. It's only fair."

Grout was beginning to shake.

"I don't care no more," he said, panic rising in his voice. "Please, just let me tell you. It's the Phoenix. He's in a cell. I've seen him. I've seen what they're doing to him. It's torture. He ain't goin' to live unless someone does something and does it quick."

He began to cry.

"It's OK, Grout. It's OK." Ruby Q put her hand on his arm. "It's very brave of you to tell us. Very brave, indeed. Isn't it, Will?"

Will didn't answer. He didn't hear her. He was thinking only, The Phoenix lives! Truly lives. He was exultant and equally, furiously, desperately intent to keep him that way.

"This is your chance, Grout, to make good," Will said coldly to Grout. "Take me into Dekaydence, show me where the Phoenix is. Help me get him out of there. Will you do that, Grout?"

Grout nodded, fighting his sobs.

"You have to realise we may die in the process, Grout. But we'll do so saving a good man who is fighting for our planet and much else besides. Do you understand?"

Grout took a deep breath.

"Yes," he said. "I understand."

56 ASHCAN CALL AT DEKAYDENCE

In the sentrybox at the tradesmen's entrance to the Palace of Dekaydence, MacNoodle was snoozing when the haggoids, Ross and Cromarty, began yarking and yattering fit to bust.

MacNoodle sat up with a start. Had he heard knocking or merely dreamt it?

"Here you are, you wee noise-bags," he said, throwing a few magazines and empty crisp packets into the air. The haggoids jumped up, devouring them, faster than lightning. "Now be quiet, boys. Let your daddy get a wee bit of shut-eye."

He checked the time, and groaned inwardly: 3 a.m. Would these deliveries never stop? He didn't have to look outside; he knew that scores of men and vans, trucks, bikes and lorries were filling the concourse, queuing to unload goods to be transported to the new Mall.

He'd already done two shifts, here in the temporary warehouses. Goodness only knew how the other Red Tartans were getting on in the thick of it, in the new Mall. Even MacGluten and his three boys had been called out of the kitchens to help.

He settled back into his chair and shut his eyes.

There was that knocking again.

He opened one eye, then the other. It wasn't a dream.

"Can no one read nowadays?"

He got up and spoke through the intercom.

"You need to see someone over there for official delivery business." He indicated into the dark and the rain.

"Sorry, guv'nor," said a Welsh voice. "But this ain't a delivery. We're collectin'."

"Collecting?" MacNoodle frowned. He'd had no notification of a collection.

He hit a button and gradually got a dim glow of light. Wasn't that typical, he sniffed, not a politician on their feet and jabbering when you needed one.

He squinted into the gloom.

A dark, bearded young man in a claret suit emblazoned with gold braid, and a claret hat and tie with a golden D, stood before him, a matching claret-red taxi-coach behind him.

MacNoodle recognised the livery. The Ashcan was the talk of the Tartan Bunker, the Tartans' café.

The young man held up a sheet of paper.

MacNoodle squinted at it, recognising the official Dekaydence stamp. But there was nothing to say who they were collecting, or where from.

"What's all this about, then?" MacNoodle enquired.

"Authorisation from the guv'nor, Lord di'Abalo himself," said the young man, pointing to an indecipherable signature below a yard of small print. "Did no one tell you?"

MacNoodle shook his head.

"No, everyone's busy on the launch. All leave and tea-breaks have been cancelled. I've never known anything like it."

"Typical," said the young man. "The likes of you and me are always the last to know. We only got the call a half-hour ago."

"Aye, you're not wrong there, laddie." MacNoodle nodded. "What are you collecting and where from?"

"We were told Level 18. Room 9a. I've no idea what we're collecting."

MacNoodle frowned.

"Ah! MacMinor's on duty there. But chances are he won't have heard about this – our electrics are haywire, and the phones keep re-routing to India. Here, take this map, else you'll never find your way. The Black Tartans who should be on duty down below have got eye strain, an allergy to the dark, would you believe?"

"Ta, mate."

"Do me a favour?" said MacNoodle, quickly leashing up a haggoid. "Take one of these wee boys to MacMinor. He'll be feeling a tad lonesome. And one of these lads is bound to cheer him up."

"OK," said the young Ashcan driver. "Mustn't separate man and his beastie."

"You are a kind boy," said MacMinor, opening the door and thrusting the leash into the young man's hand. "This is Ross. I've switched him to friendly mode. So he'll be fine. Really."

He watched the young man and haggoid step into the taxi-coach and drive up to the main door of Dekaydence HQ.

MacNoodle tried to contact MacMinor but once again the ad'um misdirected. After he'd caught up on Bhupi's family news, he reflected on the Ashcan business. Lord di'Abalo had authorised the collection. And in a hurry. So, MacNoodle decided, the Ashcan must have been called for Phlegm. With the Mall launch imminent, there was no time for his lordship to organise anything else for his old butler. And perhaps the underground room was the only clear space to put the body? Shame the old boy would miss all the fun of the launch but he'd had a good innings. He had been looking exceptionally peaky. How old was he? MacNoodle remembered sadly that the butler had joked with him only recently that he was as old as the hills, if not older.

57 OUTSIDE DEKAYDENCE

"What's going on?" Will demanded of Grout. The two, with Ruby Q, were hiding in the shadows in the road opposite the Palace of Dekaydence HQ, surveying the concourse, which was a flurry of activity amidst delivery vans and articulated lorries.

Grout shook his head. He'd no idea what was going on but he hoped the large crowd might persuade Will and Ruby Q to change their minds about getting into Dekaydence and leave him to get back to work. He imagined Rallan would be fretting about where he was — after all, he was fretting where he was. And he expected to be swooped on by an Eye-Spy or a Black Tartan at any moment.

He did want Ruby Q to meet up with her dad and he did want to help free the Phoenix but he realised he wasn't madly keen to be a hero. Let alone a dead one. More important, one without a job.

"Guess what?" said Ruby Q, checking her ad'um. "Breaking news is that the launch of the Mall is happening the day after tomorrow. The same day as ..."

She stopped, remembering the Face's words.

"As what?" said Will, knowing full well, having heard the Face's words.

Are you going to tell him about the rally, or shall I?

"Er, the same day as a friend's birthday," said Ruby Q.

He's a Real GeeZer. A violent. He won't be invited. But it won't stop him going if he finds out.

"All these deliveries must be for the launch," said Ruby Q.

"And all this chaos makes it an ideal time for us to get in," said Will.

"It means I've got to get back to work, ASAP," Grout mumbled.

"So, let's get on with it, and get in there," said Will.

"You don't understand," said Grout. "If the Mall launch is the day after tomorrow, they'll need me, urgent. I can't let them down and I can't afford to lose my job."

"You tell us a man's life hangs by a thread, you want help to save him, and then you—" Will said furious.

"Hang on," Ruby Q interrupted. "Grout's right. He has to get back to work. Alarm bells may already be ringing because he's not around."

"My god, two wimps!" said Will, angrily. "I'm talking a man's life!"

"Listen," said Ruby Q, calmly. "If Grout promises to take me in to see my dad on another day, maybe the day after the Mall launch, then I'll help you. I'll come with you to help free the Phoenix. OK?"

She looked at them both.

"Suit yourself," said Will, shrugging.

"Sounds good to me, Miss Cooper," said Grout, eagerly.

"So what's the new plan, Grout?" Will asked, condescendingly.

Grout's head slumped into his neck, and he stared at his feet for inspiration.

"I've got a pass but you haven't. So—"

"Yes?" said Will, impatiently.

An idea came into Grout's head.

"We sneak in through that Fountain of Fire in the middle of the concourse."

"How?" said Will. "It's about 30 feet high and I'm not flameproof. Are you flameproof, Miss Cooper?"

"Watch the Fountain," Grout continued, ignoring Will's manner. "There are nine pillars under the bowl. They move every nine seconds, on an axis of 27 seconds. Like a revolving door. We must follow the sequence three times – or we'll be crushed against the next pillar."

Ruddy hell, Ruby Q. To know that, he must've done this before with some other mugs, now possibly deceased.

"What about the concourse? It's awash with floodlights," said Will.

"There'll be a power cut any moment."

"How long for?" said Will.

"A few minutes, sometimes longer. But MPs don't stop talking for long."

"Surely you've got a back-up generator?" said Will.

"Yes, but we've a new state-of-the-art fuseboard, which shuts down if there's the tiniest fault anywhere in the system. Which there is, and the electricians are having to search and test miles of cable. Dekaydence building maintenance is going mental 'cos it's affecting the computers in the office, the games in the Palace ..."

"The lights have gone out! Quick, let's move!" said Will.

I feel sick and totally unfireproof, Ruby Q.

Cool it!

58 BODYNAP

The lights inside Dekaydence HQ were flickering. The young Ashcan driver decided to be on the safe side and use the fire stairs rather than the lifts. The three glass floors above ground appeared all but empty and the few Tartan guards, Red and Black, that he encountered in the corridors nodded knowingly or gulped nervously.

Was it his uniform or the sight of the haggoid unsettling them? Either way, he wasn't bothered. Quite the reverse. There was work to do and best it were done quickly. Without interruptions.

He made mental calculations of the width, angles and height of each turn on the stairs, the width of corridors and the ease of the doors to ensure a trouble-free exit. It was important to look assured and professional at all times.

Reaching the 18th floor underground, the map wasn't immediately clear as to which direction he should take. A gently snoring Voice Map on a wall behind him awoke with a start.

"Can I help you, sir?"

"Mr MacMinor?" enquired the young Ashcan driver.

"Straight along the corridor, turn left and left again."

"Thanks," said the young driver, and was off down

the corridor before the Voice Map could draw breath, or electricity, to ask more questions.

Suddenly the haggoid yowled, the noise echoing through the corridor and unsettling the young driver for a moment. The haggoid began to pull on its leash. As they turned a corner, the young man saw why.

At a distance, sitting behind three sets of heavy iron gates stretching the width of the corridor, was a short stocky Red Tartan guard whose anxious, sorrowful expression burst into a broad beam as he set eyes on the haggoid.

"Rossie!" he called out, rushing to unlock the doors. "You wee, mad metal monster. Come and give your uncle Mac a wee nip on the leg."

The young driver had to use considerable muscle power to restrain the yowling haggoid from pulling him off balance.

"Mr MacMinor?" said the young driver, as the Red Tartan struggled with the last door.

"Aye, that's me," said MacMinor, finally throwing open the door.

As MacMinor dropped to his knees to greet the haggoid, it jumped up and sank its teeth into his arm. MacMinor winced, but continued to hug the beast, stroking it behind its leather ears and tweaking its active radio aerial tail.

"It's a fine specimen, if I might say, sir," said the young driver, handing over the leash, and trying to control his impatience to get to work.

"Aye, he is that," said MacMinor, who, suddenly

recognising the uniform, lowered his voice. "What are you doing here?"

The young driver touched his hat.

"Mr MacNoodle asked me to bring you your lad, to keep you company. But actually I was sent for. Orders from Lord di'Abalo. To collect a body."

The young driver produced the document he'd shown MacNoodle.

In the gloomy light, MacMinor squinted and blinked at the document, taking in the seal and the signature and not much else in the very small print.

"My, oh, my." MacMinor nodded thoughtfully. "Who is it?"

"I've no idea," said the young driver. "I only know it's in Room 9a. Do you know?'

MacMinor shrugged.

"No, no one's tells me anything. I'm standing in for those hypochondriacs, the Black Tartans. But I've seen no one. I don't know how many people are here. Or who they are. Or where. Who feeds them, when or what? That's the way this entire place operates: don't ask questions. Och, well, at least I'm out of the wet."

The young driver nodded.

"I do understand but if you don't mind, I have to press on. Another collection after this one."

"Yes, of course. Apologies," said MacMinor, taking a key from a set on his sporran. "Follow me."

★ ★ ★

The room beyond the heavy wooden door appeared to be empty. While MacMinor stood nervously at the doorway, holding tight to the haggoid's leash, the young driver stepped inside.

It wasn't a normal cell but a large, dark chamber, like a large dining room in a stately house, lit by a lone flickering bulb. Fading tapestries of hunting scenes were hanging on the wood-panelled walls. A table, which would have comfortably seated a dozen or more, was covered in a patina of disturbed dust and dining chairs were scattered all over the place.

Several upturned buckets lay discarded on the floor, which felt sticky to the young driver. He quickly realised why: it was covered in blood.

He took a step further in and then saw it. The body of a young man, lying still, in a crumpled heap on the floor. He steeled himself and carefully walked round it. The face was swollen with cuts and bruises, the eyes puffy and closed. The once strong, handsome face now had the colour of parchment, the pallor of death. He leant closer. To check for a sign of breath, and for a pulse.

He stood up quickly.

"Right, Mr MacMinor," he said, briskly. "If you stand to one side, I'll get him loaded up. Best we put him out of his misery as soon as possible."

"Oh, dear, oh, dear," said MacMinor. "Stop it, Ross."

The haggoid was yattering, unsettled by the scent of blood.

"My, my!" said MacMinor, watching in awe as the young driver activated a small piece of metal to unfold into a stretcher, which divided in two. He then gently scooped up the body, levitated the stretcher and headed for the door.

"Oh, my," MacMinor said, as the haggoid strained to get at the fresh blood and dragged him into the room.

"Thanks, Mr MacMinor. And if you don't mind me saying, hope not to see you in a long time," said the young driver. "Have a nice Dekaydence Day."

"I'll second that, laddie," MacMinor replied. "Have a nice Dekaydence Day."

But the young driver was already away down the corridor, retracing his steps, and using the control to manoeuvre the stretcher.

The concourse was abustle as the young driver approached the Ashcan whose back doors opened to receive the stretcher. The young driver jumped into the Ashcan and drove off.

"We have much work to do," said a dark-eyed young man, wanding the Phoenix's body and watching the results on a monitor.

"Yes," replied the young driver over the intercom, the Welsh accent gone. "But we've got him out."

"I have to tell you it looks bad," said the dark-eyed doctor.

The young driver bit his lip.

"*Alevei*. He'll be OK."

"*Insha'allah*," said the dark-eyed doctor. "As God would wish."

59 INSIDE DEKAYDENCE

"OK, we're in. Now what?" said Will.

"We're on a secret staircase, on the ground floor," said Grout. "See, I've carved a 'g' in the brickwork. I've carved a number on all the floors, about the height and size of my hand, for when the lights pack up. I've never met or heard anyone on these stairs but you never know, so watch out. Go down to level 18. There's a handle – a door will slide across into the wall and you'll come out behind a tapestry. Opposite is Room 9a. If you want to check it out first, go into the next-door room, Room 8. There are spy-holes at about knee height. OK?"

"Yep, see you around," said Will, briskly, and set off down the stairs.

"Where are you going?" Ruby Q asked Grout.

Grout shrugged, nervous that she'd change her mind and decide to go with him.

"Up two levels," he muttered.

"Don't worry, Grout, I'm not coming with you. Not tonight anyway, but ... is that where my father is?"

"Yep," said Grout. He hesitated. "Suite 13."

All at once, he'd felt he had to give her something.

"Thanks, Grout, and good luck," she said, and went to follow Will.

"I'll come for you the day after the launch," said Grout.

She turned and smiled at him.

A thought came into his head.

"Er, could you do me a favour?" he called after her.

"If I can," she said, turning to him.

He took a key from his pocket.

"If you heard sommat had happened to me, will you come back here? It's my project, see. I can't tell no one else. It's on Level 19, Room 29. You'll know what to do with it."

"Come on!"

She heard the impatience in Will's voice.

"Look, I'd better go," she said, taking the key from Grout. "Room 29."

She hesitated.

"If you think it'll distract my father, don't tell him you've seen me. But don't forget, Grout, the day after the launch. Take care."

He watched her go. The more he learnt about people, the more they reminded him of the modern fuseboard. The slightest emotional hiccough, and that's it, they're kneecapped, incapacitated. It was happening to him, wasn't it? Why else would he have given a complete stranger the key to his project?

"There 'e is!" cried Innit, interrupting a bottle of champagne to sound off at the picture on the security camera. "What's he doing 'ere? I told those Tartan guards."

"Yes, but you lost Exhibit A, the film evidence, together with Exhibit B, the sound element," said Bodkin, hitting the zoom button on the control panel and freeze-framing a shot. "Anyway, this ain't the time to fire no one. All of us is on double shifts. Grout's on a triple."

"He probably set up the equipment to self-erase," Innit said, and sniffed.

"Or maybe you drank too much and switched it off, accidental like," said Bodkin.

"'Ere, whose side are you on?"

"See that," said Bodkin, peering curiously at the screen. "His jacket's all black at the back. Like it's been burnt. See!"

"So much hot air comes out of his arse, I ain't surprised!" Innit said sulkily.

"We'll get him, In, don't you worry. He's on my personal to-do list: keep an eye on Grout, preferably two."

"You're a mate, Bods," said Innit, blowing his nose on a piece of headed Dekaydence notepaper. "How about coming for a spin in the old Ashcan? I could show you what happens. You see, I don't like it when I'm not believed, Bods, I get real upset, even when I am lying 'cos I am good at it, aren't I? But this time I'm telling the truth about Grout coming out of the Face's house, with that carrot-topped bint, and I don't see why those amateur liars should get away with it."

60 HUNKY HISSES

Hunky Doré was waving his hands in exasperation. All six of them.

Dressed in a six-sleeved Dekaydence T-shirt, tight trousers and cowboy boots, his hair thick with thin metal foil strips, an anti-virus face mask tipped down on to his throat, the singer was standing on the massive stage at the centre of the Mall amidst a chaos of scene builders, painters, lighting technicians and others busily working on the set for the launch.

"I tell you, man, you can't pull the wool over my eyes, this auditorium is out of kilter," he said vehemently to the world-famous Parisian designer of the Mall and much else besides. "And I am a-mazed that you can not see it. Totally a-mazed."

The taut face of Claud Canapé grew tauter.

Hunky Doré jabbed three forefingers into the dark auditorium.

"I can see them, man. I know they're out there."

"What is out there, exactly?" Canapé regarded Doré through narrowed eyes, and spoke through a narrower mouth.

"Three seats more in that section than in any of the others."

"So?" Canapé's eyes and mouth narrowed further.

The singer clutched his head with six hands, and hollered.

"You don't get it, man, you just don't get it. It means I'd be performing to those extra seats more than to anyone else. And I can't do that, man, I just can not do it. I need equilibrium. It's essential to my performance. Understand? E-ssen-tial."

Claud Canapé pursed his lips.

"And another thing," said the singer. "Don't you feel this entire building is listing? Because it is: it's leaning heavily to the north-east. Now, I ain't got no problem with it listing to the north-west. But I can not do the north-east. It destroys me. I can't get my head round it. So, sort it, man. Just sort it. OK?"

Before Canapé could answer, Hunky Doré had walked off, pulling the face mask over his mouth, heading for a clutter of young assistants waiting to check the colour progress of his hair, his underarm temperature and much else besides. But suddenly something caught Hunky Doré's eye and he lifted the mask.

"Hey, Schneeky baby," he called to Petty Masters's assistant, who was rollerblading through the stalls.

Schneek looked up and grinned.

"Hi, HD."

"Take me to that little woman of yours!" the singer cried, wriggling all 30 of his fingers. "I need to give her a cuddle. A six-hander whopper ... Now! D'you hear me?"

61 GONE BEFORE BUT ...

"Miss Cooper!" Mr MacMinor gasped as Ruby Q opened the door to Room 9a. "What on earth are you doing here?"

"Mr MacMinor! I ... er ... I'm doing background stuff about the launch and how work's going, etcetera. I was in the concourse, wandered into Reception, sort of came down here and ... er, I thought I heard voices ... "

"Which you did," said MacMinor. "What a wonderful coincidence."

"Hello, Ross," said Ruby Q, walking from the room towards what looked like MacMinor's desk in the corridor.

"I cannae thank you enough, Miss Cooper," confided Mr MacMinor. "I didna know what to do. This mad wee beastie got over-excited, the door banged shut, it cannae open from the inside, the key fell out in the corridor ... I tried using my ad'um but it kept re-routing to India. Really nice gentleman, Mr Bhupi, but he wasn't in any position to help me. I was that worried ... "

"What were you doing in an empty old room, Mr MacMinor?" Ruby Q affected a casual manner in a tad louder voice, as she saw Will move swiftly into the next room. The haggoid saw Will, too, and began to yatter, its ears and tail pricked to alert.

"Be quiet, Rossie, you've caused enough trouble for one night." MacMinor scolded the beast. "Och, it is an empty room now but ... a few moments ago ... I can tell you, you know what they're like here, Miss Cooper. And now you work wi' us, don't you? You're on side."

"Yes, Mr MacMinor. I'm not here to tell tales about you. Or Ross."

MacMinor nodded fervently as he poured tea from a flask.

She took the mug he offered and saw that his hands were shaking.

"There was this young lad," he began, and took a handkerchief from his sporran. "Och, it was terrible. Terrible. Brings tears to your eyes. But he ..."

"What happened, Mr MacMinor?"

"Someone from the Ashcan came to take away his body."

Over the guard's shoulder, she saw Will beckoning her urgently.

Ruby Q leant forward.

"Mr MacMinor, this meeting between you and me never took place. You never got locked in the room. So no one knows what happened, not even Mr MacNoodle. So no one need be reprimanded ever. Is that OK?"

MacMinor nodded, and smiled shyly.

"Yes, Miss Cooper. Thank you, Miss Cooper."

"I'd better go now, Mr MacMinor. I'll see you soon, I'm

sure. At the Mall."

"Yes, you will, Miss Cooper. Take care, now."

"Will! Mr MacMinor said—"

"I heard. My ad'um does long range."

"What now?"

Will was thinking.

"Even if we ran, the Ashcan will have gone by now. But we must find him. Whatever's happened to him, I want to know, I want to see it with my own eyes. I want to remind myself what we're up against. And listen to this, Miss Cooper — earlier this evening a Dekaydence Guide working at CCM offered me a chocolate. She told me if I took it, it'd make Tommo happy."

"But you said your brother was ..."

"Yes, but no one's ever recovered a body. So how can I be sure? Nothing in this age of Dekaydence is for certain, is it?"

"OK, let's start at Reception," said Ruby Q. "Somewhere, they'll have the Ashcan's contact details."

"You don't have to do this," said Will. "You could go to your father."

She bit her lip.

"It might unsettle him ... I ... Well, I do want to help you."

"Even though I'm a Real GeeZer?"

"Yes. But you've just lost your best operative. I didn't always like what he did, but you had to admire him, didn't you? And I imagine you feel devastated."

Will said nothing, and was only dimly aware that he was fiddling with the remnant of a red and gold feather he'd found in the room. He was remembering his first days as a young schoolboy at Note. His first ever time away from home. Tommo and Tommo's friend had been showing him the ropes. And when his father had died, and then later, much later when Tommo had been lost, his brother's friend had supported and encouraged him.

He missed sorely the best operative the Real GeeZers had but, more, he missed the young man who'd been like a brother to him over many years. They were one and the same young man, the Phoenix.

"Let's get out of this place, Miss Cooper," Will said, suddenly. "I need to breathe what passes for goddam fresh air in this godforsaken city."

They set off up the steps.

62 WHERE IS EAST?

"East?" said the Face into her ad'um.

Within the silence from the other end, the Face detected anxiety.

"East is east," she said, "and west is west, and ..."

She paused.

"And mother's milk is always best," a young voice said, softly.

"Who is this?" said the Face.

"I am East's sister," said a girl. "East is ... isn't ... She's gone."

"What do you mean, gone?"

"She's disappeared. No message. No idea where or why. No ... no body. Nothing."

"How long ago?"

"Six days."

"We must hope," said the Face, awkwardly.

"Yes. Can't do much else, can we?" The girl sighed.

"In the meantime, about the rally," said the Face, briskly. "For a guarantee of good behaviour, Dekaydence has organised free camping and food for all *bona fide* marchers on Friday and Saturday night in Hyde Park, and free transport in and around London."

"Fantastic. But it's odd, isn't it, Dekaydence behaving

so kindly?"

"They must be up to something but whatever it is, it's too late to call off everything."

"Can't worry about what we don't know," said the girl. "We'll see you in the park. Good luck with your speech."

"Thanks," said the Face. "Oh, can you take back the three young lads East sent to me? They need more training and I haven't got the—"

"East didn't send you anyone. I know that for sure."

"They brought weapons," said the Face, slowly.

"GeeZers don't do weapons, or have things changed?"

"No, nothing's changed." The Face reflected. "Only they brought her ring."

"Oh," said the girl.

For a moment, both were silent.

"I'll be in touch," said the Face, brusquely.

She was glad that her minder was by her side, and had gleaned enough to know that action had to be taken. And fast. They listened for noises in the house. Two of the three young men were sleeping soundly in the next room; the third was on guard duty at the front of the house. She sent a text to Jack to get the hell out of the place in five minutes, giving her and Hilli time sufficient to shin down a drainpipe outside a back room and make their escape through the shadows.

It was only later she remembered: the GeeZer who'd gone to the aid of the young man shot during the raid in the underground. Who'd had to be dragged away by a minder. It'd been East. Reckless with her own safety, determined only to help the boy on the ground.

The Face felt pride that she was made of sterner stuff. She felt also a tinge of regret that it had to be thus.

63 CANS OF WORMS

"Hello, is this the Ashcan department?" Ruby Q spoke softly into the telephone.

She was crouched under the desk at the deserted Dekaydence reception so as not to be seen, and had an eye on the intermittent service provided by the security cameras, inside and outside the building.

"Hello, luv," said a male voice. "What you doin' on Reception this time of night? Shall I come over with a bottle?"

"No, thanks. I'm working, same as you," Ruby Q retorted, in the manner she assumed the bright young receptionists adopted when talking to cheeky young chaps.

"'Xactly," the young man agreed heartily. "And I got another 12 hours to do. So, what can I do you for, princess, before you get too lonesome?"

"I need the name of a young man you collected from here a few hours ago."

The young man laughed.

"We didn't do no collection."

"But—"

"All our vans are off the road, babe. Have been for 24 hours. Maintenance problems. Hang on a bit."

Ruby Q frowned.

"You there, princess?"

"Yes, what news?"

"Apparently, we might have one on the road but don't get your hopes up."

There you are!

"Really?" Ruby Q's heart jumped.

"Yes, but it'll be a stolen vehicle. An operative failed to return the van to HQ and somehow it's disappeared. We wouldn't have known but someone rung in. They tried to hail it and the driver didn't stop. That's against our rules, it's a sacking matter."

"Gosh – do you know the name of the operative?"

"Why do you want to know? Is it your man, d'you reckon?"

"I haven't got a man. No, Signor di'Abalo wants to know ..."

"Lummy! Hold on, hold on. Here it is. His name is Bright. Innit Bright."

"Did you hear that?" said Ruby Q, rushing back to the secret staircase, where Will was waiting.

"Doesn't help us, does it?" said Will, gloomily, slumping against the wall.

Ruby Q frowned.

"I think it does," she said.

"How?"

"I think someone else has got here before us and

rescued the Phoenix."

"What makes you think that?" said Will.

"I think they may have used an Ashcan."

"I don't understand. What's the significance of an Ashcan?"

"You work for CCM and you don't know?" said Ruby Q.

"No," said Will. "Should I?"

"There's a rumour that it's a crematorium on wheels."

"What?" said Will, aghast.

"Yes. It operates as a taxi but it's said to be a culling device, exterminating the elderly and infirm, or anyone who's a financial drain on society. Another cost-cutting idea from CCM."

"I don't believe it," said Will, shaking his head. "How evil—"

"Indeed. Equally, what better way to break into Dekaydence than to use a Dekaydence vehicle? Especially one that anyone in the know will want to avoid."

"It doesn't help us track it down. And we don't know what condition the Phoenix is in."

"No," said Ruby Q. "But I imagine there aren't many people who know who the Phoenix really is. Less who'd care so much, and risk so much, to try to save him. I think the people who have taken Phoenix will know his connection to you. You'll get word before too long."

Will hesitated. He thought of telling her about the Phoenix. The boy he'd been before he'd been a fighter.

But he held his tongue.

"I pray it's good news," he said, at last. "So what now, Brains?"

Ruby Q blushed deeper.

"Get your lot to attend the march peacefully?"

Will shook his head.

"No can do. We work alone. The less each one of us knows the better."

"You could say something, supporting it."

Will hesitated. He wanted to tell her of his doubts on the subject of global warming but this was neither the time nor the place.

"I'll think about it," he said. "In any event, I'll see you at the Mall launch?"

"Yes," said Ruby Q. "I'll be at the launch – in a few hours."

"Perhaps it's time to go our separate ways," said Will.

Ruby Q nodded.

"I'll go through the fire exit at Reception when the electricity packs up again."

"You'll be OK?"

"Yeah, I got a pass. Gives me permission to be out after curfew. I'll catch an all-night bus. It stops near my house."

"Not an Ashcan."

"No, not an Ashcan. What about you?"

He paused, deciding what to tell her.

"I think I'll go back underground."

Ruby Quby, don't ask any questions.

She restrained herself.

He held out his hand.

"Thanks for giving me hope. About the Phoenix."

"'S OK," she said. "I may not be right."

He frowned.

"It's just knowing what's happened to him."

"I think you'll hear soon enough."

"But I don't know anyone," he said, racking his brains.

"There's Cage," said Ruby Q. "And if you stop to think, there may be others."

You've gone all mystic.

No, I've gone logic. And you've been gone a long time.

63.5 INNIT IN IT

"Innit! Wake up, man! You're in big trouble," cried Bodkin, banging the controls.

Innit returned from oblivion, with difficulty, to find he'd finished his bottle of champagne and Bodkin was making a great deal of unnecessary noise.

"What?" Innit struggled to open his mouth.

"Gawd and Bennett, Innit, what you done? Not returning an Ashcan for repairs? Not stopping for a passenger? You'll be for it now, mate."

"Who said?" said Innit, waking up.

"I heard that bint talking to a bloke at Ashcan HQ. An Ashcan's been stolen. Someone didn't return it to HQ. And that someone they know is you!"

"That's not right, mate," said Innit wearily.

"Which bit exactly? " said Bodkin.

"Well, it's right that an Ashcan was stolen. But it was mine. However, truth to tell, Bods, I got another one stashed away."

"O, my gawd!" exclaimed Bodkin. "You gotta take it back, mate. Pronto. Tell them you recovered the one that got stolen. Maybe they'll never notice that another's missing. Come on, Innit, get up. Go get your other Ashcan. Now."

"Ain't you comin' with me?" said Innit, rising unsteadily to his feet.

"No," said Bodkin. "I told you I'm on a double shift."

"I thought you was my mate?" Innit whined.

"I am," said Bodkin. "But I got work to do here. For the launch, which is happening any pestilential moment, remember."

64 A VERY CLOSE ENCOUNTER

While Ruby Q was anxious to get home, Will had other ideas. He ran to the bottom of the secret staircase, hoping to find an exit into the network of underground tunnels – and the mysterious Dekaydence train.

He ran his hands along the brickwork. Nothing. Disappointed, he sat down, leaning against the stairwell. He was thinking of the Phoenix and his brother Tommo when something sharp dug into his back. He turned and shone the light from the ad'um on to a small metal handle in a small wooden door. He tried the handle. It was stiff but ...

He opened the door and his heart sank. It was only a broom cupboard, with a few ancient brushes and a rusting dustpan. He was closing it when he felt a gust of chill air. He wondered ... He crawled into the cupboard. And heard a noise. A distant rumbling. It could be the Dekaydence train.

He closed the door behind him and crawled deeper into the cupboard towards light pouring through a large slit in the brickwork. He pulled away the cover of rusting mesh, scanned the view, and climbed through the slit, slithering down the wall to the floor.

And there it was: the train. Growling gently, like a lion

ready to pounce. He crawled closer. There was a lot of metallic noise. A few voices. He crawled closer. There were a few people on the train. Dekaydence Guides, he supposed. But the noise was coming from a motley crew of people shifting huge urns and loading them into two carriages.

Will bided his time. He moved closer and closer to the train. Until ...

"'Ere, mate," said a young man with strong beery breath, and a clipboard. "Take that little 'un. Put it in the section marked 'Private Kitchen'."

Will picked it up and carried it into the carriage. BeerBreath happily ticked a box.

"Do I detect treacle pudding?" said Will, attempting blokey amiability.

"Put your tongue back in," said BeerBreath, warningly. "It's a special. For the King himself."

"Really?" said Will, genuinely surprised.

"Yeah," said BeerBreath. "Now, shift the King's custard vat."

"Right," said Will.

"Black Tartans pulled you off the streets, too?" said BeerBreath, conversationally, without giving Will the chance to answer. "Me and my mates were down the pub a few hours back. But the money's not bad and now the Black Tartan supervisor has gone sick, I'm in charge and I get more dosh. But look over there, they're that desperate for help, they even dragged in that tiny scrapling."

Will followed the direction of his nod.

A grubby young lad in a cap and rough baggy overalls was carrying several large boxes into a carriage, and then running back to the kitchens for more.

"He's an hard worker, give him that, though," said BeerBreath.

"Right, we're nearly done," he said.

"What now?" said Will.

"Get on board," he said, then louder for the benefit of the others. "All aboard. First stop the Mall."

Will joined the throng clambering on to the train.

"If that's the first stop, what's the second?" he asked the grubby young lad who'd sat down beside him.

The young lad turned to look him full in the face.

"Home."

Will stared in horror at the lad.

"My god! What the hell are you doing here?" he whispered, harshly.

Indigo smiled sweetly, and bent forward to whisper a reply.

"Much the same as you I expect. Spying."

There wasn't time to talk further. They arrived at the Mall and worked solidly for several hours, unloading deliveries into the lifts before it was time to move on. To the Royal Palace.

Will stood close to his young cousin, unloading food on to hi-speed carriers, when he saw a group of Dekaydence

Guides leaving the Palace's kitchens. His eyes met those of a tall young man, who grinned at him. Will frowned. He'd seen this face before. On the train. In dreams and nightmares. And somewhere else ... He stared at the boy. Leaner, taller, softer ... Whatever the changes, this was Tommo! This was his brother. Not dead, not killed but the next worse thing – he'd been turned into a Dekaydence Guide. But he was still Tommo! But what had they done to him? Will realised that he must get him away, immediately. He had to stop him boarding the train – he had to take Tommo home.

He felt a restraining hand.

"You can't do it!" Indigo held tight to his arm.

"What do you mean?" he said, angrily, under his breath. "Do you know who that is?"

"Yes, I do," she snapped back. "But you can't take him away, not yet."

"What are you talking about? That's my brother, Tommo, a prisoner in Dekaydence."

"Yes, but they haven't killed him, have they?"

"As good as."

"OK, but look at him. He's deliriously happy. He's got all his happy-clappy friends around him. He hasn't a clue who he really is. You'll be a stranger to him. Why should he believe anything you say?"

Will stared at her, and then at Tommo laughing and joking with his friends.

"I never thought of that ..."

"There has to be an antidote," said Indigo. "That's what you must get hold of. That's the best way to help Tommo. Get the stuff that'll release him from whatever they've done to him. Don't take him till you know you can make him that promise."

Will said nothing.

"Listen," said Indigo. "Go home. Leave the convoy. You've got work to do before the Mall launch. And there'll be all hell to pay if you don't show. I'll stick with the convoy, and keep on eye on Tommo for as long as I can. No one will miss me: they'll all be far too busy with the launch. OK? Deal?"

The train was growling.

"All aboard!" cried BeerBreath. "All aboard!"

Will ran his fingers through his hair, shaking his head.

"I can't think straight. I want Tommo home in Scotland, with his real friends. But perhaps you're right, the state he's in, maybe he couldn't handle it. It'd destroy him and I can't afford to lose him again."

"Quick, Will. You have to decide."

"OK, I'll try it your way. I'll go home and get on with stuff before ..." he said, and turned away from her.

"Hey, man?" shouted BeerBreath.

"He says he's had enough, guv," said Indigo. "He's going home."

"Well, I hope he knows his way out of this maze."

When she looked back, she saw Will scanning the windows of the carriages. Staring, searching for Tommo.

For the first time in her life, she saw fear in his eyes.

65 GROUT RETURNS

Grout heard the raised voices before he entered the room. When he opened the door, he saw Rallan, hunched up on the floor, rocking to and fro, his head in his hands. Piccolo was standing in front of him, keeping at bay Bodkin, who was holding a syringe. A Red Tartan guard stood ready to intervene; Phlegm hovered in the background, by a trolley of refreshments.

They all turned to look at him, and he nodded.

"Morning," he said, cheerfully.

"Where the 'ell you been?" said Bodkin, accusingly.

"Out," said Grout, calmly taking off his jacket. "What you up to?"

"Drummer man's having a breakdown, I'm here to help him through it."

"He was alright earlier. What's happened?"

"Whatever's wrong, he doesn't need Dekaydence drugs inside him," Piccolo said, angrily.

"I'd go with that," said Grout, calmly. "Let's get back to work and see how we go. I'll give you a shout, Bods, if there's trouble."

"We've got minus three seconds to get this stuff out and—!" cried Bodkin.

"I know, Bods," said Grout, soothingly. "But it's alright,

honest. The work's nearly all done. Ain't that the case?" he added, nodding at Piccolo.

"Yes," said Piccolo, curtly.

Phlegm coughed.

"If I may say something, Mr Bodkin?"

"What?" snapped Bodkin.

"At this eleventh hour, a job done is what matters most."

Bodkin glowered; standing down was not in his make-up.

There was a knock at the door, and a Black Tartan guard entered.

"Mr Bodkin, Mr MacCavity needs to speak to you as a matter of urgency."

Inwardly, Grout sighed with relief, while wondering why MacCavity, the head of Dekaydence security, would want to talk to a minion such as Bodkin.

"Where the hell have you been?" Piccolo demanded, after the others had departed, and Grout had returned to the control room to adjust sound levels.

"Out," said Grout, reverting to his old, sulky self.

"We've got a deadline and you go prancing off, without so much as a by your leave."

"There wasn't a deadline when I went out. You know that. Anyway, that's why I'm back. So, let's get on, shall we?"

"Fine by me," Piccolo said sharply, turning on his heel.

Grout hesitated.

"What's up with him?" he asked.

Piccolo turned, and glared at him.

"Homesickness. If you can understand that," he said, sarcastically. "He's been locked up in this damn place far too long. He's had enough. And for what it's worth, I think he's slowly going mad."

Piccolo slammed out of the control room and walked across to Rallan, standing alone, lost and confused. He took the older man's arm and gently guided him towards their desk.

Grout watched Rallan's retreating back, hunched and defeated. He recalled the courage and strength of the big man who'd been the mainstay of the others when they'd been prisoners underground. Keeping up their spirits, never complaining. Grout felt a muddle of emotions, among them a sense of shame that he'd been party to the imprisonment.

He left the control room and went across to the desk where Piccolo and Rallan were sitting, and knelt before Rallan.

"For God's sake, don't upset him any more," Piccolo mouthed sternly.

"Mr Cooper," Grout began loudly, mouthing his words deliberately.

Rallan smiled at him.

"I've seen your daughter," said Grout.

Rallan looked puzzled.

"At home."

Rallan frowned, and looked confused.

Grout tried again.

"I went to your house and I saw your daughter, Ruby Q Cooper. I told her that you were here ..."

A light came into Rallan's eyes.

Piccolo looked taken aback.

"She is coming to see you," Grout continued. "The day after the launch. I'm going to collect her and bring her here to see you. Secretly. No one else must know. Do you understand, Mr Cooper?"

"Hell's teeth," Piccolo muttered, aghast.

"My little girl?" Rallan said softly. "I'm going to see my little girl?"

Tears began to trickle down his cheeks.

"Yes, you'll see her soon, Mr Cooper. Very soon," said Grout, reassuringly. "But no one must know. D'you understand? No one must know."

Piccolo exhaled deeply.

"You're a dark horse, Grout. How you going to manage it?"

Grout shrugged.

"That's my business," he said, surprising himself with his unusual brusqueness. "Now, let's get back to work and get this stuff done and off to the musicians."

66 MALL CONTENTS AND OTHERS

All was quiet on the Mall's vast stage, and all was dark within the Mall's cavernous arena but for one spotlight high in the ceiling, focussed on a figure seated nonchalantly on a bar stool and dressed in expensive black trousers and black cashmere sweater, fingers supporting the forehead of a troubled mind.

"To be ..." Randall Candelskin enunciated, lifting his head slowly and allowing his gaze to travel round the thousands of empty seats. "Or not to be ..."

He took a breath.

"Time's up!" shouted a voice in the darkness.

Suddenly all the lights went on and the noisy business of set building, lighting design and general stagecraft returned to vigorous, deadline-driven life. People were shouting directions to one another; music from many airwaves exuded from portable radios and ad'ums; there was whistling, singing and cursing. A distracted Canapé ran one way, a headphoned Schneek rollerbladed another.

"Excuse me," Candelskin shouted, shielding his eyes and addressing the dark front stalls as well as the workmen. "I'm in the middle of a sound check."

"Dahling," shouted the voice in the stalls. "You had

nine seconds and filled them beautifully. But we simply must move on ... Thank you. Next!"

Tight-mouthed, Candelskin tossed his head and walked off stage, nose in the air. When he had that person's name, he'd make sure the remainder of their career was spent in an end-of-the-pier show, preferably at a resort where the end of the pier was already missing. Oh, yes. Being back in the Dekaydence fold felt good. So potently powerful.

"Hey, honeybud, will you stop sticking those pins in my rear end?" said Hunky Doré. "Drives me wild, d'you hear? Now, I ain't got much time before the show begins so I want this sorted. Will you marry me?"

A box of pins fell on the floor.

"Sorry," said Schneek, scrambling to pick up the pins, scattered far and wide.

"Did you hear me, honeybud?"

"I heard you," said Petty Masters, adjusting HD's trousers and stuffing more crackers into her mouth. "Tell me, how many women have you proposed to today?"

"That is not fair, and-or it's irrelevant. It's you I want as my wife. Think of it, honeybud, our babies will each have my six arms, and your great artistry. By the time they're in their teens, we'll be turning out quality clothing like nobody's business. What d'you say?"

"And what if they have my short stubby arms? And your artistry?"

"Mmm," said Hunky Doré, as he thought for a moment. "I got it! A musical troupe, which fits into a trunk. Honeybud, the savings we'd make on tours ..."

"What is it with you and money?"

"Let me tell you, I don't want any mother of my children going short like my mama had to do. Why else d'you think I came to this godforsaken country? To have the Professor give me two pairs of good, strong flexible arms, save me paying out for bass and rhythm guitars. I do all the guitar work myself, for myself, and for my future wife and children."

"OK, HD, you're on," said Petty.

The box of pins fell on the floor. Again.

"Sorry," said Schneek, scrambling to pick them up.

"I'm on what, honeybud?" said Hunky Doré, bemused.

"You're on, as in it's on – I'll marry you," she said.

Hunky Doré swept her up in his six arms.

"Halle-lujah!" he cried.

"Hal-le-lu-jah!" he repeated, as he danced round the room with Petty Masters in his muscular embrace until he felt a twinge and then a burning sensation in one of his adopted arms.

"Don't bother taking a seat, this won't take long, Mr Bodkin," said MacCavity.

"Right-ho," said Bodkin, loosening his collar.

MacCavity nodded to the Black Tartan to wait outside and sat back in his chair to regard Bodkin long and hard.

"So," MacCavity began slowly, as he fed titbits to the cat-sized black spider sitting in a large cage behind him.

Bodkin felt himself sweating, particularly in the cleft of his bottom.

"I'm interested in your worldwide sales figures," said MacCavity, holding up a computer printout. "Tell me, Mr Bodkin, how many home-made replica liz'oids called Colin have you and Mr Innit sold?"

Bodkin wiped his sweating hands on his trousers.

And this female version," MacCavity continued. "The MaggaThatcha. When are you hoping to release that, given your considerable workload here?"

Bodkin gave a sad but knowing smile.

"I think it best, Mr MacCavity, if you ask the mastermind behind it."

"Who is?"

"It's Grout, sir. He plays the innocent thicko but he is, in reality, Mr Big. I'm surprised you didn't know that already, sir."

BREAKING NEWS

HOME   NEWS   MUSIC   VIDEOS   DIARY   BLOG

Some two dozen women barricade themselves into an elderly people's ward in our local hospital. And I'm talking not flimsy ribbons and bows but serious concrete and iron barricades which are brought in by about twenty men. The ten elderly patients who are awake watch proceedings with increasing interest. Needless to say, but I shall anyway, there are no nurses about for a good thirty minutes before the alarm is raised.

By then, and with the time it takes for the police to arrive, call for reinforcements and jobbing builders which then prove unnecessary because the men demolish the barriers from the inside, the 30-odd invaders have done their work and stand ready to be marched away. In fact, Myra, the invader's leader, steps forward and requests, politely, that the police not bring their dirty, unhygienic feet into the ward, which has just been scrubbed from top to bottom.

One policeman makes to enter the ward but is restrained by his sergeant, who advises his men and women to look at the work that has been done.

"And it doesn't smell of bleach," marvels one policeman.

"We use only lemon juice, white vinegar and water,"

LIVE FROM AN ILLEGAL INTERNET SERVICE PROVIDER

replies Myra. "We've washed everywhere and everything. Floors, ceilings, walls, windows, lavatories, and we've replaced the curtains."

"And they've washed our hair and cut our nails," shouts one elderly lady.

"Like nurses used to do in the good ol' days!" cries another.

"And they've taken away those heavy water jugs that not one of us can lift. And brought us in jugs which have easy-press buttons to give us water."

"It's a miracle!" A patient calls out. "God bless them!"

"I feel like somebody cares!" says one elderly lady, in tears.

The sergeant surveys the scene. Maybe there are a few chips of paint missing from the doorframe but there's no real damage done. Quite the reverse. And he remembers when his elderly mother was in another hell-hole of a hospital ward. She'd been left to cry out for water, cry out to be taken to the lavatory, cry out for her spectacles, which the staff had lost and could never be bothered to recover. Whatever his input, the hospital had eventually killed her through its neglect and carelessness.

"Well, sergeant, aren't you going to arrest them?" demands the hospital's chief executive, who's just had a third five-figure efficiency bonus in as many months.

LIVE FROM AN ILLEGAL INTERNET SERVICE PROVIDER

"I think, ma'am, we'd all be better off if I arrested you," says the sergeant. "Come on, you lot."

He turns on his heel and his policemen follow him, revelling in the applause and cheers from patients and invaders alike.

"Can I have your autograph, sarge?" says one young officer. "Before they cart you off."

"We'll visit you in prison, honest we will," says another.

"No, we won't," says another. "We'll stand by you, sarge. And we'll fight anyone who comes after you, so we will."

The Phoenix lives

67 MORNING HAS BROKEN

It was after 3 a.m. and light was filtering into the night sky.

The Face was sitting alone on a bench at the top of the wooded hill overlooking London. She was watching dozens of long-tailed tits flying in and out of the blackthorn bushes and listening to the dawn chorus: the pure flutey tones of the blackbirds; the blackcap's gently loopy song; the end-of-the-pier screech of the parakeet; and the loudest voice of all, the little wren. All asserting their territory, laying their claim to survival. Not unlike the GeeZers, she thought, and all the others at the rally today.

The little wood was the Face's refuge. A place close to home, which felt like an old friend. It was for places such as this she fought.

She'd been an average student at school, with an average size circle of friends. She hadn't given much thought to political or environmental issues – until she'd seen what was happening to this little wood, how bird numbers were dwindling or had been lost through pollution, and the loss of insects and meadow flowers.

She read about species of birds and animals vanishing from the planet, about the scale of human beings' waste and thoughtlessness. And she realised that, for the most part, politicians and powerbrokers sat back and did nothing. The more she read, the angrier she became. If she'd had her way, she'd choose the extinction of politicians and powerbrokers above all other beasts of the earth. But, failing that ...

She had quit school. She'd left home – or what had been left of it. Both her father and her sister had quit home years before to pursue their dreams elsewhere. She'd exchanged friends for working colleagues, such as Cage, Will and Tommo. And she'd got on with the job of leading the GeeZers, and campaigns of peaceful disruptions. But it hadn't worked. It hadn't been enough. She'd lost Tommo, Will and Cage; and she'd lost most of her support nationwide. Now she found herself open to infiltrators. Three inexperienced young men, not sent by East, but by whom? And for what purpose? She'd given them the slip but, knowing her plans, would they appear at some point?

But maybe this rally would turn the tide. This co-production with so many other protest groups. They'd number a few thousand, she reckoned, but surely it'd make someone in authority listen. Would make someone in authority realise that all was not right.

A twig snapping startled her, and she turned round. A few yards away, by the small, long abandoned bandstand, stood the minder, arms crossed; in front of him Jack and Waat stood, hand in hand, watching her. What did they want ...?

Jack smiled, the tell-tale Martin dimple appearing in his cheek, instantly softening the Face's annoyance at being interrupted in her reverie.

"We were round the corner, seeing Mum and Dad," he said, "And I wanted to come here, to show this place to Waat."

"I didn't realise how high up we are,' said Waat, admiring the view. "It's wondrous. It looks as if the whole of London is sitting in a large teacup, and we're standing way above the rim."

Jack laughed.

The Face smiled. Waat was right. From up here on the hill, the great sprawling beloved city of London, alongside which she'd grown up, took on a different perspective. It did look miniaturised and contained within a vast bowl.

"We were going to ask you later but perhaps now's as good a time as ever," said Jack, looking at Waat who smiled and nodded.

"Ask me what?" said the Face, suspiciously.

"We want you to marry us," said Jack, grinning at Waat.

"What?" the Face exploded.

A bird flew out of a nearby tree, squawking in alarm.

"Have you been drinking? Or have you both gone more bonkers than usual?" said the Face. "The situation the world's in ..."

"We know, Face," said Waat calmly. "But whatever's going on in the world, whatever we can do or can not do, this is the right thing for us."

"You're no more than infants," said the Face, shaking her head.

"That's as maybe. And don't give us the 'I'm not registered to do this' line. We don't care," said Jack. "I got a humanist book from a charity shop – for as and when we bumped into you. Here, I've marked the pages. Should only take a few minutes."

"Witnesses?" said the Face, taking the small, battered paperback.

Jack shrugged.

"There's Hilli," he said, nodding at the minder, who gave a silent nod. "And there's Mother Nature. She'll do us nicely."

"I don't believe this, and I don't believe I'm doing this," said the Face, shaking her head. "But let's get it over and done with. We've got work to do, remember."

They stood on the rim, sunlight chasing away the usual rain and gloomy grey clouds from the sky, and the Face conducted a brief marriage ceremony. She saw the beauty of the love between Jack and Waat and, over their shoulders, the strength and magnificence of a city she had loved since childhood. They were standing among the trees, on muddy grass that sparkled with diamond drops of dew, with the songs of myriad birds surrounding and encasing them, as light as a web of feathers, and for the first time in a long while, the Face felt a sense of peace and hope. As the ceremony ended, from somewhere deep inside her she heard a voice whisper:

"As it was in the beginning, is now and ever shall be, world without end. Amen."

68 OFF-GUARD

Will found an exit that brought him on to the streets close to the Royal Palace. He wanted some time alone, some time to think. He had to find an antidote that would cure Tommo, bring him back to normal. That was assuming there was an antidote. And someone at Dekaydence he knew might tell him. But who did he know? Lord di'Abalo and Grout. The extremes of impossibility. He might've laughed if the situation hadn't been so desperate. His thoughts returned to Ruby Q Cooper: with all her contacts, might she have an idea?

He sat down on a small brick wall to take a stone out of his shoe.

For some reason, he thought of one of his dogs at home in Scotland. Oscar was a rescue dog, Alsatian crossed with Labrador and probably a lot more besides. Bright as a button, loyal and hard-working, Oscar was getting on in years. Sometimes, he'd sit and stare wide-eyed at something unknown. Sometimes, he'd wander around a room as though it was totally new to him, before choosing a spot to slump down. Ten minutes later he'd repeat the procedure; and so it might continue for an hour.

It wasn't only the memory of home and days gone by that clawed at him, it was the memory of Oscar and his inability to settle and his apparent inability to puzzle things out, which reminded Will of himself. He was searching for ways to persuade people to save the planet, he was searching for those who'd helped him and were now lost, for Cage, Phoenix and Tommo. And always he came up against a brick wall. And now he had to contain his doubts about what he was doing.

He saw the young men, but too late.

There were two of them, one white, one dark skinned, darting in and out of the shadows. One brushed into him, unsettling him, and before he could right himself, the other had knocked him to the ground. They were kicking him, in the head and the gut, calling him names, and they got his ad'um. All in a few seconds and all before one saw the Eye-Spy. They were off down the road. Will tried but was unable to get up, pain mingling with anger and despair at being caught off-guard. Before he passed out, he felt enraged by the young men, his own age, who'd done this to him, and felt a taste for revenge.

"Sir? Are you alright? Can you hear me, sir?"

He heard the voice, as if it was arriving through a tunnel. He opened his eyes.

His royal guard was kneeling beside him, checking out his wounds.

"Can you get up, sir? D'you think anything's broken?"

"No. Am fine," he managed to lie through a mouth that felt and tasted as if he'd been gargling with hot pebbles and blood.

With the guard's help, Will staggered to his feet, forcing himself to keep his balance and maintain consciousness.

"Can you make it to the car, sir?"

Will nodded without looking.

Steadied by the guard, he walked the few yards along the street to where the Mostro Marino was parked and, with help, hauled himself up on to the passenger seat. The guard climbed into the driver's seat, took a first-aid kit from the glove compartment and handed it to Will.

"I'll get the royal doctor to give you the once-over."

Will didn't have the strength to argue.

"You on your own?" Will mumbled, knocking back a painkiller.

The guard nodded.

"I thought it safer, sir."

Will looked at him, quizzically.

"I've been following you for some time, in case you needed help. Sorry, I was late tonight. HQ was calling, checking up on me."

"Do you know, I don't know your name," said Will. "After all this time."

"It's Sid, sir."

"Why did you think I might need help, Sid?"

The guard hesitated.

"I've been your guard for nigh on a year, sir. I guess at what you're doing. But I reckon it's your business, unless your safety is at risk. It's my business to keep you safe.

Tonight, I failed."

"No ..." Will began.

"But I did recover this." He handed Will his ad'um.

"How on earth ...?" said Will.

The guard shrugged.

"The Eye-Spy helped. And this."

He pulled out a Colt .45.

"The bodies are being picked up as we speak. Nothing will be said. The drivers will have scanned their foreheads and checked my security seal is authentic, and your assailants will be recognised for the scum they are, and disposed of."

Will turned to look out of the window. It'd been the wrong time, the wrong place for him and for his attackers. An accident of birth. Fate. Whatever. The ad'um appeared undamaged, and he'd survived, just, and whatever the reason for the assault, it now laid dead within the bodies of two young men.

Suddenly revenge tasted bitter in his mouth.

69 TEARS BEFORE BEDTIME

It was some time before 5 a.m. when Cage joined scores of people walking from Victoria Station, along Grosvenor Place towards the Apsley Gate entrance to Hyde Park, everyone's spirits as warm and sunny as the weather promised to be.

Cage imagined the 350-odd acres would soon be filled with hundreds, possibly thousands more. In a Panama hat and using an old walking stick he'd found in the old boathouse, Cage was wearing sunglasses to conceal as much of his face as possible – even though it'd been announced that no Eye-Spies would be on patrol in the capital that day until two hours before the evening's Royal Launch of the Mall.

He walked northward along the Broad Walk, pausing at the Joy of Life fountain where, amidst the gushing waters, two young dancers, captured eternally in bronze, held one another in a loose but tender embrace, their mutual gazes deep and intense. He thought of Waat, and what might've been, and moved on quickly to Speakers' Corner.

Already, people were on their home-made platforms, holding forth to growing crowds of listeners. Following a tradition several hundred years old: the right to speak freely.

A GeeZer, wearing a mask of a verdant globe wizening visibly, spoke passionately of the need for sustainable development in energy, food and manufacture. The need for animal as well as human rights. The need to think of future generations, as well as ourselves.

A cleric and a trade unionist demanded action to tackle poverty, injustice and climate change "to create a decent future, one bright with hope, for the many and not just the few".

Academics were debating; radical artists were performing radically, in theatre, poetry and paint. There were people from around the world accusing the leaders in their own countries of murder, for maintaining a luxurious lifestyle for themselves, which cost the lives of their own countrymen. And there were a few MPs, released on special permits, speaking out bravely in favour of issues closer to their hearts than to party policies.

There were campaigning students from universities, schools and colleges throughout the land, berating the increase in arrests for peaceful demonstration. And demanding changes from corporations which were profit-driven and ignored social or environmental needs. The time had come, they argued, to think and act in different ways – to put the needs of people and the planet before all else, before it was too late.

It did Cage good to hear the passionate demand for change come from such a wide range of people, young and old.

He walked south-west across the park, past the mosaic memorial to the Reformer's Tree, towards the Boathouse.

Everywhere, people were setting up stalls and tables, using large pebbles to secure literature against any mischievous breeze which might be lurking in the trees. He saw anarchist groups, mostly made up of older people, who'd disassembled their tables and chairs and were sitting among the debris, or handing out pamphlets to those strolling by.

Behind them, cardboard effigies of bloated bankers, Union ministers and others too unpalatable to mention were swinging from the branches of the plane trees. Among them, Cedric Cataract, the senior partner at CCM.

And everywhere there were banners and balloons, music and laughter and numerous stalls of Dekaydence delights and food.

People were queuing at the Boathouse to hire a boat or pedalo to sail on the Serpentine lake. A little girl was having a temper tantrum, refusing to wear a life jacket, as her father tried to calm her. Cage smiled. It reminded him of Taylor, who'd done much the same only a few years before. What had happened to his family? Once so close to one another, and now divided physically and philosophically.

He turned to watch the young riders, the horses' hooves turning the sand path into dusty desert clouds. There were rollerbladers, sliding, gliding gracefully along the road or, like prime athletes, weaving in and out, backwards, sideways, occasionally forwards, in small spaces between small obstacles. For some people, he thought, life went on, comfortably and easily.

It was then that he saw them. Hand in hand. Jack and Waat. Walking towards him across the grass, oblivious to his presence, eyes only for each other. He turned to face the lake, and caught sight of Ruby Q Cooper, only a few feet away. She was staring intently at Jack and Waat. And he could see the longing in her eyes.

He wanted out. He couldn't talk to Jack or Waat. And he didn't want to make polite conversation with Ruby Q. He set off in the other direction, towards the Dekaydence restaurant, when he heard someone call his name.

He kept on walking, his head down. But the voice, and then another, called to him. Within a moment Waat and Ruby Q arrived simultaneously at his side.

He saw that Jack remained at a distance. And when their eyes met, Jack looked the other way.

"It's good to see you both," said Waat. "And you look better, Cage, despite the stick. Are you feeling OK?"

Cage nodded, and smiled.

"Yes, I'm fine. And thanks for the tablets and ... everything."

She smiled.

"How are you?" he asked.

She looked from him to Ruby Q, her eyes shiny with

happiness. Slowly, she extended her left hand.

Ruby Q stared at the thin gold band on her third finger.

Steady, old girl.

"Wow, er, congratulations," she said.

Cage nodded, not trusting himself to speak.

"And there's something else," Waat said, elated. "I'm pregnant."

For a moment, neither Cage nor Ruby Q could speak.

O, b— hell!

"That's excellent," Cage said brightly. "Isn't it, Ruby Q?"

Ruby Q was nodding very fast.

"If you don't mind, Waat, we have to press on," he said. "I must talk to Ruby Q before the Face finds her. But well done. And tell Jack he's a very lucky chap."

He took Ruby Q by the arm and led her away. He didn't say anything, didn't look at her, but he knew she was crying.

70 CHEWING THE FAD

"But I'm far too young to have a sister-in-law," protested Taylor, who'd arrived on the scene with a Dek-burger. "As for being an auntie, at my age, it's practically obscene.

"That's put me right off my food. Here," she said, handing the burger to Cage. "Sorry, Ruby Q, it's got meat in it."

Meat, after a fashion. And god knows how it was treated in life and death.

"You'll get over it," said Cage, hungrily devouring the burger.

"Possibly, in several years," Taylor sniffed. "At the moment, I'm speechless. And I'm sorry, Ruby Q."

Ruby Q shrugged.

"Did you talk to Jack?" Taylor asked Cage.

Cage shook his head.

"Honestly! Families!" Taylor expostulated. "Who in their right minds would have them? I'm going to stick with cats, and occasionally take lovers."

Cage burst out laughing.

"Taylor!" said Ruby Q, shocked and amused. "I'll remind you of that on your wedding day."

Taylor tossed her head.

"Won't need to. Won't be one. Anyone want a choccy Dek-Ice?"

And so saying, she ran off to a stall.

Say something, Ruby Q. Cage needs cheering up, too.

I don't know what to say.

That's not like you.

Things change.

Ruby Q, this man is on the run. Guilty or innocent, we don't know. Brave or foolhardy, we don't know. But he's here. A Real GeeZer supporting the rally.

"Ruby Q," said Cage, abruptly. "Tonight, if you can get to Will, can you give him a message?"

"Yes, of course, but can't you ...?"

"I can't get through. And ... others have tried. Perhaps his ad'um is broken or bugged, I don't know."

"OK, what's the message?"

"Tell him the Phoenix lives."

"What? Really? Not just through other people?"

"No. The Phoenix is safe and being cared for."

"Is he ... OK? Only, we heard ..."

"He is having the best of medical care. I can say no more."

Wow! What a relief! Sounds as if it was friends who rescued him. But there's no need to burden Cage with what you and Will attempted to do.

"How is Will?" said Cage.

"He's troubled," said Ruby Q. "He's worried about you and the Phoenix and now it appears Tommo is alive and living in Dekaydence."

Cage stared at her.

"And another thing," said Ruby Q. "I think you need to talk to him soon. He's doubting what he's doing."

"What do you mean?"

"He believes climate change is natural, not man-made. I don't think he believes any more in the work of the Real GeeZers."

Cage said nothing. And for a while they walked together in silence.

"I wonder," he said at last. "How much more blood and tears will be shed, how many more lives will be lost before the struggle is over?"

Ruby Q said nothing.

"Is that what you're thinking?" he asked.

Ruby Q said nothing, simply stared into space.

How wrong can he be, Ruby Q? I know you're thinking only of Jack.

71 JOLLY BOATING WEATHER

Catgut leant over the fence separating the garden from the paddock to watch his wife in the open shed tending the goat, which was recovering from an upset stomach.

"How's he doing?" said Catgut, trying not to breathe in the smell of goat dung, while attempting to summon up enthusiasm for the animal which meant a lot to his wife but little to him.

"Much better," said Lady Catgut, smiling as she stood up. "He's got the hump with me, though, for keeping him cooped up. But I told him, it's for his own good; there might be something in the paddock which disagrees with him."

She scratched the goat's crop as she spoke, and the look on the goat's face changed from one of love to adoration.

"Are you alright, Catgut?" said Lady Catgut, shading her eyes against the early morning sun as much as at the state of her husband's attire. "You're up extremely early, and you're wearing your waders with your cricketing blazer."

"Yes, dear," said Catgut. "I've come to invite you to a weekend in London,"

Lady Catgut gave a peal of laughter, which reminded

Catgut of their first meeting, when he'd fallen head over heels for that infectious, bubbling laugh before he'd met her or even set eyes on her.

He smiled.

"You can not refuse, Henrietta. Your dear friends Edwina Gardening-Fork (pronounced Spade) and Young Miss Burgess telephoned to say that as the forecast predicts a spell of hot, sunny dry summer weather they are sailing the boat to London for a few days."

"For the rally?"

"Yes," said Catgut.

"Are you up to something, Catty?"

Catgut shrugged, trying to look innocent and failing miserably.

"Come on, I know you too well, what are you planning?"

Catgut tossed his head in the air.

"I'm going to the Mall launch."

"They'll never let you in!"

"They'll have to. I want to see Piccolo."

"Catty, darling ..."

"Etti, my mind is made up. And I want you to come too. You want to see Piccolo, too, don't you?"

"Yes, of course, I do," Lady Catgut replied. "But there's Billy and the rest of the menagerie. And I can't telephone people at such short notice to ask for help."

Gleefully, Catgut rubbed his hands together.

"Edwina thought of all that. Last night, she rang

whatever her name is who comes in to help you and she's coming to stay. In fact, she should be here any moment. Gives you time to throw a few things in a bag."

"But, Catty ..." Lady Catgut protested, wondering how Cage would fare should he return and find her gone.

"No buts," said Catgut, beaming and humming. "I know you want to see Piccolo, and this is the way we can do it."

"Have you been bullying the girls to take you?" said Lady Catgut.

"No," Catgut said vehemently. He shuddered. He stood a better chance fighting, naked and unarmed, a crazed liz'oid than he would bullying either of the "girls".

72 WATCH THE BIRDIE

At about 7 p.m. after a day of sunshine and cheer, the GeeZers and other protestors in the Peoples' Rally began to move from Hyde Park to the Gig-in-the-Square where the Face was to open and close the Power to the People Party at Trafalgar Square, which was to be packed with speeches, comic acts and music from actors and artists.

The Face was standing on a long platform with others, watching thousands of people file past through the gates, on their way to join the crowd heading across Hyde Park Corner into Constitution Hill, past the Queen Victoria Memorial, along The Mall and into Trafalgar Square.

Some carried banners, some had children perched on their shoulders, and many were shouting good-naturedly as they marched along handing out leaflets to any passers-by. There were cheers and there were songs. Waves of them, with new words woven into popular songs, such as the National Anthem or, as it was called now, the new National Anthem.

> God save our gracious Earth!
> Long live our noble Earth!
> God Save our Earth!
> See it victorious, happy and glorious.

Long live our noble Earth!
God save our Earth!

From a distance, on a low branch of a tree, Cage watched the Face. She waved from time to time, or made a fist, or shook the hand of someone or patted another vigorously on the back. No one recognised her but he saw her cheeks were aglow and her eyes alight with pride at the success of a long and peaceful day. The gig would be the icing on the cake.

And all this conducted without police or Tartan guards. Or Eye-Spies.

He was about to shimmy down to join the marchers when he saw a hand reach out of the crowd, grab the Face and drag her into the crowd, which rippled with the disturbance and then closed around her. He peered into the mass but he couldn't find her. Over-enthusiastic peaceful supporters, he concluded with a smile, demanding she join the swell on the march. He'd see her later. Hear her speech. Maybe say hello, for old times' sake, even if it meant he'd get an earful.

He was distracted by a noise in the tree. Looking a few feet above his head, he saw a large eye staring back at him. He caught a glimpse of the sleek dark body of a bird. It blinked and blinked again, making whirring and clicking noises, which was when he realised. It wasn't a bird, it was a camera. He tried to dislodge it with his stick, and failed. It simply took more pictures, at a faster rate.

Quickly, he slithered down the tree and threaded his way into the moving crowd, heading for the exit.

He consoled himself that he'd been wearing his hat and sunglasses but he couldn't shake off the thought that it was unlikely to be the only camera in the park.

73 WHY IS THERE A DOCTOR IN THE PARK?

"Is your friend alright?" said someone in the crowd close to Comprendo.

"Yeah, she's fine, doll," said Comprendo, breezily.

"If you're sure," said the Concerned Stranger. "She does look most unwell."

"Yeah." Comprendo nodded. "She's not good in the sun, you see, 'specially when she's had a bellyful of Dek-o-Dregs. I told 'er before, that stuff's lethal."

"Only I do have medical experience. In fact, I'm a doctor."

"That's nice," said Comprendo, swallowing hard. "But ... she's me sister, see, and somewhere I got me two brothers and we're taking 'er home to my dad who's a specialist actually. But thanks for askin'."

He turned away as best he could, given he was supporting the Face's limp body and one of her arms was hanging heavy on his neck. He glanced around and discreetly plucked the sedation dart from her wrist.

Two lads carrying ice creams at head height shoved their way into the crowd. He shot them a fierce look.

"Crikey," said the first one. "You scored quick. We were only gone a minute."

"We wanted to get you an ice cream," said the second,

"but we couldn't decide what flavour you'd—"

"Crikey," said the first one, examining the Face more closely. "Where'd you find her?"

"Never mind," snarled Comprendo. "Give me your ice creams and take a hold of her, one each side, before my back gives out. She needs support. Like the rest of us."

"So which hospital does your father work at?" said the Concerned Stranger.

The two lads looked at one another, blankly.

"What ...?" they said, in unison.

"East Kilbride," Comprendo said quickly.

"Well, how's that for a coincidence?" said the Concerned Stranger. "So do I."

Comprendo raised his eyes to heaven.

And then he heard something. Something which, for a moment, made him forget everyone and everything else. It was something that had the same effect on everyone else.

The drums sounded first, like thunder announcing a storm. Then a host of trumpets, as if out of the heavens. Then the cymbals. And trombones. All proclaiming Copland's "Fanfare for the Common Man".

Everyone in the street stopped, and everyone in streets beyond and throughout the capital stopped whatever they were doing and looked to the sky and saw something emerging above the Houses of Parliament, on the south bank of the river.

The lasers, which had spindled and hidden the new Dekaydence Mall in shades of grey, red and black, were fading and falling away slowly, like broken chains, to reveal an immense titanium globe, circumnavigated by seven rings the colours of the rainbow. At the pinnacle was a great glass crow's nest held in place by a golden column fashioned in the shape of an ornate letter D.

"Ruddy hell," murmured one of the lads by Comprendo's side, as the crowd gasped and applauded.

"Yeah," said the other, gawping at the awesome sight.

"Right, come on," said Comprendo. "We've got to get her back to base."

"Are you sure about this, C?" said the first lad. "No one asked us to get her."

"No, but we lost her, and I want to be ahead of the game, like Innit. So, we'll all get extra Brownie points. Or cash, as we ordinary mortals call it."

Suddenly, a flock of thousands of steely black birds appeared in the sky, high above the globe, creating a huge dark, dense cloud. Just as suddenly, the flock turned, appearing to disappear in the sunlight, turning back, reformed, to spell out the words: *The Dekaydence Mall: Royal Launch Tonight at 8*. And disappearing and re-forming yet again to spell out: *Be there or nowhere!* Then the birds flew in and out of the sunlight, creating shooting trails of light.

There were cheers and more applause – except from Cage, who was staring at the birds. He'd seen them flying out of Hyde Park. Certainly, they'd looked like birds, they flocked like birds, but he'd heard the whirring and the click of their wings. They weren't birds, they were cameras taking thousands and thousands of pictures.

74 BREAD'N'WATER ...
AND TOAST

Bread'n'Water were playing the opening number of the Gig to an enthusiastic crowd of people packing Trafalgar Square, while the performance was relayed live on the sides of buildings in the Strand, Charing Cross Road, Whitehall and all round the capital to those unable to reach the square.

At the back of the stage, Jack hoped he'd misheard Hilli, the Face's minder.

"Honest, I was away a moment, for a quick leak. Got back, and she'd gone."

"Where?" said Jack. "Did she say where she was going?"

"No, she wasn't going anywhere," Hilli insisted. "Except here."

"So what d'you think has happened?"

Hilli looked uneasy.

"Well, I reckon she's been kidnapped or ..."

"Oh, no!" Waat put her hand to her mouth.

"Who'd kidnap her? And why?" said Jack, guessing the answer.

Hilli shrugged.

"It must be them three thugs. The ones who said they were sent by East."

Jack nodded.

"I s'pse so. But who's behind them? Dekaydence?"

"It'd suit them to scupper this do, wouldn't it?" said Hilli.

Jack frowned.

"Yes, and yet they've been unusually helpful. It doesn't add up."

"Shouldn't we contact the police?" said Waat.

"No point, we can't be sure who's on our side," said Jack. "No, our priority is to keep the show on the road. She worked hard for this. It mustn't crumble because she's not here. She'd be furious about that."

"So what do we do?" said Waat, as the applause at the end of Bread'n'Water's song began to die down.

"There's no option, is there?" said Hilli, looking at Jack, who exhaled a long deep breath.

"Wish me luck, Mrs Martin," said Jack, "for my first public engagement."

Waat looked at him in wonder.

"Should I say 'Break a leg'?"

"Better not. Don't want to tempt fate."

Jack grinned, a dimple appearing in his cheek. He kissed her and ran up the steps on to the stage. It would be the last time she saw him.

"What have you done with East, you despicable little squirt?" the Face demanded of Comprendo, her hands clenching and unclenching restlessly.

"Nuffink!" Comprendo retorted.

"Then where is she? How did you get her ring? Tell me that, you lying toe-rag!" And unable to contain her anger, she grabbed hold of Comprendo's lower jaw.

"Let go of me, you crazy bint!" Comprendo cried, struggling to free himself. "Do something, boss!"

"Yeah, right," said a young man, unenthusiastically, leaning unsteadily against a wall in the spare, bleak room.

The Face released Comprendo, and rounded on the young man.

"And who the hell are you?" she shouted.

"Wouldn't you like to know, Ms Face?" Innit sneered through a vale of alcohol, and slumped to the floor.

"Who is he?" she demanded of the two lads cowering in the corner.

"That's Innit, ma'am," one blurted out, nervously.

"Yeah, he's the one who sent us to work for you," said the other. "He gave us the ring. We dunno where it came from. Honest, ma'am."

"So how did you get hold of the ring?" The Face rounded on Innit.

Innit belched in her face.

"I got it from her bedside table." He smirked up at her.

"You ...!"

The Face stood, speechless.

"Yes, but that table is in his nan's house," said the first

lad, pointing at Comprendo.

"East's alright," said Comprendo. "I should know, she's me cousin. Straight up. Eighteen times removed, by marriage. She's just a bit ... tied up."

The Face looked from one to the others.

"Innit wanted us to keep an eye on you, to get in the good books of this lot," whispered the second lad. "He works for them, you see."

"You mean ... ?" said the Face.

"Yeah, Dekaydence," whispered the first lad.

The Face nodded.

"And then Comprendo decided to go it alone," said the second lad. "Said we'd make more money by delivering you directly into their hands."

"Yes," said the first. "Comprendo said we needed to cut out the middle man, who was getting a bit unreliable. If you takes my meaning."

"You mean, miserable—!" the Face began.

"We're all out of work," Comprendo interrupted. "That's the honest truth. Have been since we left school. Like our mums and dads. Shut down the mines, factories, local shops. What we supposed to do, eh? Even if the dole office could be inclined to get off its arse, there ain't no work out there."

"Right," said the Face. "This calls for action."

She banged hard on the locked door.

"If we get out of this hell-hole, you three can come and work for me. And you answer to me, and me alone.

Understand?" said the Face. "And don't waste time thinking you'll get money out of Dekaydence for me or East. You won't. You'd be lucky to get a thank-you for telling them about this drunken renegade, working in their midst."

There was a bump.

All four looked round.

Innit lay prostrate on the floor, his eyes shut, his mouth wide open as he snored loudly.

"I'll put them back in the cells, sir," said McCarbon, saluting.

"No," said MacCavity, looking through the one-way glass. "Get the Face back to Trafalgar Square now! Give her this bag of Dekaydence goodies, with an apology from his lordship. Tell her we'll find and release the girl, East."

"And the others, sir?"

"Get the address from the hoodlums, where East is being held. And release Innit. Get someone to tail him. See where he goes. Who he meets."

"Anything else, sir?"

"Advise the Red Tartans, who don't read their texts, that if anyone else attempts to surrender themselves, or get themselves arrested, ignore them, at all costs. Else they'll suffer another pay cut."

"Yes, sir." McCarbon saluted again. "It is odd, though, isn't it, sir? I mean, freeing the Face. I thought the GeeZers were the enemy."

"His lordship's order. And we're trained not to think, Mr McCarbon," said MacCavity. But he knew precisely what McCarbon meant.

"There's no need for a temper tantrum, Catty," said Lady Catgut, after her husband gave the side of the barge a furious kick.

"I disagree, Etti," said Catgut, annoyed. "I promised to take you to tonight's Royal Mall Launch and at no point did the 'girls' inform me that this old rust-bucket would take several days to arrive in London."

"The Wey and Arun Canal Trust have worked a miracle to restore London's lost route to the sea and that's the time they estimate," said Edwina Gardening-Fork (pronounced Spade), as she stepped up from the galley on to the deck. "Besides, Catgut, I don't recall you informing me that you were going to gatecrash a party to which I know you've not been invited."

"No, neither do I," said Young Miss Burgess, at the wheel. "Otherwise I'd have packed a posh frock and come with you."

Catgut kicked out at the side of the boat.

"I hope you're still taking your tablets, dearest," Lady Catgut said, softly.

"If by that, Etti, you're inferring that I'm losing it," said Catgut, icily, "you are right. But I'd prefer you didn't discuss my medical history in front of others."

"We're not the least bit interested in your medical history," said Young Miss Burgess. "But we are interested in food. Here, try one of these."

She held out a plate of sandwiches.

Catgut hesitated, hovered and swooped on three before Young Miss Burgess offered the plate to Lady Catgut.

"I'd ruddy swim if—" Catgut muttered.

"Forget that, dear boy. Remember Bournemouth?" Edwina said cuttingly.

Catgut sat down with his back to the girls, looking furiously at the riverbank.

Lady Catgut wished she were at home with her goats.

"Can I borrow you for a moment, Henrietta?" said Young Miss Burgess. "I'd like your opinion on the engine."

Lady Catgut smiled, grateful for her friend's attempt to distract her.

"I'll polish the flag and keep an eye on him," said Edwina Gardening-Fork, nodding at Catgut. She lowered her voice. "How do you put up with him, Henrietta?"

"It's called 'love', dear," Young Miss Burgess said briskly. "Personally, I'd stick to cats."

Henrietta laughed.

BREAKING NEWS

HOME NEWS MUSIC VIDEOS DIARY BLOG

All the shops in the high street have been robbed at least once and nearby houses are now being burgled and their cars broken into. But the police don't show any interest. Oh, except when someone pulled a gun in one of the bigger stores, which has since closed down. Oh, yes, there was another time, more recently, when they dropped by to tell the local estate agents to take down the balloons outside their window – in case a balloon escaped and a child ran after it and into the road.

Durgh? said the local community.

Then a young teenager is beaten up in broad daylight. He's asked to view mugshots at a police station, not his local branch but at one some distance from where he lives. Oh, and he's asked to attend a fortnight after the incident because mugshot identity takes place only once a week and that's the first available appointment.

Durgh! say the local community.

And then they say:

No, we're not having this. We're not having people coming in and stealing from us, running out of our shops with a new TV, a suntanned body, a head of highlights, threatening our livelihoods and now our lives. If no one will do something to help us ...

LIVE FROM AN ILLEGAL INTERNET SERVICE PROVIDER

There is a meeting. The hairdresser, the butcher, the supermarket manager and the beautician organise it. It's decided that every person working in each and every shop finds at least 18 friends to help out. Within a week, several hundred people are on a rota. So are four dozen dogs. Word gets around. Members of a local archery club sign up; so do members of a boxing club at a local school, available only after school hours. A handful of keen photographers within the local Women's Institute organise themselves – no one else would dare to – and position themselves in premises above the shops.

The robberies begin to subside. The local paper does a story. The nationals it pick up and run with it. Other high streets across the country follow suit. Schools adapt the idea for themselves, so does public transport. They become safer places. Yes, there are times when pictures are taken, when arrows bring down a target, and trespassers and the innocent are carried off to police stations and, yes, sometimes to hospitals, and to jail. But, gradually, little worlds become greatly safer. And all because of one small high street. And one rather large hairdresser with guts.

It can be done. And it can be done – by you.

The Phoenix lives

LIVE FROM AN ILLEGAL INTERNET SERVICE PROVIDER

76 MALL HAUTEUR

"Gosh, look at the time. I must go, Taylor, I've got to get to the Mall. Tell Jack he was brilliant and enjoy the rest of the Gig."

"Text me when you're back from the Mall. I want to know every detail. Shame you'll miss all this lovely warm weather."

Careful, Ruby Q, you're pushing against the flow. As usual.

I'm late. And remember, the editor's made the Mall my main assignment today.

I know. But was your speedy departure more due to the crowds cheering, applauding and hollering for Jack?

Don't be silly.

Or could it be that you couldn't cope with the adoration pouring from Waat's eyes as she looked at the father of her child?

Stop it!

He did well, the Dimpled One. And it wasn't just that drool-worthy dimple.

He wasn't bad. But I thought the Face was supposed to be doing the opener.

Perhaps she got the date wrong.

You're being silly again.

Yes, but I do silly really well, don't I? Ouch, pesky backpacks. Why do they fill them with cement?

Hurry up. And be quiet. All this chatter is slowing me down. And I must focus on the Mall.

It's humungous! It makes the Houses of Parliament opposite look like a doll's house. Not a bad idea given some of the small-minded contents.

Amazing. A titanium globe with huge portholes of mosaic glass, which glitter in the sunlight, and a glass and gold crow's nest. It's like a flying boat in the skies.

That's nice. Good copy for the paper. Get that down, girl, before you forget it.

Quiet. Look at the seven rings circling the globe, in the seven colours of the rainbow.

Oh, wow! The Orbees, they're flying straight into the rings and disappearing! No doors. Nothing. Just straight in.

They're anti-gravitational, remember.

Yes, and we could've been on one.

Yes, and I prefer to walk. This summer's been such a wash-out, it's a real treat to have a warm, sunny day. Let's walk along the Embankment and cross the river at Westminster Bridge. I'll change into my party dress and do my hair.

That won't make a scrap of diff— Ouch, that hurt.

★ ★ ★

The Great Globe sat at the centre of wide, tree-lined sand avenues, each with a feature of a fountain or a sculpture. Rainbow-coloured marble steps led up to four massive entrances, each worked in a different metal, stone and glass.

Ruby Q made her way to the west entrance, where dozens of discreet ID/DNA turnstiles stood ready to check in visitors and direct them to the shopping level appropriate to their status – very poor, poor, lower middle income, middle, upper middle income, rich, super-rich.

For tonight, the stiles weren't in operation. And guests arriving for the pre-Royal Launch party were met by smiling Dekaydence Guides in rainbow-coloured suits who exchanged their invitations for virtual souvenir brochures, and a Dekaydence ad'um for the few who didn't have one. It was an occasion when anyone who was anyone was there, along with others who didn't feature in celebrity gossip columns and were thus judged to be no one special.

"Please make your way to the central lift and ... Have a nice Dekaydence Day!" said the beaming Guides, with East European accents.

Ruby Q walked into the vast circular entrance hall, the size of three football pitches. Immediately to her left and right there were lifts and stairways to the upper floors, with more discreet ID/DNA scanners to prevent any visitor trying to gain access to an "inappropriate" floor.

Yuk and muk! Who'd have birds inside a shopping mall?

Ruby Q squinted at a sleek dark bird, high above her head.

That's no bird, that's a camera.

What?

But Ruby Q was transfixed by the shopping mall, with boutiques and cafés all the way round the outer ring, cafés done out in black and white, and a vast black and white chequered floor. And huge sensaroundaround walls, showing the Mall's stage.

Look, Ruby Q. The White Room!

It's a bar, though, isn't it? An in-house joke and a bar.

We'll be spending our time here on this very poor level, so shall we head up in the world for tonight?

Good idea. There's a tour in 30 minutes, and I've got the virtual brochure.

Wow, three huge circular glass lifts across the arena, with a fantastic jungle in the middle. Travelling from top to bottom of the globe.

Wow, look at the magnificent Masaccio ceiling at the pinnacle. Worth being rich just to get close to it.

Everything is done in white, even the mock Greek columns. And the central floors are glass, so, in theory, you can see the painted ceiling from every floor.

Look, the furniture is different at every stage. White plastic on the ground floor, for the very poor; laminated wood for the poor; decking for the lower middle incomes;

bronze for the middle incomes; silver for the upper middle incomes, gold for the rich; and platinum for the super-rich. And the design goes from the ornate at the bottom to the expensively simple at the top. Canapé has really gone to town. Oh, we're nearly there.

The Crow's Nest. Certainly, it's got a selection of skinny, batty-looking women.

No sign of Will. So I'll go and get changed.

I'm coming with you. I don't like the look of those birds and I'd swear they don't like the look of me.

77 BROTHERS IN ARMS

Cataract was having a wonderful evening, dining at his club with his younger brother, Wiggins, a respected King's Counsel.

It was a regular six-monthly date, fixed in stone. Nothing could entice him away from this date, not even the launch of the Dekaydence Mall. Not that he'd declined the invitation, simply decided not to tell anyone. Some time tomorrow he'd contact di'Abalo's office and explain a sudden 24-hour bug of some sort had kept him away. Apologies and all that.

No, tonight was his evening for fun, the evening he let down his hair. Or would've, if he'd had any.

By the end of their hors d'oeuvres he and Wiggins had sketched out a new law. By the middle of the main course it was detailed and completed. All complaints made to government, hospital, education and justice departments in writing, email or by phone would be ignored, officially. There'd be no acknowledgement of any kind and, thus, no redress. After a few brandies they toyed with the idea of directing all complaints to a non-existent ombudsman in the Orkneys, who could double up as Father Christmas.

They guffawed their way through a jolly decent second bottle of red wine. Then an ash-dry Sancerre with pudding; claret with the cheese; then brandies. By which time they'd reintroduced capital punishment for not being able to spell.

"I presume your operation went well?" Wiggins enquired, a glint in his eye.

"Remarkably well, thank you, Wiggins." Cataract smiled contentedly. "Good we have a brilliant surgeon in the family. Who comes with his own excellent clinic."

"Technically, Gerald is my wife's family," Wiggins corrected his brother.

"Yes, but the Bartlett-Evanses are always marrying into our family."

"Or we are into theirs," Wiggins pointed out gently.

"Put your wig back in the box, Wiggins, and have another drink," said Cataract. "I've got a little scheme you might be interested in."

"Sounds 'citing, Cedric. Do tell." Wiggins held out his glass and giggled.

The party in the Crow's Nest was light-headed with Dekaydence champagne, cocktails and canapés as well as the marvellous warm weather. Excepting those with toupées or elaborate hairdos, many ventured on to the balcony to admire the magnificent views over London, several spotting Her Majesty the Queen in her back garden, sitting with her feet up, knitting and reading the newspaper.

You can brush up nicely when you've a mind, Ruby Q.

I thank you.

Yikes, hold on, there's a breeze blowing up. The others are going in.

I like it. It reminds me of the wind off the sea. Buckets and spades. Ice cream.

Steady.

Yes, and my last clear memory of my mother.

Sorry, old thing.

Whatever happened ... I miss her. I see other people with their mums. And I miss having a mum. I miss my mum.

Maybe—

Don't. If she'd wanted to contact me, she's had every opportunity. If she were dead, we'd have heard. But I have to recognise that for me she might as well be dead. And the same must go for her. I'm giving up searching for her, there is no point.

Oh, dear. What about your aunt?

Same conclusion.

Oh, dear, but you'll be seeing your dad tomorrow night.

Yes, I can't wait!

No sign of Will. And we're being summoned to the Grand Opening.

We'll see him at the party afterwards.

Will you look at that? The shopping mall has become a gigantic arena. The entire central lifts have disappeared and from the middle-income level upwards, the edge of each shopping mall walkway has grown a balcony of raked seats. Thousands of them, all facing the empty stage.

Guess what? The brochure shows that visitors on the three lower levels can watch shows only on huge monitors.

That's a bit lower-levellist, isn't it?

Yes, and money-ist. The brochure implies that it's because poor people don't have more than a three-second attention span and have to eat every 18 seconds. That's why the lower levels are awash with the new DEN, or Dek-Eco-Nomic, range of food. And all the floors are washable.

Blimey. Bleach-ist as well.

Ssshhh, the lights have gone out. The show is about to begin.

They sat in pitch-black darkness. An excited low hum of chatter mingled with the sound of waves, lapping gently on a beach. A voice began to speak, a voice entwining the enchanting music of Eire and the beauty of Italy, and an excited, expectant hush fell across the audience.

"In the beginning God created the heaven and the earth. And the earth was without form, and void; and darkness was upon the face of the deep. And the spirit of God moved upon the face of the waters.

"And God said, 'Let there be light: and there was light.'"

A soft creamy light from a large crescent moon and cascades of stars enveloped the arena and the audience saw that the stage was covered in moving water. There were gasps, a few muffled screams, until all realised the water lapped only to the edge of the stage before retreating. Over and over again. All was well and under control.

How silly, thought many with embarrassment, to think it would be otherwise. They were, after all, in Dekaydence.

A huge globe began to rise slowly from the waters. It split asunder, each segment returning to the ground to become a swathe of land within the waters.

The light turned golden as a golden orb dominated the sky. Tiny creatures crawled out of the water on to the land. Small plants appeared. Flowers. Then trees, which became forests. A warm breeze wafted through the air, carrying the scent of syringa, jasmine and the damp moss of ancient woodland.

A blue whale leapt up, out of the waters, splashing those in the front rows of the middle-income level, who recovered their shock sufficiently to join in the applause. Creatures, big and small – on land and sea – began to appear, with colourful butterflies and singing birds fluttering and flying over the heads of the audience.

There were drums, a fanfare of trumpets and from the remains of the globe arose a young man and a young woman, naked but for a discreet arrangement of flowers and leaves. They gazed into one another's eyes. Then, turning, the woman picked an apple from a nearby tree and presented it to the man, with a coy look. The man took the apple, smiled and was about to take a bite when he remembered his gift for the woman. He reached into the folds of his finery and pulled out ... a singing Dekaydence credit card. The woman took it and clutched it to her bosom, looking dreamily up into the stars.

There was laughter and applause, in equal measure.

Ah!

No. Sexist rubbish!

OK, OK, anyway the scene is changing.

The forests became cities of skyscrapers. The woods

became housing estates. Everywhere people, and their vehicles, covered the land, the seas and the air. Everywhere there was noise. The sounds of nature were replaced with car horns and a constant hum of traffic, loud music and louder talk.

There was a loud bang above the heads of the audience and a small aircraft appeared to crash through the ceiling. There were screams as it did a twirling dive-bombing descent then an acrobatic spinning, swooping tour of the arena before flying out through the ceiling.

There was shock, and more applause.

Their anti-gravitational stuff is amazing.

I think it's scary.

You can be such a girl!

Yes, surprising, isn't it?

The scene's changing again. Ooh, pretty luxurious stuff.

There were parties, wild with gold, silk and marble, Old Masters, and Dekaydence champagne; barbecues frizzling on sunny, exotic sandy beaches. There were beautiful people in designer clothes draped on designer furniture in appliance-packed kitchens; drawing rooms with cinema walls; and canopied bedrooms, with maids and butlers on 24/7 attendance. Beautiful people footling in indoor swimming pools; or playing tennis on underfloor-heated courts, surrounded by snow. Everywhere there were discreet signs advertising where all these goods and more were available – Dekaydence. Suddenly, the sky again went black, the noise stopped.

Some people clapped, thinking it was the interval, before the magical voice spoke again.

"It is time now for you to choose your faith or following," said the voice. "Examine the control panel on your armchair, press the button that suits you best and you will see me as you want."

The puzzled audience examined the buttons: Christianity, Islam, Secular, Hinduism, Buddhism, Sikhism, Judaism.

Coo, what's this about, Ruby Q? Is it in the brochure?

No, it says only Back to Basics.

What's that mean?

Who knows? But I'll press Christian.

Sparkling dancing rainbow lights appeared high above them, surrounding a dense cloud, descending slowly towards the centre of the arena. A thunderclap broke the silence, lightning shot across the arena from one side to another as the clouds dispersed and, in the midst of the rainbow lights, the figure of a man became clear.

Randall Candelskin!

Dressed from head to foot in white and gold, he looks like a dictator.

No, he looks like the Archbishop of Canterbury.

Or the Pope. Try another button, Ruby Q.

Crikey, it's still Candelskin but he's wearing a long beard and a big black hat.

He's a rabbi. Press another button. Try Secular ...

Wow, a Maccaroni suit. Let's try another ...

Sikhism ...

A distar.

Another ...

No, wait. He's lifting up his arms. A sure sign he's about to speak. I'll switch back to Christianity to be on the safe side.

"Friends, Londoners, countrymen, lend me your ears ..."

Haven't I heard that before?

Sort of. Sshhh!

"I am here tonight to welcome you to Dekaydence, to this Mall of marvels, this palace of pleasure, where you can buy anything you want, from a cup to a castle, from a mutt to a moat. You can sweat in a state-of-the-art gymnasium or luxuriate in a health spa within the exclusive Dekaydence five-star hotel. You can travel on a virtual holiday to anywhere in the world. You can watch the latest movie, enjoy a concert, or savour a snack or a banquet. You can use a Dekaydence bank, a Dekaydence supermarket, get Dekaydence insurance for your health, your car or your cat. You can even arrive here, as most of you did tonight, by an Orbee, which brings you straight into your own personal level of shopping, courtesy of your ID/DNA card or your personal Dek'card.

"And now, because time is precious for us all, Dekaydence offers you the opportunity to pray to your god, here on site. There are virtual areas for prayer for all. For individuals and groups. All with Internet connection for virtual confession. And for making donations. With a variety of packages for holding virtual celebrations, big or small, gaining you vouchers to spend on your Dek'card, and redemption points against a time in hell or your chosen equivalent.

"As many of you know, I have lived in the darkest place of all. In a prison, where my head and my heart touched the extremes of despair. I considered taking my own life. Yes, I did but ... my hand was stayed. I had the kind support of Lord di'Abalo, who supplied me with religious writings, and I was visited by religious leaders seeking my professional marketing help and guidance. But in doing so they all brought in their god, their pathway to light and to heaven. My hand was stayed and I was redeemed.

"And so I stand here before you as the Ambassador for each and every faith. And to be fair, for those of no faith, which is a place I also know well.

"I shall be here in this place of Dekaydence. I shall be with you always in Dekaydence. God Bless You. Or not. As you choose."

The drums and trumpets sounded as Candelskin walked and waved his way around the arena, touching those nearest who leant towards him for a blessing. There were loud cheers, which grew louder as fragrant petals, along with Dekaydence vouchers, fell softly from on high on to the appreciative audience.

"How does he do it?" said the Editor, sitting behind Ruby Q. shaking her head.

"All of a sudden, I believe in reincarnation," sighed the Suit, sitting beside her.

"Must be going, old chap," said Wiggins, his head nodding on his chest.

"How about a little cocoa, Wiggi-woo?" said Cataract, enticingly.

Wiggins started, and looked around furtively to see if anyone other than he had heard mention of a childhood name he thought better left in the nursery. But most diners had departed and a few waiters only remained, laying tables unenthusiastically for the next day's luncheon.

"Not tonight, alas, Cedric," he said. "Elspeth thought it'd be a hoot to drive up overnight to Durham and treat the twins to a slap-up breakfast. I told her we'd be lucky to find them awake, let alone in their own beds, but ..."

They walked down the stairs together in a convivial mixture of tired small talk and inebriated giggles.

"Excuse me, Mr Cataract ..."

A young man at Reception held out a coat.

"You left it here last week and—"

Cataract snatched the coat and walked off, without a word.

The young man was staring at Cataract's retreating back with barely suppressed fury when he felt money being pressed into his hand by the other old man, who was holding a finger to his lips.

"Car's outside, Cedric. Can I give you a lift?" Wiggins called to his brother.

"No thanks, Wiggi-woo."

"Rain! What a surprise," said Wiggins. "Not what the BBC forecasters said."

"Probably the heat of the day," said Cedric.

"Care to change your mind about a lift?"

Cataract shook his head.

"No. Surgeon says it's good to walk. And I've got the Churchill." He tapped the elegant walking stick on the ground. "Besides, I like storms."

He walked off.

"*Arrivederci*, Wiggi-woo!" Cataract cried into the summer's night.

"Toodle-pip, Cedders," cried Wiggins. "Thanks for the meal. My shout next month. Mind the marchers."

Wiggins took a deep breath of fresh air and hurried off in the opposite direction. Cataract's refusal of a lift would free him of the chore of fumigating the car. Elspeth was right as usual: Cataract was beginning to smell.

Despite the sudden onset of rain, the Gig was swelling with supporters in the square and nearby roads. Some way through the second Bread'n'Water set word was going around that the Face had arrived.

People began turning round, nudging and pointing to

each other and cheering so that the band stopped their song and began a quickly revised anthem:

> "God Save Our Gracious Face
> Long Live Our Noble Face
> God Save Our Face
> Send her Victorious, Happy and Glorious
> Long to Reign Over Us, God Save our Face ... !"

The crowd cheered as they carried the Face shoulder high towards the set. Cage watched Jack run on to the stage to greet her and to introduce her. She stood there, aglow with pride, surveying the mass before her.

"Yes, we can do it!" she shouted, raising her fist. "Yes, to peace! No, to bloodshed!"

The cheers grew louder, the crowd adopting her fighting fist and chanting along with her.

"Yes, we can do it!"

"Yes, we can do it!"

The Face called back:

"Because we can!"

"Because we can!"

The crowd took the hint:

"Because we can!"

"Because we can!"

The Face turned to the band's lead singer, and Bread'n'Water broke into song: "Here's to the day."

★ ★ ★

Cataract felt his legs were heavier than ever. Since the operation they *were* heavier, but perhaps it was the alcohol, the rain, the late hour or even, heaven forefend, his age that were combining to slow him down.

He pushed away such negative thoughts and started to hum to himself when suddenly he screamed out in pain, convinced one leg was about to break in two.

He looked down and froze.

Two mad, black beady eyes stared back into his. It was a damnable liz'oid.

He tried to shake it off. He used his stick to prise it away. But the thing clung on tight and the pain grew worse. It didn't take its eyes off him as blood slithered from its metal jaws. His blood. The pain made him dizzy; he thought he might be sick. He forced himself to breathe deeply, to rise above it. If only he could reach his ad'um, call for help, a cab, Wiggins ... He was startled by a loud voice.

"Colin!"

A young man ran up, pressing frantically at a remote control. Finally, giving up in exasperation, he pulled a bottle of ketchup from his jacket and thrust it into the liz'oid's jaws.

The liz'oid released its grip; Cataract thought he might pass out.

"Sorry, mate," said the young man, bending down to put a pink collar on the 'oid. "That's a nasty wound you got there but ..."

The young man looked up slowly, his eyes glinting brightly. Cataract's heart sank. His secret was out, and to a man he recognised but couldn't place, and wouldn't trust to add up two and two.

"Show me your ID, mister," said the young man, slowly standing up.

Cataract reached into his coat pocket. He reached into another pocket. An inside pocket. A jacket pocket. His trouser pockets. Not only did he not have his card, his keys and his wallet, everything had gone. It had to be those young rogues at the club. He'd sensed all along they had it in for him. Just wait until ...

The young man had a supportive arm round his waist. He was helping him across the street towards ... Perhaps, he'd been wrong.

As soon as Cataract saw it, he struggled and it came to him where he'd encountered the young man. He was the Ashcan driver who'd taken his bridge friends.

"Do you know who I am? And what I could have done to you?" he said, realising his voice was thin and weak, as was the rest of him.

Innit laughed.

"That's what they all say. I thought you might be more ... creative, given what you've done. And I bet that didn't come on the National Health." He nodded at Cataract's lower limbs. "Look, old man, face up to it, your time's up. But don't fret. I'll take good care of you afterwards. You gone to all that trouble to keep your good fortune from the banks, and change your old bones for ones of gold ... Well, I won't let you down. I'll be drinking a toast to you every day."

Cataract was trying hard to recall tips from a *Practical Guide to Accountancy and Difficult Customers* when a thought occurred to him: if he survived this ordeal he'd perform a good deed. But what...? He had it! Any company with a call centre abroad would be taxed heavily. He reminded the god with whom he was bargaining of the bonus: the taxes raised would fund people on the dole to fly off to jobs in foreign call centres. Surely that would do it for god?

80 MALL DISCONTENT

Will sat in the Royal Box, alongside Lord di'Abalo and the President of the Union. The doctor had checked him out and advised him to rest but ... Reluctantly, he'd had to use make-up to conceal the cuts and bruises. But he'd delivered a speech, cut the gold and black ribbon officially opening the Dekaydence Mall, and spoken to a few selected VIPs during the brief interval. He was aware of Ruby Q Cooper in the distance, trying to catch his attention, but his mind was elsewhere.

He'd left the King and a Royal Palace, quietly uneasy as to the whereabouts of the King's granddaughter, the Princess Indigo. It wasn't like her to stay out all night and Will fretted that she'd stayed on too long in Dekaydence HQ. He tried not to imagine what might've happened to her ... If Sid hadn't had a day's leave, he'd have confided in him but ... He shouldn't have agreed to her proposal. But the wild waif was a persuasive and determined young woman.

During the interval, he was aware that people were peering through the portholes at the lightning and the rains. So much for summer, people were complaining. A Voice in the Air requested everyone be seated, at which point he was ushered back into the Royal Box to loud cheers, which he acknowledged with a wave and the now familiar grim smile.

The second half began. From one end of the arena to the other, hundreds of lithe young athl'oids made of fire, water, wind or ice were creating vast live tableaux of pictures, of words, and of moving creatures.

Could it be, Will wondered, that among them was Tommo? He wanted to grab di'Abalo by the throat, denounce him and his company before everyone, but what could he say? What evidence could he produce?

It was time for the main set.

A circular stage rose from the centre of the arena, with four waterfalls erupting in the colours of sapphire, ruby, amethyst and emerald. Somewhere a band began playing the opening bars of "Mall Content" and a huge cheer went up as the four Studs and Sluts emerged dry from the four waterfalls, two boys and two girls dressed in a Petty Masters elegance of black.

The audience gasped as a fireball erupted in the centre of the stage, and there at its fiery core stood Hunky Doré, in a figure-hugging short-sleeved red leather catsuit, his blond locks wildly electrocuted into the air like a halo round his face. He stormed on to the stage, waving and blowing kisses to all and sundry with all his six hands. Then he adopted a pose, entwining his six hands and six arms around himself and a microphone, and burst into song, drawing a roar of approval and whistles from the audience.

MALL CONTENT

All that glisters can often be gold
What ever rubbish that you have been told
All the stuff that's up for grabs
I tell you it's utterly fab.

I just wanna spend dosh
And ... not get the dross
I'll forever be yours, yours eternally,
Eternally.

I've been working my fingers to the bone
The 60 digits that I own
Now I'm here to spend my cash
Want the clobber to make a splash!

And I just wanna spend dosh
And ... not get the dross
I'll forever be yours, yours eternally,
Infernally.

Dekaydence is in my dreams
Dekaydence is in my dreams
Dekaydence is in my dreams
Dekaydence is in my dreams

All that glisters can often be gold
What ever rubbish that you have been told

'Cos I just wanna spend dosh
And … not get the dross
I'll forever be yours, yours eternally,
Infernally. Eternally, Infernally.

Infernally. Infernally.

"And don't forget, folks!" he called out. "You can hear this song all over again on the website www.dekaydence. com."

What was that noise, Ruby Q?

I dunno. But it felt like the whole globe moved. And why are they rushing Hunky Doré and the Studs and Sluts off the stage?

A Voice coughed, discreetly, over the Mall's sound system.

"Your Royal Highness, honoured guests, ladies and gentlemen, please sit back in your seats and relax as your automatic safety belt holds you snug in your seat," said the Voice, with calm authority. "We are experiencing a spot of rough weather. Please remain seated until you hear a further announcement. Thank you."

What does it mean, "rough weather"?

I don't know, but that roaring noise is getting louder and …

Agh! Flamin''eck!

Something has hit the globe! We're listing …

Out of interest, what's the music they're playing to keep us calm?

Debussy's '*En bateau*'.

Of course! Just what we need!

"Where are we going?" said Rallan.

"To the top floor," Piccolo said.

"Why?"

"All staff told to report immediately to the top deck of their building."

"Where's Grout?"

"He'll join us in a bit. He has to get something urgently from his workshop."

"Has he gone for Ruby Q?" Rallan said, eagerly.

"I don't think so," said Piccolo. "Come on, Rallan, we've got to move fast."

"Bassard! What d'you want?"

"Nothing, but we've got to get out of here," said Grout.

"Why? You've never let me out before."

"I know but this is an emergency."

"So you can do more experiments on me? Get lost!"

"Look, I could inject you, knock you out, and stuff you into that cage. Alternatively, you put on this cloak and you ..."

"Alright, alright. I'll come quietly. But one day I'll get my own back, bassard, for getting me into this mess."

★ ★ ★

"What's happening?" Will asked.

"It's speculation at this point but it's thought to be a tsunami," said di'Abalo.

"What?"

"Yes, strange, isn't it, in this part of the world? But it could be caused by a meteorite or ... Whatever, it's due any moment."

"What news from outside?" Will tried to sound calm.

"We've alerted everyone we could. All our buildings, the Royal Palace, government departments, schools, hospitals ..."

"What about the Gig, the people on the rally ...?"

"We were about to send out Orbees, with loudhailers, but the strong winds have beaten them back."

"Oh, my god."

Di'Abalo sighed.

"You'll be reassured, sir, that the King's office has replied to reassure us that all is well."

Will nodded. But what of Indigo? he wondered. And Tommo? Cage and the Face? And the thousands of people out on the streets ...? And the Phoenix, wherever he was?

Innit, dragging the failing but heavy weight of Cataract, had reached the Ashcan when he heard the roaring sound.

The yowling liz'oid jerked its lead from Innit's hand and

jumped into the van, the door slamming.

"Colin!" Innit shouted. Unable to reach his keys or the remote, he kicked the door. "Good boy, Colin, open the door! Ketchup, ketchup! Come on, boy, if I don't get you home quick, my name will be ..."

The roar grew louder. Someone screamed.

He looked up and saw a 30-foot wall of water heading towards him.

In Trafalgar Square, the Face was midway through her speech when they heard the noises. A rumbling, a crashing and a terrifying crunching, as windows were broken, doors wrenched from their hinges, and buildings were felled.

There was split second only to wonder. A split second for Cage, high up in a building, to see the Face grab hold of Jack before they, and hundreds of others, were swept away in the waters.

For Cage there was all the time in the world to cry out, over and over again, "Waat!"

"Good God, Edwina, what's happening? Am I drunk or are we going backwards at some speed?" said Catgut, clutching the side of the boat, which was bobbing about on the mounting water.

"I don't know, Catgut, I leave the technology to Young Miss Burgess. I manage the window boxes, housework and the flag."

"There aren't any window boxes," said Catgut, peering over the edge.

"What?" thundered Miss Gardening-Fork, stumbling across the deck to see a bright red geranium join its fellows under the rumbling waters. She turned on her heel, intending to have words, when Young Miss Burgess and Lady Catgut emerged, hurriedly and in their life jackets, from with the engine room.

"What on earth ...?" Edwina began.

"I don't know, dear, but this is not a time for questions. Put on your life jacket. You, too, Catgut. Now!" Young Miss Burgess said briskly. "Hold yourselves ready, at my command. We may have to abandon ship."

81 TO THE RESCUE

"I can't stand this any longer," said Ruby Q, undoing her seat belt and standing up.

You're right. So, where are we going? Oh, lorks! The Royal Box! Don't argue with the guards, please, Ruby Q!

"A stranger demands to see you, Lord di'Abalo," said a Red Tartan guard.

"Miss Cooper," said Lord di'Abalo, seeing Ruby Q in the doorway. "Please, do come in."

"There's no time, Lord di'Abalo. We can't just sit here, watching the TV monitors, seeing people die."

"You're right, of course, but what do you suggest? The emergency services appear to be doing all they can."

"We could use the Orbees," said Ruby Q. "We could pick up survivors and bring them back here."

"But we have no piloting guides here."

Will stood up.

"If the Dekaydence Guides can use them, so can we," he said.

"Your Royal Highness, the King would not—" the President began.

"Miss Cooper is right. It's the least we can do," Will said firmly.

"Alright, if you insist," said Lord di'Abalo. "Head

for the Orbee station on this floor. MacCavity will run you through the operations. We'll ask the audience for volunteers to follow your example. I am proud and humbled to know two very brave people. Good luck."

No sooner had they left than the President put his hand to his mouth.

"And if you lose them?" he said.

Lord di'Abalo turned to the President with a curious slow smile.

"A tragedy, of course, but the main objective has been achieved, hasn't it, Mr President?" he said. "We've eliminated a number of tedious, interfering, rebellious young people and, with your Presidential influence, we win lucrative rebuilding contracts which enrich us both."

82 MEN OF NOTE REUNITED

"Oh, my god," said the young man, tears in his eyes, as he looked out from the penthouse of the apartment building on the Embankment.

"Gods have nothing to do with this, my brother," said the second young man.

"We must do something to help."

"We are," said the other, looking at the closed bedroom door behind which the Phoenix slept.

"Yes, but look out there. Hundreds of bodies. Men and women, young and old. And children. All enjoying a summer's day. Innocents. All drowned. Hundreds, no, probably thousands. Their bodies left for the birds. And the mess, the destruction, the debris everywhere. The terrible, dreadful waste."

"Seen or unseen, there is always death, there is always debris, always waste."

"Yes, but there will be survivors and we are doctors, we must go out and help."

"I know but ..."

He looked at the bedroom door. Now it was open. And the Phoenix stood there, leaning on the lintel.

"I feel I've been asleep for years," he said groggily.

"You look better. How do you feel?"

"Better, thanks to you, Men of Note."

"You are our brother," said the other one, with a smile and a dismissive shrug.

"Whatever our faith," the Phoenix concluded with a nod. "And I thank you."

The Phoenix studied their faces.

"But I sense something is amiss?" he said.

When they told him what little they knew, he urged them to do what their heads and hearts dictated. He would be fine, he assured them. They were to worry about him no longer. They were to take care of themselves.

When they'd gone, he made his way, unsteadily, to the bathroom, showered and dressed. He made himself a cup of sweet tea, and sat down to think and plan his next and, most likely, his last assignment.

"There's something I must tell you, " said Ruby Q, as she and Will hurried to the Orbee docking station. "I saw Cage in Hyde Park. He told me to tell you that the Phoenix is alive and safe. He would've called you but he thinks your ad'um may be bugged. Cage is OK, too. Well, he was a few hours back."

Her voice trailed off.

"We have to hope, " said Will. "It's the only way to get through."

"And take action," said Ruby Q.

"Yes," said Will. "Come on, let's get going."

"There's MacCavity. Shall we travel together or alone?"

"I'd welcome your company, Miss Cooper, but we can pick up twice as many people with two Orbees."

"You're right but how about we travel in convoy? And if we start at Trafalgar Square and then head for Dekaydence HQ? I'm so hoping my father is there."

"Di'Abalo said all staff were ordered to the top floor of their building, so everyone should be fine," said Will, praying fervently that Indigo and Tommo would be there too.

★ ★ ★

They flew low over the floodwaters, now as calm as milk after the three big waves. Mostro Marinos and Ashcans were out in force, wading through the waters, disposing of dead bodies and picking up the injured, who were clinging to lampposts, branches of trees, any bit of debris that helped keep a head above the waters.

They made several trips to and from Trafalgar Square, picking up survivors who settled in the Orbees, mostly in a silent shock. A few cried quietly; one young man moaned constantly about his sprained ankle and a lost ad'um.

When they eventually reached Dekaydence HQ, they saw a mass of people crowded together on the top floor desperately waving to them.

The two Orbees flew in close to the balcony.

"Thank goodness the Palace of Dekaydence was closed today because of the Mall launch," said one, clambering into an Orbee. "Otherwise there'd be thousands of dead children."

That is lucky.

"Yes," said Ruby, peering into the crowd, searching for her father.

"Ruby Q!"

She heard Rallan's voice before she saw him being guided to the front of the crowd by Piccolo. He was laughing and weeping with joy as he stepped into the Orbee and enveloped his daughter in a bear hug.

"Dad!" she exclaimed. "I can't believe it! I can't believe it!"

She was sobbing, tears cascading down her cheeks. For a time, she thought the world stood still.

He looks good. But you can catch up later. For now—

OK, OK. Give me a break.

She prised herself away.

"Dad—"

"You've got work to do. Understand," said Rallan. 'We can catch up later."

He smiled and sat down close to her. He looked around, expecting to see Piccolo, and then realised he was still in the building. Rallan waved and called, but Piccolo's focus was elsewhere.

"Don't worry, Dad, we'll come back for him," said Ruby Q.

Will looked up, and saw Piccolo staring at him, intently.

It'd been nearly a year since they'd last seen one another.

"Pix," Will muttered under his breath, and then called out, loudly. "PIX!"

But Piccolo had disappeared into the crowd.

Will would've gone after him but the work wasn't done.

When Piccolo saw Will, he froze.

Will was an arm's length out of reach. So close and yet so ...

He couldn't forget the vow he'd made to the god he

wasn't convinced was there or listening but ...

The bottom line was, he'd struck a deal. To stay away from Will, in order to keep him alive. And he didn't dare risk breaking that vow.

A large unusual boat sounded its deep horn and drew up.

"Piccolo!" Is Piccolo Smith there?"

Piccolo frowned. It was the voice of Lady Catgut but how ...?

From within the diminishing crowd he saw Will's loaded Orbee depart and made his way to the front.

"Piccolo!" Lady Catgut cried.

"Thank God!" muttered Catgut.

"Well, are you coming aboard, young man?" said Edwina Gardening-Fork.

Piccolo hesitated.

"Yes, but I have a friend ..."

"Get him, quickly!" said Lady Catgut.

He looked around, nudged his way through the mass and grabbed hold of Grout, who was holding the arm of a small, hooded figure.

"Come on, Grout. This way to freedom ..."

Recovering from his surprise, Grout nodded at the figure beside him.

"I got me experiment ..."

Piccolo hesitated.

"I'm sure one more won't matter. Come on, Grout."

"But—" Grout began.

"No buts ... It's time you had a taste of heaven."

As he said the words, Piccolo remembered Bianco's promise to take him to the Promised Land. Will and Bianco. Lost to him for ever. He must move on.

"Three stowaways coming aboard, Lady C!" he cried.

84 THE BIRD TURNS

In the ivory room overlooking the river Thames, the black cat and the white had brought down the metal perch on which the large black bird was chained.

Eyes glinting, a death rattle in their throats, the cats crawled towards the bird, which had been injured in the fall. The bird beat its wings and the cats hesitated but sensed a frailty. They slinked forward, their sleek bodies low, two long intents of muscle and motive.

But they stopped again. Something had unsettled them.

The bird's wings were widespread and still, only a breeze from the open balcony doors ruffled the feathers. One cat uttered a loud piteous miaou and retreated slowly, paw by nervous paw. A split second later, a flash of lights, the colours of a rainbow, streaked through the balcony doors, striking the bird's perch. The cats screeched and ran for cover behind the settle.

The bird rose into the air, its chains falling to the ground. It flew from the room, soaring briefly into the sky as if celebrating its release, before flying fast towards the flooded earth. As it did so, a strange bough of fire and the dark hues of red, black and gold appeared overhead and flew directly at it.

The bird sensed that it was too late for it to react.

But in that moment before the final moment, in a whisper of air between the bird and the bough, a wall of rainbow light exploded suddenly like fireworks. The dark bough faltered and the bird flew on.

There was much work to be done. There were souls to be saved but first there were people. And time was short, Bianco knew - for them as well as himself.

BREAKING NEWS

There's no film for this story. I tell you it with my own voice because I saw it with my own eyes. I had a camera but I prefer that the pictures remain in my memory, for her sake.

She was a woman. She was visiting her brother in jail. It's not an irrelevance to add that he was there on a trumped-up charge. As she left the prison to return home, the woman was bundled into a car by two policemen, drugged speedily to stop her cries and struggles, and driven to an empty house in the city. There, she was raped by one of the men, the event filmed by the other. The rapist boasted he'd get away with this crime because he had family in high places. He was right. The woman? As is the custom for bringing the shame of rape into a household, she was killed.

I can hear your questions crying in the wind and travelling to me from thousands of miles away as well as a few metres from where I'm standing. And the loudest questions of all, which howl and scream above the others in order to be heard. How can this man walk free? Where did this happen?

You want to feel safe. I understand. Don't we all? I tell you, this happened here in my country. But equally it is

LIVE FROM AN ILLEGAL INTERNET SERVICE PROVIDER

happening in yours. Oh, yes, trust me. Now is not a time for complacency.

Ah, and there on the breeze arrives the little question, which wriggles and niggles for an answer: if I know all this, if I saw it taking place, why didn't I intervene to stop it? Why? I was in a car across the street on my way to work. I saw them take her, forcing her into a police car. Something didn't look right. I tried calling the police and when I couldn't get through I followed the car at a distance. When they took the woman inside the house, I called the police again. I got through this time and gave them the address and prayed they were quickly on the scene. I waited, seeing the reflections in the downstairs mirror. A police car drove by, hesitated but did not stop.

I prayed that the woman's ordeal would soon be over.

When they dragged her out and put her into the car, I did try to follow but the car travelled too fast. Two days later I heard that the woman had been killed.

I'd taken pictures, which I'd hoped to give to the police to help them with their enquiries, but I knew it was pointless. I have friends and family who are policemen, who are honourable and true. Alas, I have learnt that sometimes this is not enough.

By chance, the wife of the rapist was an acquaintance of good and mutual friends. Luckily, she had been summoned urgently to her mother's house when the six of us called. When we arrived, disguised, late one night and in a not irregular power cut, the rapist, who had been drinking heavily, as was his habit, positively welcomed us into his home. In fact, when we stripped him of his trousers and taped his mouth, he thought it was a hilarious game, even when we donned long surgical plastic gloves. Of course, he had to be held down while we cut off his member with a cheese wire. It was a pretty poor specimen, as we'd been advised. We placed it in a tumbler on the mantelpiece alongside a red and gold feather.

I thank you for reading this story of a woman, who could have been your mother, your sister, your girlfriend, your wife, your friend. Or mine. Think of her as such, rather than a stranger. Think of her of living nearby, rather than in a far-away land.

In telling you this story, I hope to awaken within you a desire to do good in the world, and more, a desire to fight evil. Recently, I read of the work of a young man in the north of the Union, who is said to have died fighting for justice. So, if I may, I commit this story to the worldwide movement that continues his campaign.

Fight, for the sake of those you love, as well as for strangers. It can and must be done.

The Phoenix lives

LIVE FROM AN ILLEGAL INTERNET SERVICE PROVIDER

AUTUMN

85 CAGE

"Are you OK walking up all these steps?" Cage asks Waat as they climb the hill. "If you're cold, you can have my coat."

"I'm pregnant, Cage, not an invalid," says Waat. "Stop fussing and relax."

"Sorry," says Cage.

They sit down on the bench looking out over London, the sounds of rebuilding the city dense and continuous in the late summer sunshine.

"It doesn't look any different from up here, does it?" Waat muses. "No one would guess what happened."

Cage nods but says nothing. He's thinking of the few inches of space separating his body from that of Waat. Even if she takes his hand, which she does from time to time, there will always be that space. The space belonging to Jack. And it always will belong to him, even though Jack is dead.

Cage finds it hard to accept that his brother no longer exists, except in memories. And that his body has never been recovered. Every time he thinks, Jack is dead, it feels like a punch in the chest. His father takes solace in drink; his mother has become withdrawn. Meryl returns home when she can, to be with her mother; Kane rings regularly from the US. Meanwhile, Taylor climbs a tree and weeps alone.

Waat, who's come to live at the Martins' home, has quietly taken over running the household. She sits with his mother. And with Taylor. She listens to his dad. She is kindness personified. She says nothing but Cage senses her loneliness, her confusion, her shock. He thinks Ruby Q Cooper is grieving in the same way.

It is too early to say what will happen to the GeeZers, Real or otherwise. There have been rumours that the Face is alive. Nothing more. But everything is in limbo. People are still searching for the dead, and grieving for those lost. There has been no news of the Phoenix. No news from anyone. Not even Will.

Cage is still wary. He visits the house increasingly, has even stayed over. He lives with guilt, even though he heard that the policeman he thought he'd killed had actually been wounded superficially and had made a full recovery. Officially, he's still a wanted man but no one has come after him and because he yearns to be with Waat ...

He hopes the baby will be a boy. If it is, Waat will name him Jack. He wants to be close to the boy, as he was close once to his brother, and he would like to be close to Waat. But he knows things between Waat and him will never change. He will always be Jack's brother, a friend, albeit a close friend. There will always be that space.

86 INNIT AND BODKIN

Innit's face is greyer than the sheets on his national health hospital bed and the bandages on his head and bits of his body.

Bodkin sits by his side, not sure what to say. He's never encountered this dejected side of Innit. Hardly surprising; Innit's never experienced it either. He decides not to mention Grout's promotion. He is keen to tell Innit about the fine chavnasium he's joined, and the fit girlie members, the Stink Bombes, even if their perfumes do bring on his asthma.

Bodkin lifts the cage, which he's smuggled past the nurses, on to his knees. He checks the coast is clear and leans forward.

"In," he whispers. "I got Colin in 'ere. Say hello to Colin, In."

Innit shakes his head, once, almost imperceptibly, very slowly.

"Go in, In," Bodkin urges.

The liz'oid makes a loud noise and Bodkin hurriedly checks the muzzle is in place. He sees a tear trickle down Innit's cheek and Bodkin surprises himself by reaching out and putting a hand on Innit's.

"I am sorry, In," says Bodkin. "But you kept your job.

That's good."

"But I ain't got her," Innit wails. "Why did she go and get drowned? She only went out to get Colin another bottle of ketchup. It ain't fair, Bods, it ain't fair."

The patients and visitors in the ward are quiet, and avert their eyes.

Bodkin wriggles uncomfortably in his chair.

"I know, In. But it's what she would've wanted. Getting Colin his ketchup."

"No, it firkin' isn't!" Innit cries. "She'd have wanted to live. She wanted to have kids. Get more Colins. And a farm. Silly bint but—"

"I know, In. I know," says Bods.

"No, you don't, Bods," Innit sobs. "I think I loved Jezza. No, I know I loved her. I must do 'cos I wouldn't feel like this if I didn't."

"You don't think it's the food?" Bods suggests. "Hospital food is …"

He senses the old Innit temper about to flare and adds, "No, no silly of me. But you got me, old man. You got me."

"Yeah," Innit says, flatly. "I got you, Bods."

Init sneezes. It's the disinfectants in the lavatories. Or the vintage dust.

"Bless me," he says, mournfully.

"You can't do that now, In," says Bodkin, looking around, nervously.

"What you talking about?" says Innit.

"You have to be certified to bless someone," says Bodkin.

Innit snorts.

"I think you need certifying, Bods."

"No, honest, In," says Bodkin. "If you want to be blessed, even if you sneeze, you have to use a properly certificated religious registrar. It's one of the new regulations from the HOH, His Overall Holiness, Randall Candelskin."

"Is that so?" says Innit, as that part of his brain which has lain comatose for months stirs with interest and imagines the sound of multi-faith cash registers ringing for him.

87 PETTY AND HUNKY

"How's she doing, Mrs Doré?"

Petty Masters does a double take: will she ever get used to her new name or status?

She is wearing her household frock of forest hues, multi-layered with built-in pockets and bags, which today are full of fruit, books and antiseptic wipes. You can't be too careful these days.

She walks across to the neighbouring bed in the private Dekaydence clinic, which is occupied by the wild man who's become her husband.

"She's asleep but the doctor said she's doing fine. Thanks to you, HD," she says, and leans over and plants a kiss on his cheek.

"Hey, honeybud, I didn't perform the operation," says Hunky Doré. "You gotta thank the ol' Professor. And what else d'you expect me to do? She's your sister, so she's my family. Besides, that arm was hanging off me, doin' nothin'. And I've got plenty others."

"The Professor says your new arm will be ready next month, so we could've waited."

"Hell, no. What if she woke up and found ...?"

"It's going to be a colour-coding shock for her finding she's got a new black arm instead of her old white one,"

Schneek mutters.

Petty glares at him.

"I think I'll take a little nap, honeybud." Hunky Doré yawns, and stretches his five remaining arms. "Me and anaesthetics don't get along that well. But take a look at this crochet jacket I've been working on. See what you think."

Schneek stares aghast at Hunky Doré's pink and orange creation and sneaks a look at Petty Masters, to see if love has affected her judgement.

"It's delightful," she says, examining it closely.

Schneek sighs inwardly with relief: thank goodness, she hates it.

Petty Masters kisses HD again, promising to see him a little later. She turns to leave and looks anxiously at her sister.

"If she wakes up, HD, tell her what's happened. Tell her she's safe. Where I am, etcetera. And if she appears a bit forgetful, remind her of her name — it's Verona."

"Sure thing, honeybud." HD laughs. "But she's a fit young woman, despite what's happened to her. And she looks like a fighter to me. Not some dipsy girlie who's flaky about her own name."

Petty Masters nods and smiles, as she leaves the room.

"You're taking a risk, aren't you?" Schneek whispers, when they're in the corridor. "Bringing her here, into Dekaydence."

"They'll never know unless someone tells them,"

Petty growls at Schneek. "And she needs the best care possible."

She's edgier than usual because the day before her wedding she stopped eating cream crackers, and the withdrawal symptoms are almost unbearable.

She and Schneek struggle to get through the 30-odd of HD's people camped in the corridor, talking to the outside world and one another on their ad'ums. She grits her teeth; none of these retainers is necessary. Not least the six stylists each in charge of a different colour on HD's head of hair. She'll have words with HD later. Better still, she thinks, she'll contact her godfather, the accountant. She hasn't spoken to him in years but ...

"Does HD know who your sister is?" Schneek asks.

"Not yet."

"When we had the wedding ceremony around the beds," says Schneek slowly, "and your sister signed as a witness, I never did get to see what name she used."

Petty glares at Schneek.

"So," he says with a grin, "I take it she didn't use her more popular identity and sign in as the Face?"

88 MACNOODLE AND MACMINOR

"What's that you're reading?" MacNoodle asks MacMinor.

"It's the Open University prospectus," MacMinor replies, nonchalantly.

"You won't find many cheap weekend breaks in Bognor in that," MacNoodle snorts.

"That's fine wi' me," says MacMinor. "I don't want to go to Bognor Regis. I want to go to Florence. I've signed up to study the history of art, so I have."

"You, study? Art?" MacNoodle is aghast. "Is the Professor treating you for something I should know about?"

MacMinor puts down his book.

"We lead a very sheltered life, you know," he says quietly. "We need to get out more."

"Speak for yourself!" MacNoodle retorts.

"Aye, I shall 'cos I'm the only one who can," MacMinor agrees. "So put the kettle on for our tea while I take Rossie and Cromarty for their constitutional."

He gets up, puts the prospectus on the table and leaves the room.

It isn't long before MacNoodle picks up the book and flicks idly through the pages, sniffing disapprovingly from time to time. Then something catches and holds his eye. And holds it some more. Checking no one is watching, he makes notes. He'll phone later and he'll enrol to study "Managing in the workplace". He likes the sound of it. Very much. He wants to show those Black Tartans a thing or two. He quite fancies a desk, and a life not subjected to the tantrums of the new weather. He imagines a place in management. An inflated Dekaydence pension. And a Mostro Marino of his very own.

89 LORD DI'ABALO AND CANDELSKIN

Randall Candelskin stands centre stage on the podium at Trafalgar Square, leading mourners in the Memorial Service for the victims of the tsunami. He spreads his arms wide as though embracing not only the crowds in the square but also the many millions around the world who are watching this spectacular gathering of the good and the great, including the King, Will, Indigo, the President of the Union, many crowned and uncrowned heads of state also affected by the tsunami, and the head of the United Nations.

The newly elected President of the USA is here also, on his first official outing. He smiles and waves to the crowd, and some note that his skin appears to change colour in the bright sunshine from white through pink to yellow to brown to black.

Candelskin speaks of the tragedy, the number of deaths, the number unaccounted for, and promises that those assembled here today commit their countries to "green" policies, commit to save the planet from environmental collapse. The crowds, at home and abroad, cheer. There is music and singing. Many GeeZers, worldwide, weep and cheer, hug and applaud, believing their long campaign has won through. But there are Real GeeZers, such as North, who don't believe for one moment that this promise will be kept; they know they will need to be vigilant. And there are those such as Will who believe the whole thing is a fabricated farce stitched to an economic bandwagon.

Candelskin speaks of aid for the homeless, the end of poverty, global healthcare and much more besides. He speaks with authority, passion, and with a new strength, composure and dignity. His performance outshines the performance of any one else called to speak from around the world. It is his greatest performance to date. The cheering crowd tells him this, as does the rapturous applause, which calls him back for three encores.

At the reception afterwards in the Royal Palace there are a number keen to shake one of Hunky Doré's six hands but everyone wants to shake the hand of Candelskin.

"The new Messiah," mutters the King, discarding uneaten his favourite treacle sponge pudding with extra custard.

Lord di'Abalo is in a corner with the Professor.

"He's doing rather well, I think," says the Professor, nodding not at Candelskin but at the newly elected President of the USA, who is smiling and waving at everyone outside the dense cordon of security guards surrounding him.

"Yes, Herr Professor," says Lord di'Abalo. "And the ever-changing multicoloured skin is a masterstroke."

The Professor smiles stiffly but proudly.

Di'Abalo smiles.

"There is one thing," he says. "The President may be a puppet but I do think our game plan might be served better if you removed the stamp on the back of his neck saying 'Made by Dekaydence'."

90 PICCOLO AND GROUT, AND THE CATGUTS

Piccolo and Grout live in at Dekaydence during the week and have passes to stay with the Catguts at weekends and holidays. Piccolo relishes being back with the Catguts, where he is spoilt. At first, he is jealous of Grout, who is similarly indulged. But after the two sit down together one night and talk into the small hours about their family backgrounds, Piccolo realises they have much in common. In fact, though he hasn't realised it yet, Piccolo is beginning to treat Grout like a friend. Possibly, even a brother.

Catgut has become less spiky. For the first time Lady Catgut can recall, he is happy to listen to the opinion of others. And take it. She feels that Catgut and his music are enriched by the young men's presence, and by their interest in and respect for him. In fact, Catgut has upgraded his recording studio, on Grout's advice, and, much to his surprise, Piccolo has learnt a great deal about technical musical matters. Lady Catgut thinks of Cage and worries about him, and looks for news of him. One day, she hopes (and prays) she'll see him again. But she watches her husband, Piccolo and Grout and her heart almost bursts with pride and joy. Her boys, she purrs to herself. Her three musical boys.

Well, three and a half. Because, of course, there's the other one. The wee hooded figure brought by Grout, which constantly clutches a case to its bosom.

At first the creature keeps itself remote, sleeping in a shed next to the goat, and eating only late at night when all except Grout have retired. One night Lady Catgut hears a high-pitched voice ranting at Grout. Catgut tiptoes downstairs to investigate and the secret is out. Its hood off, Catgut recognises the miserable creature, which shrieks and takes off at speed but stops in its tracks when Catgut calls out its name.

A day or so later, Nigel joins the family for breakfast and moves into the spare room. Nigel agrees reluctantly that his state of being is due to the Professor, as he reacted badly to the miniaturisation process employed to transport the musicians from their underground prison. He accepts grudgingly that he owes his life to Grout who kept him alive somehow after he was taken off the life-support system attached to the hospital incubator.

But he's still angry that Grout's trial antidote went wrong.

Nigel, already prone to eczema, came out in great scabs – not of skin but of metal. Another reason Grout held him secure underground. Poor Nigel. The metal scabs clunk whenever he moves. Terrible for anyone but for a violinist, especially a sensitive first violinist, a sheer and utter nightmare.

Lady Catgut's kindness is softening his anger. She calls

him Nigellus, her Roman soldier, and she makes him laurel wreaths to wear on his head, with herbs and flowers such as lavender and jasmine that she knows will sooth his troubled, albeit part-metal brow.

The four men muddle through, mostly in harmony. Each odd and different and a loner at heart, yet each relishing the company of the others.

Occasionally, they share their joy in music in a performance outside on the flower-filled terrace for Lady Catgut and the "girls", Edwina Gardening-Fork (pronounced Spade) and Young Miss Burgess, who applaud as though the quartet had actually invented music.

At other times, Lady Catgut teaches Piccolo and Grout about animal husbandry. Piccolo has developed a soft spot for the pig, Montezuma; and it appears the feeling is reciprocated. Grout has got used to Billy the Goat sitting happily on his lap, except when it's foot-trimming time. Nigel sits at a distance away but Lady Catgut knows he is getting much less anxious because, just occasionally, he leaves his beloved violin in its case in his room.

At night, in his room under the eaves and the stars, Piccolo dreams of his dead father and of Bianco. And he dreams of Will, who calls to him from a boat. In the dream, Piccolo waves back. And sometimes, not often, he boards the boat and they sail away together.

91 WILL

"They told me the move was temporary. That we'd live in the summerhouse until the Palace dries out. But they lied," the King tells Will. "They've moved in a few exiled monarchs, distant relatives I could do without, some government health and safety departments that no one else will harbour. Meanwhile, that man Candelskin has commandeered my apartment, including the Armageddon Conservatory. And I'm convinced that someone is up to something in the cellars. What can I do, Will? What can I do?"

There are tears in the old man's eyes, as well as impotent fury.

Will is interested in the goings-on in the cellar but he can do nothing to help the King. He has no answers because he has no power.

He also has no work: Cataract is in hospital, in Intensive Care, which means his job at CCM hangs in the balance.

Living conditions in the summerhouse are cramped and he sees he gets under the feet and skin of the King. He would like to return to Scotland, the estate and his books. But as Tommo is happy living with Indigo ...

He can do next to nothing to help Indigo who's moved to the country, where she's learning to farm real food when others are farming Dekaydence chemical "food". Secretly, she's caring for Tommo, while waiting for Will to find an antidote. How he is to achieve that he has no idea. But he visits her and Tommo. With Sid's help. And well away from prying eyes, the four of them picnic occasionally by the river in the sunshine of a late summer. These times remind Will of his old life in Scotland, when Tommo would take him fishing on the loch. When Tommo had been Tommo. One day, he tells himself, he must find that antidote. He must get back the real Tommo.

Recently, he has met with Cage and sat with him in his grief. Will promises to see him again, and soon. He has also attended a school reunion and met with two old Noteians, who told him a recovering Phoenix had left them while they had worked in the aftermath of the tsunami. But none has seen him or heard a word since. The three promise to keep in touch. And Noteians keep their promises.

Will has handed over the leadership of the Real GeeZers to North because he no longer believes in the cause. He is not much concerned that he hears no news of the GeeZers, or of the Face.

His focus is elsewhere. He has read much, is reading more and has concluded that the majority of people are deluded or misguided into thinking man is to blame for climate change. Man is responsible for destroying the environment, he believes, for leading an unsustainable life, which impacts hugely and dangerously on people worldwide. But it's clear to him that climate change is caused by natural elements such as the sun, over which man has no control.

He believes passionately that carbon footprints are a meaningless, empty notion, funding an entire industry of greenhouse gasbaggers and enabling governments to raise lucrative taxes – until fossil fuels run out, Will reads, within 10 or 20 years, when uranium, an essential for nuclear power, will also be running out.

These people are too busy trying to solve last year's problem, he realises, to give any thought to what the next fuel is to be. It reminds him of the hysterical tulip mania, which gripped Holland in the 17th century when tulips sold for tens of thousands of guilders.

Will is convinced humans cannot stop climate change. Climate changes are a normal reality for a dynamic planet. If you did want to stop climate change you'd have to stop sunspots, tides, orbital wobbles, meteorites, volcanoes, ocean currents, comets, continental drift, sedimentation, erosion, weathering and life itself. You'd have to be a god, not a human.

Will wants to research more. To find answers and weapons in natural science, not computer models which, he believes, are manipulated into delivering the "correct" green doomsday message. It's made him think about the tsunami and wonder about its cause. It wasn't a natural phenomenon for the northern hemisphere so ... He puzzles and thinks and wonders, and stretches the bounds of possibility: could it be that Dekaydence played some part in the event, by design or accident ...?

And then he gets a call from Lord di'Abalo.

"Until we know Cataract's state of health, I wondered if you'd like to work with me," di'Abalo enquires.

Will is taken aback. It is a chance to explore and experience real power. It is a chance to contact Grout and discover if there is, or could be, an antidote for Tommo. It is a chance to find the White Room, the place where youngsters are turned into Dekaydence Guides. Perhaps discover the reason why. Will wants desperately to study but recognises the opportunity for what it is. It's an offer he cannot refuse.

92 THE PHOENIX

The Phoenix climbs to the top of the hill, which overlooks the sea. The sun is setting and a broad band of burnt ochre rises through yellow to cream stretching round the horizon between the sea and a deepening blue sky. The wind is fresh on the Phoenix's face as he walks with some difficulty down the cliff to the isolated cottage where the lights are already burning.

The Phoenix is not fully healed. He knows that, in some areas, he never will be. But he has been waiting for this moment for a long time. Over and above the time he has been living wild and rough a mile or so away. He has been preparing and checking constantly the occupancy of the cottage from the hills above. Now is the moment, he has decided.

His old strength is returning; his ruthlessness never deserted him.

Should this be his last deed, he will be content.

He disposes of the two guards outside with sedation darts and uses his key to open the side door.

The TV is blaring out noise and pictures. Men and women cavort naked across the screen. A man in navy pyjamas sits in a huge armchair, drinking champagne as he ogles the screen.

The Phoenix cocks a gun.

The President of the Union turns.

"I wondered when you'd turn up," he says, turning back to the screen. "God, your face looks a mess. What have you been up to? No, don't tell me."

"Some of your friends, Father. Took against me. Can't think why. They—"

"I don't wish to know any more. What do you want? Food, money drugs? A ministerial post? I can arrange 'most anything. Now that I'm the President of the Union, in case you missed the news."

The Phoenix sits down in the chair near the President, fiddling with the gun.

The President scowls.

"Stop playing with that thing. How many times have I told you? Guns are dangerous. And where have you been? Hanging out with your old Noteian reprobates in a treehouse? D'you know, your sister keeps asking what I've done with you."

"Where is she?" says the Phoenix.

"How do I know? She never tells me. Maria prefers the company of others to mine. Like you. So, what have you been up to?"

"This and that."

"And what do you want?"

"Justice."

"Oh, god, what now? Has your breakdown got you into more trouble? You need a good lawyer or what?"

"No, thanks. This is to be homespun justice, Father."

"Ah, and what am I to blame for? Working my arse off seven days a week to send you and your sister to the best schools in the country? Working my arse off to give you organic food, designer clothes, the very latest of gadgets, pets ...?"

"Which you killed, Father," the Phoenix says.

"Stuff and nonsense."

"You killed the puppies, and took pleasure in doing so. I saw it with my own eyes, Father. And now I know you've framed an innocent man for a crime, that should be laid at your feet. It wasn't Cage Martin who blew up Number 10 Downing Street. It wasn't Cage Martin who killed my mother and my brother. You did, Father. They died to satisfy your ambition, they died to get you a huge sympathy vote, to get you elected as President."

"Where do you get this drivel?"

"In a conversation between di'Abalo and Candelskin, which fingers you."

"What?" The President looks startled.

"As you planned, Father, Note has given me excellent contacts. We overhear everything."

"You always thought you were better than me, didn't you?" snarls the President. "Like your damn mother."

"Stop it, Father, or I'll stop you."

"You're just like her. Arrogant. Opinionated ... "

"Which made it OK to kill her? What about Josef? He was six years old."

"I ... He wasn't supposed to be there," the President says quietly, and stares at the floor, thinking of the child who had been most like him.

"You have to face the consequences, Father. Rough justice for rough injustice," says the Phoenix.

The President nods slowly. He lifts his head to look mournfully at his son.

"Jesus!" The President calls out the given name of his son as he reaches for the alarm button.

The young man, better known as the Phoenix, fires the gun.

93 RUBY Q

Ruby Q peers through a microscope fixed in the side of a bath full of clear liquid.

"Can you see anything?" Grout asks excitedly.

"Yes," says Ruby Q. "A bath full of water."

"And?"

"Well, a drop of water looks like a giant waterfall."

"Yes, yes," says Grout impatiently. "Anything else?"

Ruby Q is puzzled. She knows Grout well enough to know that he doesn't do practical jokes but she's already seen the bathtub is full of water and nothing else. She moves the microscope to scan the waters until ...

"Oh, my!" she says.

"What is it?" Grout asks, almost squeaking with joy.

"There must be hundreds, no, thousands of ... what are they, Grout?"

"Workers," says Grout, happily. "Millions of miniature nan'oids, or nans."

"And what on earth are they doing?"

Ruby Q moves away from the bath and looks into the waters. In a moment or two and before her very eyes a tiny blob of bright yellow plastic turns into a rubber duck, which bobs about on the water, quacks, and then begins transmitting a performance of *The Marriage of Figaro*.

"What's it all about, Grout?" Ruby Q asks.

"The liquid in the bath contains all essential elements and the nans assemble from that anything you like. A camera, a radio ... Soon they'll go out to find underground faults in cables and mend them and go into the human body to repair injuries or destroy tumours."

"Why did you want me to see this?"

Grout blinks back to the present; his mind is now often thinking how this technology might help Nigel and Catgut and the other shrinking IoU musicians.

"I didn't. It was Lord di'Abalo's idea. He thought you'd be interested to watch how the project develops."

"I wonder why. I'm not the paper's science correspondent," says Ruby Q.

Grout shrugs. Understanding people has never been his strength.

Ruby Q returns home. She sits in her bedroom, alone. She is overjoyed to have her father home. Technically, this home belongs to Grandmother Elsa who, although she says nothing, makes them aware that they're a disruption to her life. Even though Rallan is her son.

Ruby Q realises that her father is seriously deaf, which he acknowledges, and that his mind is going, which he does not. He's determined to return to work and has gone off on a lecture tour. Alone. Which concerns her but ...

Her thoughts soon turn to Jack. She feels she's lost him twice: to Waat, and to death. Though she recognises that he was never her Jack, except in her imagination. At the moment she can't cope with her own grief, let alone Taylor's. So they see little of one another. It's easier to feel guilt.

For some reason, she doesn't cry. She's curious why that is. Is it because she's busy at the newspaper? Where she's learning much and doing well? Perhaps.

Thoughts of her mother and her aunt have become buried in work and more pressing worries about her father so one day, when she is working and listening with half an ear to Grieg's Piano Concerto No. 1, she is shocked to get a call from Aunt Lily.

"How are you?" says Aunt Lily.

Ruby Q wonders why the concern now; it's been some time since the tsunami.

"I ... I'd like to get to know you," says Aunt Lily, falteringly. "And I'd like you to visit me in Florence."

"What's made you change your mind?" says Ruby Q, curious but wary.

"I've not spoken to your mother in years," says Aunt Lily. "But in my dotage I realise I ..."

Ruby Q hopes her aunt isn't changing her mind.

"You see, Ruby Q," Aunt Lily continues slowly, "all these years, I realise I've been punishing you for a great wrong done to me by your mother."

Ruby Q thinks about the great wrong done to *her* by her mother but says only, "What did my mother do to you?"

"You don't know?" Aunt Lily asks, tentatively.

"No," says Ruby Q.

"Well, Ruby Q, she stole from me."

"Heavens," says Ruby Q. "It must've been something pretty important."

"Yes, it was."

There is another pause.

"Can you tell me what it was?" Ruby Q asks.

Again, Aunt Lily hesitates.

"It concerns you ... And I worry—"

"If it concerns me then I want to know, Aunt Lily. I'd rather hear it from you than stumble over it by chance."

Or hear it from Grandmother Elsa.

That's for sure. And where have you been?

You've been doing fine without me. But I thought I'd better pop back.

So, do you know what this is about?

Shhh! Listen.

Aunt Lily takes a deep breath.

"Your mother stole from me the man to whom I was engaged."

"Oh," says Ruby Q, thinking of herself, Jack and Waat. "That must've been awful. I—"

But her aunt hasn't finished.

"Your mother stole from me the man who is your father," says Aunt Lily.

Ruby Q frowns.

"I never knew you were engaged to my father, to

Rallan," she says.

"I wasn't. I'm talking about the man who is your real father."

"My real father?" Ruby Q repeats. She feels decidedly wobbly.

Steady, Ruby Q.

"You mean, she never told you." Somehow Aunt Lily manages to sound suspicious and surprised.

"No," says Ruby Q. Her heart is beating fast. She swallows before she asks, "Who is my real father, Aunt Lily?"

"I wish I could say this as I held your hand." Aunt Lily struggles to suppress old and mixed emotions fighting for release in her voice. "I wish I could say this after we'd known one another and loved one another for years."

Ruby Q's heart is throbbing fit to bust. She feels like a cornered animal sensing it faces terrible injury or maybe death.

Her aunt speaks strongly and firmly.

"Your father is Lorenzo di'Abalo."

If her hands are shaking, Ruby Q isn't aware of it. If her aunt is calling her, she hears only a noise in the far distance. She can't – doesn't dare to – speak. She skims the surface of the news. It makes a kind of sense. The speedy wedding of Rallan and Angelica. Her family's disapproval. Mrs Wedding Guest trying to tell her what she saw was going on. Was this why her mother eventually ran away? Did Rallan know and never tell her? Does di'Abalo have any idea?

Ruby Q has only just accepted that she has lost her mother who didn't love her. Now she discovers that she is the child not of a good man but a man of great evil.

Rallan was her rock. He cared for and about her. He introduced her to books, to music and animals, inspiring her to love them all. They laughed at the same things. He gave her confidence in herself and what she did. And who she was. But now ...

She is di'Abalo's child. She carries his genes. What might she be capable of?

Whatever happens, Ruby Quby, remember Rallan has been the real dad in your life. He's been there for you, always. Whatever is to come, hold on to that truth. Do you hear me, Ruby Q?

Ruby Q shivers. She is scared of the unknown. Who is she now? Where does she belong and to whom? Her head and heart stumble about in a dark fog, empty of everything except walls of acute pain and seemingly unending shock. She catches sight of herself in the looking glass.

I'm looking in the mirror. I'm there, but only in part. Will I ever be complete?

The third book in the Chronicles of Dekaydence
is due out in 2011.

While you're waiting,
you might want to ...

Hear the music

Listen to an extract

or

Go behind the scenes of

DEKAYDENCE

at
www.dekaydence.com